THE AUTHOR

THOMAS CHANDLER HALIBURTON was born in Windsor, Nova Scotia, in 1796. He studied at King's College and was called to the bar in 1820. He practised law in Annapolis Royal and represented that constituency in the provincial assembly from 1826 to 1829. Named a judge of the Inferior Court of Common Pleas in 1829, he was elevated twelve years later to the Supreme Court of Nova Scotia.

Haliburton began his writing career as an historian. In the 1830s he turned to humorous and satirical fiction to express his Tory opinions on political and social questions. In 1835 he contributed to Joseph Howe's journal *The Novascotian* a series of satirical sketches entitled "Recollections of Nova Scotia." Their popularity led him to expand them into *The Clockmaker; or, The Sayings and Doings of Samuel Slick, of Slickville* (1836). He published a second series of sketches in 1838 and a third in 1840.

In 1856 Haliburton retired and moved to England, where he represented Launceston in the House of Commons from 1859 to 1865.

Thomas Chand[died   ]orth, Middlesex, England, i

THE CLOCKMAKER

OR

THE SAYINGS AND DOINGS OF
SAMUEL SLICK, OF SLICKVILLE

THOMAS CHANDLER
HALIBURTON

AFTERWORD BY
ROBERT L. McDOUGALL

New Canadian Library edition copyright © 1993 by McClelland & Stewart Ltd.
Afterword © 1993 by Robert L. McDougall.
This New Canadian Library edition 2007.

Library and Archives Canada Cataloguing in Publication

Haliburton, Thomas Chandler, 1796-1865
    The clockmaker, or, The sayings and doings of Samuel Slick of Slickville / Thomas Chandler Haliburton ; with an afterword by Robert L. McDougall.

(New Canadian library)
Originally published: Halifax, N.S. : J. Howe, 1836.
ISBN 978-0-7710-9625-9

    I. Title. II. Title: Sayings and doings of Samuel Slick, of Slickville.
III. Series.

PS8515.A38C5 2007   C813'.3   C2007-903183-8

We acknowledge the financial support of the Government of Canada through the Book Publishing Industry Development Program and that of the Government of Ontario through the Ontario Media Development Corporation's Ontario Book Initiative. We further acknowledge the support of the Canada Council for the Arts and the Ontario Arts Council for our publishing program.

ANCIENT FOREST FRIENDLY

Typeset in Garamond by M&S, Toronto
Printed and bound in Canada

McClelland & Stewart Ltd.
75 Sherbourne Street
Toronto, Ontario
M5A 2P9
www.mcclelland.com/NCL

1 2 3 4 5   11 10 09 08 07

ADVERTISEMENT

The following Sketches, as far as the twenty-first No. originally appeared in "The Novascotian" newspaper. The great popularity they acquired, induced the Editor of that paper to apply to the Author for the remaining part of the series, and permission to publish the whole entire. This request having been acceded to, the Editor has now the pleasure of laying them before the public in their present shape.

Halifax, December, 1836.

CONTENTS

THE CLOCKMAKER

SLICK'S LETTER

[After these Sketches had gone through the press, and were ready for the binder, we sent Mr. Slick a copy; and shortly afterwards received from him the following letter, which characteristic communication we give entire. – Editor.]

To Mr. Howe,

Sir. – I received your letter, and note its contents. I aint over half pleased, I tell you; I think I have been used scandalous, that's a fact. It warn't the part of a gentleman for to go and pump me arter that fashion, and then go right off and blart it out in print. It was a nasty dirty mean action, and I don't thank you nor the Squire a bit for it. It will be more nor a thousand dollars out of my pocket. There's an eend to the Clock trade now, and a pretty kettle of fish I've made on it, hav'nt I? I shall never hear the last on it, and what am I to say when I go back to the States? I'll take my oath I never said one half the stuff he has set down there; and as for that long lochrum about Mr. Everett, and the Hon. Alden Gobble, and Minister, there aint a word of truth in it from beginnin to eend. If ever I come near hand to him agin, I'll larn him – but

I

never mind, I say nothin. Now there's one thing I don't cleverly understand. If this here book is my "*Sayins and Doins*," how comes it yourn or the Squire's either? If my thoughts and notions are my own, how can they be any other folks's? According to my idee you have no more right to take them, than you have to take my clocks without payin for 'em. A man that would be guilty of such an action is no gentleman, that's flat, and if you don't like it, you may lump it – for I don't valy him nor you, neither, nor are a Blue Nose that ever stept in shoe leather the matter of a pin's head. I don't know as ever I felt so ugly afore since I was raised; why didn't he put his name to it, as well as mine? When an article han't the maker's name and factory on it, it shows its a cheat, and he's ashamed to own it. If I'm to have the name I'll have the game, or I'll know the cause why, that's a fact? Now folks say you are a considerable of a candid man, and right up and down in your dealins, and do things above board, handsum – at least so I've hearn tell. That's what I like; I love to deal with such folks. Now spose you make me an offer? You'll find me not very difficult to trade with, and I don't know but I might put off more than half of the books myself, tu. I'll tell you how I'd work it. I'd say, "Here's a book they've namesaked arter me, Sam Slick the Clockmaker, but it tante mine, and I can't altogether jist say rightly whose it is. Some say it's the General's, and some say its the Bishop's, and some say its Howe himself; but I aint availed who it is. Its a wise child that knows its own father. It wipes up the Blue Noses considerable hard, and don't let off the Yankees so very easy neither, but it's generally allowed to be about the prettiest book ever writ in this country; and although it aint altogether jist gospel what's in it, there's some pretty home truths in it, that's a fact. Whoever wrote it must be a funny feller, too, that's sartin; for there are some queer stories in it that no soul could help larfin at, that's a fact. Its about the wittiest book I ever seed. Its nearly all sold off, but jist a few copies I've kept for my old customers. The price is just 5s. 6d. but I'll let you have it for 5s. because you'll not get another chance to have one." Always ax a sixpence more than the price, and then bate it, and when Blue Nose hears that, he thinks he's got a bargain, and bites directly. I never see one on 'em yet that didn't fall right into the trap.

Yes, make me an offer, and you and I will trade, I think. But fair play's a jewel, and I must say I feel ryled and kinder sore. I han't been used handsum atween you two, and it don't seem to me that I had ought to be made a fool on in that book, arter that fashion, for folks to laugh at, and then be sheered out of the spec. If I am, somebody had better look out for squalls, I tell you. I'm as easy as an old glove, but a glove aint an old shoe to be trod on, and I think a certain person will find that out afore he is six months older, or else I'm mistakened, that's all. Hopin to hear from you soon, I remain yours to command,

SAMUEL SLICK.

Pugnose's Inn, River Philip, Dec. 25, 1836.

P.S. I see in the last page it is writ, that the Squire is to take another journey round the Shore, and back to Halifax with me next Spring. Well, I did agree with him, to drive him round the coast, but dont you mind – we'll understand each other, I guess, afore we start. I concait he'll rise considerable airly in the mornin, afore he catches me asleep agin. I'll be wide awake for him next hitch, that's a fact. I'd a ginn a thousand dollars if he had only used Campbell's name instead of mine; for he was a most an almighty villain, and cheated a proper raft of folks, and then shipped himself off to Botany Bay, for fear folks would transport him there; you couldnt rub out Slick, and put in Campbell, could you? that's a good feller; if you would I'd make it worth your while, you may depend.

THE TROTTING HORSE

I was always well mounted; I am fond of a horse, and always piqued myself on having the fastest trotter in the Province. I have made no great progress in the world, I feel doubly, therefore, the pleasure of not being surpassed on the road. I never feel so well or so cheerful as on horseback, for there is something exhilirating in quick motion; and, old as I am, I feel a pleasure in making any person whom I meet on the way put his horse to the full gallop, to keep pace with my trotter. Poor Ethiope! you recollect him, how he was wont to lay back his ears on his arched neck, and push away from all competition. He is done, poor fellow! the spavin spoiled his speed, and he now roams at large upon 'my farm at Truro.' Mohawk never failed me till this summer. I pride myself, (you may laugh at such childish weakness in a man of my age,) but still, I pride myself in taking the conceit out of coxcombs I meet on the road, and on the ease with which I can leave a fool behind, whose nonsense disturbs my solitary musings. On my last journey to Fort Lawrence, as the beautiful view of Colchester had just opened upon me, and as I was contemplating its richness and exquisite scenery, a tall thin man, with hollow cheeks and bright twinkling black eyes, on a good bay horse, somewhat out of condition, overtook me; and drawing up, said, I guess you started early this morning, Sir? I did, Sir, I replied. You did not come from Halifax, I presume, Sir, did you? in a dialect too rich to be mistaken as genuine Yankee. And which way may you be travelling? asked my inquisitive companion. To Fort Lawrence. Ah! said he, so am I, it is *in my circuit.* The word *circuit* sounded so professional, I looked again at him, to ascertain whether I had ever seen him before, or whether I had met with one of those nameless, but innumerable limbs of the law, who now flourish in every district of the Province. There was a keenness about his eye, and an acuteness of expression, much in favor of the law; but the dress, and general bearing of the man, made against the supposition. His was not the coat of a man who can afford to wear an old coat, nor was it one of 'Tempest & More's,' that distinguish country lawyers from country boobies. His clothes were well made, and of good materials, but looked as if their owner had shrunk a little since they were made for him; they hung somewhat loose on him. A large brooch, and some superfluous seals and gold keys, which ornamented his outward man, looked 'New England' like. A visit to the States, had perhaps, I thought, turned this Colchester beau into a Yankee fop. Of what consequence was it to me who he was – in either case I had nothing to do with him, and I desired neither his acquaintance nor his company – still I could not but ask myself who can this man be? I am not aware, said I, that there is a court sitting at this time at Cumberland? Nor am I, said my friend. What then could he have to do with the circuit? It occurred to me he must be a Methodist preacher. I looked again, but his appearance again puzzled me. His attire might do – the colour might be suitable – the broad brim not out of place; but there

was a want of that staidness of look, that seriousness of countenance, that expression, in short, so characteristic of the clergy.
I could not account for my idle curiosity – a curiosity which,
in him, I had the moment before viewed both with suspicion
and disgust; but so it was – I felt a desire to know who he could
be who was neither lawyer nor preacher, and yet talked of his
circuit with the gravity of both. How ridiculous, I thought to
myself, is this; I will leave him. Turning towards him, I said, I
feared I should be late for breakfast, and must therefore bid
him good morning. Mohawk felt the pressure of my knees, and
away we went at a slapping pace. I congratulated myself on
conquering my own curiosity, and on avoiding that of my travelling companion. This, I said to myself, this is the value of a
good horse; I patted his neck – I felt proud of him. Presently I
heard the steps of the unknown's horse – the clatter increased.
Ah, my friend, thought I, it won't do; you should be well
mounted if you desire my company; I pushed Mohawk faster,
faster, faster – to his best. He outdid himself; he had never
trotted so handsomely – so easily – so well.

I guess that is a pretty considerable smart horse, said the
stranger, as he came beside me, and apparently reined in, to
prevent his horse passing me; there is not, I reckon, so spry a
one on *my circuit*.

Circuit, or no circuit, one thing was settled in my mind;
he was a Yankee, and a very impertinent Yankee, too. I felt
humbled, my pride was hurt, and Mohawk was beaten. To
continue this trotting contest was humiliating; I yielded,
therefore, before the victory was palpable, and pulled up. Yes,
continued he, a horse of pretty considerable good action, and
a pretty fair trotter, too, I guess. Pride must have a fall – I
confess mine was prostrate in the dust. These words cut me to
the heart. What! is it come to this, poor Mohawk, that you,

the admiration of all but the envious, the great Mohawk, the standard by which all other horses are measured – trots next to Mohawk, only yields to Mohawk, looks like Mohawk – that you are, after all, only a counterfeit, and pronounced by a straggling Yankee to be merely 'a pretty fair trotter!' If he was trained, I guess that he might be made do a little more. Excuse me, but if you divide your weight between the knee and the stirrup, rather most on the knee, and rise forward on the saddle, so as to leave a little daylight between you and it, I hope I may never ride *this circuit again*, if you don't get a mile more an hour out of him. What! not enough, I mentally groaned, to have my horse beaten, but I must be told that I don't know how to ride him; and that, too, by a Yankee – Aye, there's the rub – a Yankee what? Perhaps a half-bred puppy, half Yankee, half Blue Nose. As there is no escape, I'll try to make out my riding master. *Your circuit*, said I, my looks expressing all the surprise they were capable of – your circuit, pray what may that be? Oh, said he, the eastern circuit – I am on the eastern circuit, sir. I have heard, said I, feeling that I now had a lawyer to deal with, that there is a great deal of business on this circuit – pray, are there many cases of importance? There is a pretty fair business to be done, at least there has been, but the cases are of no great value – we do not make much out of them, we get them up very easy, but they don't bring much profit. What a beast, thought I, is this; and what a curse to a country, to have such an unfeeling pettifogging rascal practising in it – a horse jockey, too – what a finished character! I'll try him on that branch of his business.

That is a superior animal you are mounted on, said I – I seldom meet one that can travel with mine. Yes, said he coolly, a considerable fair traveller, and most particular good bottom. I hesitated, this man who talks with such unblushing effrontery of getting up cases, and making profit out of them, cannot be offended at the question – yes, I will put it to him. Do you feel an inclination to part with him? I never part with a horse sir, that suits me, said he – I am fond of a horse – I don't like to ride in the dust after every one I meet, and I allow no man to pass me but when I choose. Is it possible, I thought, that he can know me; that he has heard of my foible, and is quizzing me, or have I this feeling in common with him. But, continued I, you might supply yourself again. Not on *this circuit*, I guess, said he, nor yet in Campbell's circuit. Campbell's circuit – pray, sir, what is that? That, said he, is the western – and Lampton rides the shore circuit; and as for the people on the shore, they know so little of horses, that Lampton tells me, a man from Aylesford once sold a hornless ox there, whose tail he had cut and nicked for a horse of the Goliath breed. I should think, said I, that Mr. Lampton must have no lack of cases among such enlightened clients. Clients, sir, said my friend, Mr. Lampton is not a lawyer. I beg pardon, I thought you said he rode the *circuit*. We call it a circuit, said the stranger, who seemed by no means flattered by the mistake – we divide the Province, as in the Almanack, into circuits, in each of which we separately carry on our business of manufacturing and selling clocks. There are few, I guess, said the Clockmaker, who go upon *tick* as much as we do, who have so little use for lawyers; if attornies could wind a *man up again*, after he has been fairly *run down*, I guess they'd be a pretty harmless sort of folks. This explanation restored my good humour, and as I could not quit my companion, and he did not feel disposed to leave me, I made up my mind to travel with him to Fort Lawrence, the limit of *his circuit*.

THE CLOCKMAKER

I had heard of Yankee clock pedlars, tin pedlars, and bible pedlars, especially of him who sold Polyglot Bibles *(all in English)* to the amount of sixteen thousand pounds. The house of every substantial farmer had three substantial ornaments, a wooden clock, a tin reflector, and a Polyglot Bible. How is it that an American can sell his wares, at whatever price he pleases, where a Blue Nose would fail to make a sale at all? I will enquire of the Clockmaker the secret of his success. What a pity it is, Mr. *Slick*, (for such was his name,) what a pity it is, said I, that you, who are so successful in teaching these people the value of *clocks*, could not also teach them the value of *time*. I guess, said he, they have got that ring to grow on their horns yet, which every four year old has in our country. We reckon hours and minutes to be dollars and cents. They do nothing in these parts, but eat, drink, smoke, sleep, ride about, lounge at taverns, make speeches at temperance meetings, and talk about "*House of Assembly*." If a man don't hoe his corn, and he don't get a crop, he says it is all owing to the Bank; and if he runs into debt and is sued, why says the lawyers are a curse to the country. They are a most idle set of folks, I tell you. But how is it, said I, that you manage to sell such an immense number of clocks, (which certainly cannot be called necessary articles,) among a people with whom there seems to be so great a scarcity of money.

Mr. Slick paused, as if considering the propriety of answering the question, and looking me in the face, said, in a confidential tone, Why, I don't care if I do tell you, for the market is glutted, and I shall quit this circuit. It is done by a knowledge of *soft sawder* and *human natur*. But here is Deacon Flint's, said he, I have but one clock left, and I guess I will sell it to him. At the gate of a most comfortable looking farm house stood Deacon Flint, a respectable old man, who had understood the value of time better than most of his neighbors, if one might judge from the appearance of every thing about him. After the usual salutation, an invitation to "alight" was accepted by Mr. Slick, who said, he wished to take leave of Mrs. Flint before he left Colchester. We had hardly entered the house, before the Clockmaker pointed to the view from the window, and, addressing himself to me, said, if I was to tell them in Connecticut, there was such a farm as this away down east here in Nova Scotia, they would'nt believe me – why there aint such a location in all New England. The Deacon has a hundred acres of dyke – seventy, said the Deacon, only seventy. Well, seventy; but then there is your fine deep bottom, why I could run a ramrod into it – Interval, we call it, said the Deacon, who, though evidently pleased at this eulogium, seemed to wish the experiment of the ramrod to be tried in the right place – well interval if you please, (though Professor Eleazer Cumstick, in his work on Ohio, calls them bottoms,) is just as good as dyke. Then there is that water privilege, worth 3 or $4,000, twice as good as what Governor Cass paid $15,000 for. I wonder, Deacon, you don't put up a carding mill on it: the same works would carry a turning lathe, a shingle machine, a circular saw, grind bark, and ————. Too old, said the Deacon, too old for all those speculations – old, repeated the Clockmaker, not you; why you are worth half a dozen of the young men we see, now-a-days, you are young enough to have – here he said something in a lower tone of voice, which I did not distinctly hear; but whatever it was, the Deacon was pleased, he smiled and said he did not think of such things now. But your beasts, dear me, your beasts must be put in and have a feed; saying which, he went out to order them to be taken to the stable. As the old gentleman closed the door after him, Mr. Slick drew near to me, and said in an under tone, that is what I call "*soft sawder.*" An Englishman would pass that man as a sheep passes a hog in a pasture, without looking at him; or, said he, looking rather archly, if he was mounted on a pretty smart horse, I guess he'd trot away, *if he could.* Now I find – here his lecture on "*soft sawder*" was cut short by the entrance of Mrs. Flint. Jist come to say good bye, Mrs. Flint. What, have you sold all your clocks? yes, and very low, too, for money is scarce, and I wished to close the concarn; no, I am wrong in saying all, for I have just one left. Neighbor Steel's wife asked to have the refusal of it, but I guess I won't sell it; I had but two of them, this one and the feller of it, that I sold Governor Lincoln. General Green, the Secretary of State for Maine, said he'd give me 50 dollars for this here one – it has composition wheels and patent axles, it is a beautiful article – a real first chop – no mistake, genuine superfine, but I guess I'll take it back; and beside, Squire Hawk might think kinder harder, that I did not give him the offer. Dear me, said Mrs. Flint, I should like to see it, where is it? It is in a chest of mine over the way, at Tom Tape's store, I guess he can ship it on to Eastport. That's a good man, said Mrs. Flint, jist let's look at it. Mr. Slick, willing to oblige, yielded to these entreaties, and soon produced the clock – a gawdy, highly varnished, trumpery looking affair. He placed it on the chimney-piece, where its beauties were pointed out and duly appreciated by Mrs. Flint, whose admiration was about ending in a proposal, when Mr. Flint returned from giving his directions about the care of the horses. The Deacon praised the clock, he too thought it a handsome one; but the Deacon was a prudent man, he had a watch, he was sorry, but he had no occasion for a clock. I guess you're in the wrong furrow this time, Deacon, it ant for sale, said Mr. Slick; and if it was, I reckon neighbor Steel's wife would have it, for she gives me no peace about it. Mrs. Flint said, that Mr. Steel had enough to do, poor man, to pay his interest, without buying clocks for his wife. It's no concarn of mine, said Mr. Slick, as long as he pays me, what he has to do, but I guess I don't want to sell it, and beside it comes too high; that clock can't be made at Rhode Island under 40 dollars. Why it ant possible, said the Clockmaker, in apparent surprise, looking at his watch, why as I'm alive it is 4 o'clock, and if I hav'nt been two hours here – how on airth shall I reach River Philip to-night? I'll tell you what, Mrs. Flint, I'll leave the clock in your care till I return on my way to the States – I'll set it a going and put it to the right time. As soon as this operation was performed, he delivered the key to the deacon with a sort of serio-comic injunction to wind up the clock every Saturday night, which Mrs. Flint said she would take care should be done, and promised to remind her husband of it, in case he should chance to forget it.

That, said the Clockmaker as soon as we were mounted, that I call '*human natur!*' Now that clock is sold for 40 dollars – it cost me just 6 dollars and 50 cents. Mrs. Flint will never let Mrs. Steel have the refusal – nor will the deacon learn until I call for the clock, that having once indulged in the use of a superfluity, how difficult it is to give it up. We can do without any article of luxury we have never had, but when once obtained, it is not '*in human natur*' to surrender it voluntarily. Of fifteen thousand sold by myself and partners in this Province, twelve thousand were left in this manner, and only ten clocks were ever returned – when we called for them they invariably bought them. We trust to '*soft sawder*' to get them into the house, and to '*human natur*' that they never come out of it.

THE SILENT GIRLS

D o you see them are swallows, said the Clockmaker, how low they fly? Well I presume we shall have rain right away, and them noisy critters, them gulls how close they keep to the water, down there in the Shubenacadie; well that's a sure sign. If we study natur, we don't want no thermometer. But I guess we shall be in time to get under cover in a shingle-maker's shed about three miles ahead on us. We had just reached the deserted hovel when the rain fell in torrents.

I reckon, said the Clockmaker, as he sat himself down on a bundle of shingles, I reckon they are bad off for inns in this country. When a feller is too lazy to work here, he paints his name over his door, and calls it a tavern, and as like as not he makes the whole neighborhood as lazy as himself – it is about as easy to find a good inn in Halifax, as it is to find wool on a goat's back. An inn, to be a good concarn, must be built a purpose, you can no more make a good tavern out of a common dwelling house, I expect, than a good coat out of an old pair of trowsers. They are etarnal lazy, you may depend – now there might be a grand spec made there, in building a good Inn and a good Church. What a sacrilegious and unnatural union, said

I, with most unaffected surprise. Not at all, said Mr. Slick, we build both on speculation in the States, and make a good deal of profit out of 'em too, I tell you. We look out a good sightly place, in a town like Halifax, that is pretty considerably well peopled, with folks that are good marks; and if there is no real right down good preacher among them, we build a handsome Church, touched off like a New York liner, a real taking looking thing – and then we look out for a preacher, a crack man, a regular ten horse power chap – well, we hire him, and we have to give pretty high wages too, say twelve hundred or sixteen hundred dollars a year. We take him at first on trial for a Sabbath or two, to try his paces, and if he takes with the folks, if he goes down well, we clinch the bargain, and let and sell the pews; and, I tell you it pays well and makes a real good investment. There were few better specs among us than Inns and Churches, until the rail roads came on the carpet – as soon as the novelty of the new preacher wears off, we hire another, and that keeps up the steam. I trust it will be long, very long, my friend, said I, ere the rage for speculation introduces "the money changers into the temple," with us. Mr. Slick looked at me with a most ineffable expression of pity and surprise. Depend on it, Sir, said he, with a most philosophical air, this Province is much behind the intelligence of the age. But if it is behind us in that respect, it is a long chalk ahead on us in others.

I never seed or heard tell of a country that had so many natural privileges as this. Why there are twice as many harbors and water powers here, as we have all the way from Eastport to New Or*leens*. They have all they can ax, and more than they desarve. They have iron, coal, slate, grindstone, lime, firestone, gypsum, freestone, and a list as long as an auctioneer's catalogue. But they are either asleep, or stone blind to them. Their shores are crowded with fish, and their lands covered with wood. A government that lays as light on 'em as a down counterpin, and no taxes. Then look at their dykes. The Lord seems to have made 'em on purpose for such lazy folks. If you were to tell the citizens of our country, that these dykes had been cropped for a hundred years without manure, they'd say, they guessed you had seen Col. Crockett, the greatest hand at a flam in our nation. You have heerd tell of a man who could'nt see London for the houses, I tell you, if we had this country, you could'nt see the harbors for the shipping. There'd be a rush of folks to it, as there is in one of our inns, to the dinner table, when they sometimes get jammed together in the door-way, and a man has to take a running leap over their heads, afore he can get in. A little nigger boy in New York found a diamond worth 2,000 dollars; well, he sold it to a watchmaker for 50 cents – the little critter did'nt know no better. *Your people are just like the nigger boy, they don't know the value of their diamond.*

Do you know the reason monkeys are no good? because they chatter all day long – so do the niggers – and so do the Blue Noses of Nova Scotia – its all talk and no work; now, with us its all work and no talk – in our ship yards, our factories, our mills, and even in our vessels, there's no talk – a man can't work and talk too. I guess if you were at the factories at Lowell we'd show you a wonder – *five hundred galls at work together all in silence*. I don't think our great country has such a real natural curiosity as that – I expect the world don't contain the beat of that; for a woman's tongue goes so slick of itself, without water power or steam, and moves so easy on its hinges, that its no easy matter to put a spring stop on it, I tell you – it comes as natural as drinkin mint julip.

I don't pretend to say the galls don't nullify the rule, sometimes at intermission and arter hours, but when they do, if they don't let go, then its a pity. You have heerd a school come out, of little boys, Lord its no touch to it; or a flock of geese at it, they are no more a match for em than a pony is for a coach-horse. But when they are at work, all's as still as sleep and no snoring. I guess we have a right to brag o' that invention – we trained the dear critters, so they don't think of striking the minutes and seconds no longer.

Now the folks of Halifax take it all out in talking – they talk of steamboats, whalers and rail roads – but they all end where they begin – in talk. I don't think I'd be out in my latitude, if I was to say they beat the women kind at that. One feller says, I talk of going to England – another says, I talk of going to the Country – while a third says, I talk of going to sleep. If we happen to speak of such things, we say: 'I'm right off down East; or I'm away off South,' and away we go, jist like a streak of lightning.

When we want folks to talk, we pay 'em for it, such as ministers, lawyers, and members of congress: but then we expect the use of their tongues, and not their hands; and when we pay folks to work, we expect the use of their hands, and not their tongues. I guess work don't come kind o' natural to the people of this Province, no more than it does to a full bred horse. I expect they think they have a little *too much blood* in 'em for work, for they are near about as proud as they are lazy.

Now the bees know how to sarve out such chaps, for they have their drones too. Well they reckon its no fun, a making honey all summer, for these idle critters to eat all winter – so they give 'em Lynch Law. They have a regular built mob of citizens, and string up the drones like the Vixburg gamblers. Their maxim is, and not a bad one neither I guess, 'no work, no honey.'

CONVERSATIONS AT THE RIVER PHILIP

It was late before we arrived at Pugnose's Inn – the evening was cool, and a fire was cheering and comfortable. Mr. Slick declined any share in the bottle of wine, he said he was dyspeptic; and a glass or two soon convinced me, that it was likely to produce in me something worse than dyspepsy. It was speedily removed and we drew up to the fire. Taking a small penknife from his pocket, he began to whittle a thin piece of dry wood, which lay on the hearth; and, after musing some time said, I guess you've never been in the States. I replied that I had not, but that before I returned to England I proposed visiting that country. There, said he, you'll see the great Daniel Webster – he's a great man, I tell you; King William, number 4, I guess, would be no match for him as an orator – he'd talk him out of sight in half an hour. If he was in your house of Commons, I reckon he'd make some of your great folks look pretty streaked – he's a true patriot and statesman, the first in our country, and a most particular cute Lawyer. There was a Quaker chap too cute for him once tho'. This Quaker, a pretty knowin' old shaver, had a cause down to Rhode Island; so he went to Daniel to hire him to go down and plead his case for him; so says he, Lawyer Webster what's your fee? Why, says Daniel, let me see, I have to go down south to Washington, to plead the great Insurance case of the Hartford Company – and I've got to be at Cincinnati to attend the Convention, and I dont see how I can go to Rhode Island without great loss and great fatigue; it would cost you may be more than you'd be willing to give. Well, the Quaker looked pretty white about the gills, I tell you, when he heard this, for he could not do without him no how, and he did not like this preliminary talk of his at all – at last he made bold to ask him the worst of it, what he would take; why, says Daniel, I always liked the Quakers, they are a quiet peaceable people who never go to law if they can help it, and it would be better for our great country if there were more such people in it. I never seed or heerd tell of any harm in em except going the whole figure for Gineral Jackson, and that everlastin almighty villain, Van Buren; yes, I love the Quakers, I hope they'll go the Webster ticket yet – and I'll go for you as low as I can any way afford, say 1000 dollars. The Quaker well nigh fainted when he heerd this, but he was pretty deep too; so, says he, Lawyer, that's a great deal of money, but I have more causes there, if I give you the 1000 dollars will you plead the other cases I shall have to give you? Yes, says Daniel, I will to the best of my humble abilities; so down they went to Rhode Island, and Daniel tried the case and carried it for the Quaker. Well, the Quaker he goes round to all the folks that had suits in court, and says he what will you give me if I get the great Daniel to plead for you? It cost me 1000 dollars for a fee, but now he and I are pretty thick, and as he is on the spot, I'd get him to plead cheap for you – so he got three hundred dollars from one, and two from another and so on, until he got eleven hundred dollars, jist one hundred dollars more than he gave. Daniel was in a great rage when he heerd this; what, said he, do you think I would agree to your letting me out like a horse to hire? Friend Daniel, said the Quaker, didst thou not undertake to plead all such cases as I should have to give thee? If thou wilt not stand to thy agreement, neither will I stand to mine. Daniel laughed out ready to split his sides at this. Well, says he, I guess I might as well stand still for you to put the bridle on this time, for you have fairly pinned me up in a corner of the fence any how – so he went good humouredly to work and pleaded them all.

This lazy fellow, Pugnose, continued the Clockmaker, that keeps this inn, is going to sell off and go to the States; he says he has to work too hard here; that the markets are dull, and the winters too long; and he guesses he can live easier there; I guess he'll find his mistake afore he has been there long. Why our country aint to be compared to this, on no account whatever; our country never made us to be the great nation we are, but we made the country. How on airth could we, if we were all like old Pugnose, as lazy as ugly, make that cold thin soil of New England produce what it does? Why, Sir, the land between Boston and Salem would starve a flock of geese; and yet look at Salem, it has more cash than would buy Nova Scotia from the King. We rise early, live frugally, and work late: what we get we take care of. To all this we add enterprise and intelligence – a feller who finds work too hard here, had better not go to the States. I met an Irishman, one Pat Lannigan, last week, who had just returned from the States; why, says I, Pat, what on airth brought you back? Bad luck to them, says Pat, if I warn't properly bit. What do you get a day in Nova Scotia? says Judge Beler to me. Four shillings, your Lordship, says I. There are no Lords here, says he, we are all free. Well, says he, I'll give you as much in one day as you can earn there in two; I'll give you eight shillings. Long life to your

Lordship, says I. So next day to it I went with a party of men a-digging a piece of canal, and if it wasn't a hot day my name is not Pat Lannigan. Presently I looked up and straightened my back; says I to a comrade of mine, Mick, says I, I'm very dry; with that, says the overseer, we don't allow gentlemen to talk at their work in this country. Faith, I soon found out for my two days' pay in one, I had to do two days' work in one, and pay two weeks' board in one, and at the end of a month, I found myself no better off in pocket than in Nova Scotia; while the devil a bone in my body that didn't ache with pain: and as for my nose, it took to bleeding, and bled day and night entirely. Upon my soul, Mr. Slick, said he, the poor laborer does not last long in your country; what with new rum, hard labor, and hot weather, you'll see the graves of the Irish each side of the canals, for all the world like two rows of potatoes in a field that have forgot to come up. It is a land, Sir, continued the Clockmaker, of hard work. We have two kind of slaves, the niggers and the white slaves. All European laborers and blacks, who come out to us, do our hard bodily work, while we direct it to a profitable end; neither rich nor poor, high nor low, with us, eat the bread of idleness. Our whole capital is in active operation, and our whole population is in active employment. An idle fellow, like Pugnose, who runs away to us, is clapt into harness afore he knows where he is, and is made to work; like a horse that refuses to draw, he is put into the Teamboat; he finds some before him and others behind him, *he must either draw*, or be *dragged to death*.

JUSTICE PETTIFOG

I n the morning the Clockmaker informed me that a
Justice's Court was to be held that day at Pugnose's Inn,
and he guessed he could do a little business among the
country folks that would be assembled there. Some of them,
he said, owed him for clocks, and it would save him a world
of travelling, to have the Justice and Constable to drive them
up together. If you want a fat wether, there's nothing like
penning up the whole flock in a corner. I guess, said he, if
General Campbell knew what sort of a man that are magistrate was, he'd disband him pretty quick: he's a regular suck
egg – a disgrace to the country. I guess if he acted that way in
Kentucky, he'd get a breakfast of cold lead some morning, out
of the small end of a rifle, he'd find pretty difficult to digest.
They tell me he issues three hundred writs a year, the cost of
which, including that tarnation Constable's fees, can't amount
to nothing less than 3,000 dollars per annum. If the Hon.
Daniel Webster had him afore a jury, I reckon he'd turn him
inside out, and slip him back again, as quick as an old stocking.
He'd paint him to the life, as plain to be known as the head
of Gineral Jackson. He's jist a fit feller for Lynch law, to be

23

tried, hanged, and damned, all at once – there's more nor him in the country – there's some of the breed in every county in the Province. Jist one or two to do the dirty work, as we keep niggers, for jobs that would give a white man the cholera. They ought to pay his passage, as we do with such critters, tell him his place is taken in the Mail Coach, and if he is found here after twenty four hours, they'd make a carpenter's plumb-bob of him, and hang him outside the church steeple, to try if it was perpendicular. He almost always gives judgment for plaintiff, and if the poor defendant has an offset, he makes him sue it, so that it grinds a grist both ways for him, like the upper and lower mill stone.

People soon began to assemble, some on foot, and others on horseback and in waggons – Pugnose's tavern was all bustle and confusion – Plaintiffs, Defendants, and witnesses, all talking, quarreling, explaining, and drinking. Here comes the Squire, said one – I'm thinking his horse carries more roguery than law, said another; they must have been in proper want of timber to make a justice of, said a third, when they took such a crooked stick as that; sap headed enough too for refuse, said a stout looking farmer; may be so, said another, but as hard at the heart as a log of elm; howsomever, said a third, I hope it wont be long afore he has the wainy edge scored off of him, any how. Many more such remarks were made, all drawn from familiar objects, but all expressive of bitterness and contempt.

He carried one or two large books with him in his gig, and a considerable roll of papers. As soon as the obsequious Mr. Pugnose saw him at the door, he assisted him to alight, ushered him into the "best room," and desired the constable to attend "the Squire." The crowd immediately entered, and the Constable opened the Court in due form, and commanded silence. Taking out a long list of causes, Mr. Pettifog

commenced reading the names – James Sharp versus John
Slug – call John Slug: John Slug being duly called and not
answering, was defaulted. In this manner he proceeded to
default some 20 or 30 persons; at last he came to a cause,
William Hare versus Dennis O'Brien – call Dennis O'Brien –
here I am, said a voice from the other room – here I am, who
has any thing to say to Dennis O'Brien? Make less noise, sir,
said the Justice, or I'll commit you. Commit me, is it, said
Dennis, take care then, Squire, you don't commit yourself.
You are sued by William Hare for three pounds for a month's
board and lodging, what have you to say to it? Say to it, said
Dennis, did you ever hear what Tim Doyle said when he was
going to be hanged for stealing a pig? says he, if the pig had'nt
squeeled in the bag I'd never have been found out, so I
would'nt – so I'll take warning by Tom Doyle's fate; I say
nothing, let him prove it. Here Mr. Hare was called on for his
proof, but taking it for granted that the board would be admitted, and the defence opened, he was not prepared with proof.
I demand, said Dennis, I demand an unsuit. Here there was a
consultation between the Justice and the Plaintiff, when the
Justice said, I shall not nonsuit him, I shall continue the cause.
What, hang it up till next Court – you had better hang me up
then at once – how can a poor man come here so often – this
may be the entertainment Pugnose advertises for horses, but
by Jacquers, it is no entertainment for me – I admit then,
sooner than come again, I admit it. You admit you owe him
three pounds then for a month's board? I admit no such thing,
I say I boarded with him a month, and was like Pat Moran's
cow at the end of it, at the lifting, bad luck to him. A neighbor was here called who proved that the three pounds might
be the usual price. And do you know I taught his children to
write at the school, said Dennis – you might, answered the

witness – and what is that worth? I don't know – you don't know, faith I believe you're right, said Dennis, for if the children are half as big rogues as the father, they might leave writing alone, or they'd be like to be hanged for forgery. Here Dennis produced his account for teaching five children, two quarters, at 9 shillings a quarter each, £4 10s. I am sorry, Mr. O'Brien, said the Justice, very sorry, but your defence will not avail you, your account is too large for one Justice, any sum over three pounds must be sued before two magistrates – but I only want to offset as much as will pay the board – it can't be done in this shape, said the magistrate; I will consult Justice Dolittle, my neighbor, and if Mr. Hare won't settle with you I will sue it for you. Well, said Dennis, all I have to say is, that there is not so big a rogue as Hare on the whole river, save and except one scoundrel who shall be nameless, making a significant and humble bow to the Justice. Here there was a general laugh throughout the Court – Dennis retired to the next room to indemnify himself by another glass of grog, and venting his abuse against Hare and the Magistrate. Disgusted at the gross partiality of the Justice, I also quitted the Court, fully concurring in the opinion, though not in the language, that Dennis was giving utterance to in the bar room.

Pettifog owed his elevation to his interest at an election. It is to be hoped that his subsequent merits will be as promptly rewarded, by his dismissal from a bench which he disgraces and defiles by his presence.

ANECDOTES

As we mounted our horses to proceed to Amherst, groups of country people were to be seen standing about Pugnose's Inn, talking over the events of the morning, while others were dispersing to their several homes. A pretty prime superfine scoundrel, that Pettifog, said the Clockmaker; he and his constable are well mated, and they've travelled in the same gear so long together, that they make about as nice a yoke of rascals, as you'll meet in a day's ride. They pull together like one rope reeved through two blocks. That are constable was een almost strangled t'other day; and if he had'nt had a little grain more wit than his master, I guess he'd had his wind-pipe stopped as tight as a bladder. There is an outlaw of a feller here, for all the world like one of our Kentucky Squatters, one Bill Smith – a critter that neither fears man nor devil. Sheriff and constable can make no hand of him – they can't catch him no how; and if they do come up with him, he slips through their fingers like an eel: and then, he goes armed, and he can knock the eye out of a squirrel with a ball, at fifty yards hand running – a regular ugly customer. Well, Nabb, the constable, had a writ agin him, and he was cyphering a good while how he should catch him; at last he hit on a plan that he thought was pretty clever, and he scheemed for a chance to try it. So one day he heard that Bill was up at Pugnose's Inn, a settling some business, and was likely to be there all night. Nabb waits till it was considerable late in the evening, and then he takes his horse and rides down to the inn, and hitches his beast behind the hay stack. Then he crawls up to the window and peeps in, and watches there till Bill should go to bed, thinking the best way to catch them are sort of animals is to catch them asleep. Well, he kept Nabb a waiting outside so long, with his talking and singing, that he well nigh fell asleep first himself; at last Bill began to strip for bed. First he takes out a long pocket pistol, examines the priming, and lays it down on the table, near the head of the bed.

When Nabb sees this, he begins to creep like all over, and feel kinder ugly, and rather sick of his job; but when he seed him jump into bed, and heerd him snore out a noise like a man driving pigs to market, he plucked up courage, and thought he might do it easy arter all if he was to open the door softly, and make one spring on him afore he could wake. So round he goes, lifts up the latch of his door as soft as soap, and makes a jump right atop of him, as he lay on the bed. I guess I got you this time, said Nabb; I guess so too, said Bill, but I wish you would'nt lay so plaguy heavy on me – jist turn over, that's a good fellow, will you? With that Bill lays his arm on him to raise him up, for he said he was squeezed as flat as a pancake, and afore Nabb knew where he was, Bill rolled him right over and was atop of him. Then he seized him by the throat, and twisted his pipe till his eyes were as big as saucers, and his tongue grew six inches longer, while he kept making faces for all the world like the pirate that was hanged on Monument Hill at Boston. It was pretty near over with him, when Nabb thought of his spurs; so he just curled up both heels, and drove the spurs right into him; he let him have it jist below his cruper; as Bill was naked he had a fair chance, and he ragged him like the leaf of a book cut open with your finger. At last, Bill could stand it no longer; he let go his hold and roared like a bull, and clapping both hands ahind him, he out of the door like a shot. If it had'nt been for them are spurs, I guess Bill would have saved the hangman a job of Nabb that time.

The Clockmaker was an observing man, and equally communicative. Nothing escaped his notice; he knew every body's genealogy, history and means, and like a driver of an English Stage Coach, was not unwilling to impart what he knew. Do you see that snug looking house there, said he, with a short sarce garden afore it, that belongs to Elder Thomson. The Elder is pretty close fisted, and holds special fast to all he gets. He is a just man and very pious, but I have observed when a man becomes near about too good, he is apt, some-times, to slip a head into avarice, unless he looks sharp arter his girths. A friend of mine in Connecticut, an old sea Captain, who was once let in for it pretty deep, by a man with a broader brim than common, said to me, friend Sam, says he, "I don't like those folks who are too d–n good." There is, I expect, some truth in it, tho' he need'nt have swore at all, but he was an awful hand to swear. Howsomever that may be, there is a story about the Elder, that's not so coarse neither. It appears, an old Minister came there once, to hold a meetin at his house – well, after meetin was over, the Elder took the min-ister all over his farm, which is pretty tidy, I tell you; and he shewed him a great Ox he had, and a swingeing big Pig, that weighed some six or seven hundred weight, that he was plaguy proud of, but he never offered the old minister any thing to eat or drink. The preacher was pretty tired of all this, and seeing no prospect of being asked to partake with the family, and tolerably sharp set, he asked one of the boys to fetch him his horse out of the barn. When he was taking leave of the Elder, (there were several folks by at the time,) says he, Elder Thomson, you have a fine farm here, a very fine farm, indeed; you have a large Ox too, a very large Ox; and I think, said he, I've seen to-day, (turning and looking him full in the face, for he intended to hit him pretty hard,) *I think I have seen to-day the greatest Hog I ever saw in my life.* The neighbors snickered a good deal, and the Elder felt pretty streaked. I guess he'd give his great Pig or his great Ox either, if that story had'nt got wind.

GO AHEAD

Wh-- hen we resumed our conversation, the Clockmaker said, "I guess we are the greatest nation on
the face of the airth, and the most enlightened
too." This was rather too arrogant to pass unnoticed, and I was
about replying, that whatever doubts there might be on that
subject, there could be none whatever that they were the most
modest; when he continued "we go ahead," the Nova Scotians
go "astarn." Our ships go ahead of the ships of other folks, our
steam boats beat the British in speed, and so do our stage
coaches; and I reckon a real right down New York trotter might
stump the univarse for going "ahead." But since we introduced
the Rail Roads if we dont go "ahead" its a pity. We never fairly
knew what going the whole hog was till then; we actilly went
ahead of ourselves, and that's no easy matter I tell you. If they
only had edication here, they might learn to do so too, but
they dont know nothin. You undervalue them, said I, they
have their College and Academies, their grammar schools and
primary institutions, and I believe there are few among them
who cannot read and write.

I guess all that's nothin, said he. As for Latin and Greek, we dont valy it a cent; we teach it, and so we do painting and music, because the English do, and we like to go ahead on em, even in them are things. As for reading, its well enough for them that has nothing to do, and writing is plaguy apt to bring a man to States-prison, particularly if he writes his name so like another man as to have it mistaken for his'n. Cyphering is the thing – if a man knows how to cypher, he is sure to grow rich. We are a 'calculating' people, we all cypher.

A horse that wont go ahead, is apt to run back, and the more you whip him the faster he goes astarn. That's jist the way with the Nova Scotians; they have been running back so fast lately, that they have tumbled over a *Bank* or two, and nearly broke their necks; and now they've got up and shook themselves, they swear their dirty clothes and bloody noses are all owing to the *Banks*. I guess if they wont look ahead for the future, they'll larn to look behind, and see if there's a bank near hand em.

A Bear always goes down a tree *starn foremost*. He is a cunning critter, he knows tante safe to carry a heavy load over his head, and his rump is so heavy, he dont like to trust it over hisn, for fear it might take a lurch, and carry him heels over head, to the ground; so he lets his starn down first, and his head arter. I wish the Blue Noses would find as good an excuse in their rumps for running backwards as he has. But the bear '*cyphers*;' he knows how many pounds his hams weigh, and he '*calculates*' if he carried them up in the air, they might be top heavy for him.

If we had this Province we'd go to work and 'cypher' right off. Halifax is nothing without a river or back country; add nothing to nothing, and I guess you have nothing still – add a Rail Road to the Bay of Fundy, and how much do you git? That requires cyphering – it will cost $300,000 or £75,000 your money – add for notions omitted in the addition column, one third, and it makes even money – £100,00. Interest at 5 per cent £5,000 a year. Now turn over the slate and count up freight – I make it upwards of £25,000 a year. If I had you at the desk, I'd shew you a bill of items.

Now comes "*subtraction*;" deduct cost of engines, wear and tear, and expenses, and what not, and reduce it for shortness down to £5000 a year, the amount of interest. What figures have you got now? you have an investment that pays interest, I guess, and if it dont pay more then I dont know chalk from cheese. But suppose it dont, and that it only yields 2½ per cent, (and it requires good cyphering, I tell you, to say how it would act with folks that like going astarn better than going ahead,) what would them are wise ones say then? Why the critters would say it wont pay; but I say the sum ant half stated. Can you count in your head? Not to any extent, said I. Well, that's an etarnal pity, said the Clockmaker, for I should like to show you *Yankee Cyphering*. What is the entire real estate of Halifax worth, at a valeation? I really cannot say. Ah, said he, I see you dont cypher, and Latin and Greek wont do; them are people had no rail roads. Well, find out, and then only add ten per cent to it, for increased value, and if it don't give the cost of a rail road, then my name is not Sam Slick. Well, the land between Halifax and Ardoise is worth ———— nothing, add 5 per cent to that, and send the sum to the College, and ax the students how much it comes to. But when you get into Hants County, I guess you have land worth coming all the way from Boston to see. His Royal Highness the King, I guess, hasn't got the like in his dominions. Well, add 15 per cent to all them are lands that border on Windsor Basin, and 5 per cent to what butts on Basin of Mines, and then, what do you get? A pretty considerable sum I tell you – but its no use to give you the *chalks*, if you can't keep the *tallies*. Now we will lay down the schoolmaster's assistant, and take up another book every bit and grain as good as that, although these folks affect to sneer at it – I mean human natur. Ah! said I, a knowledge of that was of great service to you, certainly, in the sale of your clock to the old Deacon; let us see how it will assist you now. What does a clock want that's run down? said he. Undoubtedly to be wound up, I replied; I guess you've hit it this time. The folks of Halifax have run down, and they'll never go to all etarnity, till they are wound up into motion; the works are all good, and it is plaguy well cased and set – it only wants a *key*. Put this rail road into operation, and the activity it will inspire into business, the new life it will give the place, will surprise you. Its like lifting a child off its crawling, and putting him on his legs to run – see how the little critter goes ahead arter that. A kurnel, (I don't mean a Kurnel of militia, for we don't valy that breed o' cattle nothing – they do nothing but strut about and screech all day, like peacocks,) but a kurnel of grain, when sowed, will stool into several shoots, and each shoot bear many kurnels, and will multiply itself thus – 4 times 1 is 4, and 4 times 25 is a hundred, (you see all natur cyphers, except the Blue Noses.) Jist so, this here rail road will not perhaps beget other rail roads, but it will beget a spirit of enterprise, that will beget other useful improvements. It will enlarge the sphere and the means of trade, open new sources of traffic and supply – develop resources – and what is of more value perhaps than all – beget motion. It will teach the folks that go astarn or stand stock still, like the statehouse in Boston, (though they do say the foundation of that has moved a little this summer) not only to go *"ahead,"* but to nullify time and space.

Here his horse (who, feeling the animation of his master, had been restive of late) set off at a most prodigious rate of trotting. It was some time before he was reined up. When I overtook him, the Clockmaker said, "this old Yankee horse, you see, understands our word 'go ahead' better nor these Blue Noses."

What is it, he continued, what is it that 'fetters' the heels of a young country, and hangs like 'a poke' around its neck? what retards the cultivation of its soil, and the improvement of its fisheries? – the high price of labor, I guess. Well, what's a rail road? The substitution of mechanical for human and animal labor, on a scale as grand as our great country. Labor is dear in America, and cheap in Europe. A rail road, therefore, is comparatively no manner of use to them, to what it is to us – it does wonders there, but it works miracles here. There it makes the old man younger, but here it makes a child a giant. To us it is river, bridge, road and canal, all one. It saves what we han't got to spare, men, horses, carts, vessels, barges, and what's all in all – time.

Since the creation of the Univarse, I guess it's the greatest invention, arter man. Now this is what I call "cyphering" arter human natur, while figures are cyphering arter "the assistant." These two sorts of cyphering make idecation – and you may depend on't Squire, there is nothing like folks cyphering, if they want to "go ahead."

THE PREACHER THAT WANDERED
FROM HIS TEXT

I guess, said the Clockmaker, we know more of Nova Scotia than the Blue Noses themselves do. The Yankees see further ahead than most folks; they can een a most see round t'other side of a thing; indeed some on them have hurt their eyes by it, and sometimes I think that's the reason such a sight of them wear spectacles. The first I ever heerd tell of Cumberland was from Mr. Everett of Congress; he know'd as much about it as if he had lived here all his days, and may be a little grain more. He is a splendid man that – we class him No. 1, letter A. One night I chanced to go into General Peep's tavern at Boston, and who should I see there but the great Mr. Everett, a studying over a map of the Province of Nova Scotia. Why it aint possible! said I – if that aint Professor Everett, as I am alive! why how do you do, Professor? Pretty well, I give you thanks, said he; how be you? but I aint no longer Professor; I gin that up, and also the trade of Preaching, and took to politics. You don't say so, said I; why what on airth is the cause o' that? Why, says he, look here, Mr. Slick. What *is* the use of reading the Proverbs of Solomon to our free and enlightened citizens, that are every mite and mortal as wise as

36

he was? That are man undertook to say there was nothing new under the sun. I guess he'd think he spoke a little too fast, if he was to see our steam boats, rail roads, and India rubber shoes – three inventions worth more nor all he knew put in a heap together. Well, I don't know, said I, but somehow or another, I guess you'd have found preaching the best speculation in the long run; them are Unitarians pay better than Uncle Sam (we call, said the Clockmaker, the American public Uncle Sam, as you call the British John Bull.)

That remark seemed to grig him a little; he felt oneasy like, and walked twice across the room, fifty fathoms deep in thought; at last he said, which way are you from, Mr. Slick, this hitch? Why, says I, I've been away up south a speculating in nutmegs. I hope, says the Professor, they were a good article, the real right down genuine thing. No mistake, says I, – no mistake, Professor: they were all prime, first chop, but why did you ax that are question? Why, says he, that eternal scoundrel, that Captain John Allspice of Nahant, he used to trade to Charleston, and he carried a cargo once there of fifty barrels of nutmegs: well, he put half a bushel of good ones into each eend of the barrel, and the rest he filled up with wooden ones, so like the real thing, no soul could tell the difference until *he bit one with his teeth*, and that he never thought of doing, until he was first *bit himself.* Well, its been a standing joke with them southerners agin us ever since. It was only tother day at Washington, that everlasting Virginy duellist General Cuffy, afore a number of senators, at the President's house, said to me, 'Well Everett,' says he – 'you know I was always dead agin your Tariff bill, but I have changed my mind since your able speech on it; I shall vote for it now.' 'Give me your hand,' says I, 'General Cuffy; the Boston folks will be dreadful glad when they hear your splendid talents are on our side – I think it will go now – we'll carry it.' 'Yes,' says he, 'your factories down east beat all natur; they go ahead on the English a long chalk.' You may depend I was glad to hear the New Englanders spoken of that way – I felt proud I tell you – 'and,' says he, 'there's one manufacture that might stump all Europe to produce the like.' 'What's that?' says I, looking as pleased all the time as a gall that's tickled. 'Why,' says he, 'the facture of wooden nutmegs; that's a cap sheef that bangs the bush – its a real Yankee patent invention.' With that all the gentlemen set up a laugh, you might have heard away down to Sandy Hook – and the General gig gobbled like a great turkey cock, the half nigger, half alligator like looking villain as he is. I tell you what, Mr. Slick, said the Professor, I wish with all my heart them are damned nutmegs were in the bottom of the sea. That was the first oath I ever heerd him let slip: but he was dreadful ryled, and it made me feel ugly too, for its awful to hear a minister swear; and the only match I know for it, is to hear a regular sneezer of a sinner quote scripture. Says I, Mr. Everett, that's the fruit that politics bear; for my part I never seed a good graft on it yet, that bore any thing good to eat, or easy to digest.

Well, he stood awhile looking down on the carpet, with his hands behind him, quite taken up a cyphering in his head, and then he straightened himself up, and he put his hand upon his heart, just as he used to do in the pulpit, (he looked pretty I tell you) and slowly lifting his hand off his breast, he said, 'Mr. Slick, our tree of liberty was a beautiful tree – a splendid tree – it was a sight to look at; it was well fenced and well protected, and it grew so stately and so handsome, that strangers came from all parts of the globe to see it. They all allowed it was the most splendid thing in the world. Well, the mobs have broken in and tore down the fences, and snapped off the branches, and scattered all the leaves about, and it looks no better than a gallows tree.' 'I am afeared,' said he, 'I tremble to think on it, but I am afeared our ways will no longer be ways of pleasantness, nor our paths, paths of peace; I am, indeed, I vow, Mr. Slick.' He looked so streaked and so chop-fallen, that I felt kinder sorry for him; I actilly thought he'd a boo-hood right out. So, to turn the conversation, says I, Professor, what are great map is that I seed you a studyin' over when I came in? Says he, it's a map of Nova Scotia. That, says he, is a valuable province, a real clever province; we hant got the like on it, but its most plagily in our way. Well, says I, send for Sam Patch (that are man was a great diver, says the Clockmaker, and the last dive he took was off the falls of Niagara, and he was never heerd of agin till tother day, when Captain Enoch Wentworth, of the Susy Ann Whaler, saw him in the South Sea. Why, says Capt. Enoch to him, why Sam, says he, how on airth did you get here? I thought you was drowned at the Canadian lines. Why, says he, I didnt get *on* airth here at all, but I came right slap *through* it. In that are Niagara dive, I went so everlasting deep, I thought it was just as short to come up tother side, so out I came in those parts. If I don't take the shine off the Sea Serpent, when I get back to Boston, then my name's not Sam Patch.)

Well, says I, Professor, send for Sam Patch, the diver, and let him dive down and stick a torpedo in the bottom of the Province and blow it up; or if that won't do, send for some of our steam tow boats from our great Eastern cities, and tow it out to sea; you know there's nothing our folks can't do, when they once fairly take hold on a thing in airnest. Well, that made him laugh; he seemed to forget about the nutmegs, and says he, that's a bright scheme, but it won't do; we shall want the Province some day, and I guess we'll buy it of King William;

they say he is over head and ears in debt, and owes nine hundred millions of pounds starling – we'll buy it, as we did Florida. In the meantime we must have a canal from Bay Fundy to Bay Varte, right through Cumberland neck, by Shittyack, for our fishing vessels to go to Labradore. I guess you must ax leave first, said I; that's jist what I was cyphering at, says he, when you came in. I believe we won't ax them at all, but jist fall to and do it; *its a road of needcessity*. I once heard Chief Justice Marshall of Baltimore say; 'If the people's highway is dangerous – a man may take down a fence – and pass through the fields as a way of *needcessity*;' and we shall do it on that principle, as the way round by Isle Sable is dangerous. I wonder the Nova Scotians don't do it for their own convenience. Said I, it would'nt make a bad speculation that. The critters don't know no better, said he.

Well, says I, the St. John's folks, why don't they? for they are pretty cute chaps them. They remind me, says the Professor, of Jim Billings. You knew Jim Billings, didn't you, Mr. Slick? Oh yes, said I, I knew him. It was he that made such a talk by shipping blankets to the West Indies; the same, says he. Well, I went to see him the other day at Mrs. Lecain's Boarding House, and says I, Billings, you have a nice location here. A plaguy sight too nice, said he. Marm Lecain makes such an etarnal touss about her carpets, that I have to go along that everlasting long entry, and down both staircases, to the street door to spit; and it keeps all the gentlemen a running with their mouths full all day. I had a real bout with a New Yorker this morning, I run down to the street door, and afore I see'd any body a coming, I let go, and I vow if I did'nt let a chap have it all over his white waistcoat. Well, he makes a grab at me, and I shuts the door right to on his wrist, and hooks the door chain taught and leaves him there, and into Marm

Lecain's bed room like a shot, and hides behind the curtain. Well, he roared like a bull, till black Lucretia, one of the house helps, let him go, and they looked into all the gentlemen's rooms and found nobody – so I got out of that are scrape. So, what with Marm Lecain's carpets in the house, and other folks' waistcoats in the street, its too nice a location for me, I guess, so I shall up killoch and off to-morrow to the *Tree* mont.

Now, says the Professor, the St. John's folks are jist like Billings, fifty cents would have bought him a spit box, and saved him all them are journeys to the street door – and a canal at Bay Varte would save the St. John's folks a voyage all round Nova Scotia. Why, they can't get at their own backside settlements, without a voyage most as long as one to Europe. *If we had that are neck of land in Cumberland, we'd have a ship canal there, and a town at each eend of it as big as Portland.* You may talk of Solomon, said the Professor, but if Solomon in all his glory was not arrayed like a lily of the field, neither was he in all his wisdom, equal in knowledge to a real free American citizen. Well, said I, Professor, we are a most enlightened people, that's sartain, but somehow I don't like to hear you run down King Solomon neither; perhaps he warnt quite so wise as Uncle Sam, but then, said I, (drawing close to the Professor, and whispering in his ear, for fear any folks in the bar room might hear me,) but then, said I, may be he was every bit and grain as honest. Says he, Mr. Slick, there are some folks who think a good deal and say but little, and they are wise folks; and there are others agin, who blart right out whatever comes uppermost, and I guess they are pretty considerable superfine darned fools. And with that he turned right around, and sat down to his map and never said another word, lookin' as mad as a hatter the whole blessed time.

YANKEE EATING AND HORSE FEEDING

Did you ever heer tell of Abernethy, a British doctor? said the Clockmaker. Frequently, said I, he was an eminent man, and had a most extensive practice. Well, I reckon he was a vulgar critter that, he replied, he treated the honble. Alden Gobble, secretary to our legation at London, dreadful bad once; and I guess if it had been me he had used that way, I'd a fixed his flint for him, so that he'd think twice afore he'd fire such another shot as that are again. I'd a made him make tracks, I guess, as quick as a dog does a hog from a potatoe field. He'd a found his way out of the hole in the fence a plaguy sight quicker than he came in, I reckon. His manner, said I, was certainly rather unceremonious at times, but he was so honest, and so straightforward, that no person was, I believe, ever seriously offended at him. *It was his way.* Then his way was so plaguy rough, continued the Clockmaker, that he'd been the better, if it had been hammered and mauled down smoother. I'd a levelled him as flat as a flounder. Pray what was his offence? said I. Bad enough you may depend. The honble. Alden Gobble was dyspeptic, and he suffered great oneasiness arter eatin, so he goes to Abernethy for advice. What's the matter with you, said the Doctor? jist that way, without even passing the time o' day with him – What's the matter with you? said he. Why, says Alden, I presume I have the Dyspepsy. Ah! said he, I see; a Yankee swallowed more dollars and cents than he can digest. I am an American citizen, says Alden, with great dignity; I am Secretary to our Legation at the Court of St. James. The devil you are, said Abernethy; then you'll soon get rid of your dyspepsy. I don't see that are inference, said Alden; it dont follow from what you predicate at all – it ant a natural consequence, I guess, that a man should cease to be ill, because he is called by the voice of a free and enlightened people to fill an important office. (The truth is, you could no more trap Alden than you could an Indian. He could see other folks' trail, and made none himself; he was a real diplomatist, and I believe our diplomatists are allowed to be the best in the world.) But I tell you it does follow, said the Doctor; for in the company you'll have to keep, you'll have to eat like a Christian. It was an everlasting pity Alden contradicted him, for he broke out like one ravin distracted mad. I'll be d–d, said he, if ever I saw a Yankee that did'nt bolt his food whole like a Boa Constrictor. How the devil can you expect to digest food, that you neither take the trouble to dissect, nor time to masticate? It's no wonder you lose your teeth, for you never use them; nor your digestion, for you overload it; nor your saliva, for you expend it on the carpets, instead of your food. Its disgusting, its beastly. You Yankees load your stomachs as a Devonshire man does his cart, as full as it can hold, and as fast as he can pitch it with a dung fork, and drive off; and then you complain that such a load of compost is too heavy for you. Dyspepsy, eh! infernal guzzling, you mean. I'll tell you what, Mr. Secretary of Legation, take half the time to eat, that you do to drawl out your words, chew your food half as much as you do your filthy tobacco, and you'll be well in a month. I dont understand such language, said Alden, (for he was fairly ryled, and got his dander up, and when he shows clear grit, he looks wicked ugly, I tell you,) I dont understand such language, Sir; I came here to consult you professionally, and not to be ———. Dont understand! said the Doctor, why its plain English; but here, read my book – and he shoved a book into his hands and left him in an instant, standing alone in the middle of the room. If the honble. Alden Gobble had gone right away and demanded his passports, and returned home with the Legation, in one of our first class frigates, (I guess the English would as soon see pyson as one o' them are Serpents) to Washington, the President and the people would have sustained him in it, I guess, until an apology was offered for the insult to the nation. I guess if it had been me, said Mr. Slick, I'd a headed him afore he slipt out o' the door, and pinned him up agin the wall, and made him bolt his words agin, as quick as he throw'd 'em up, for I never see'd an Englishman that did'nt cut his words as short as he does his horse's tail, close up to the stump. It certainly was very coarse and vulgar language, and I think, said I, that your Secretary had just cause to be offended at such an ungentlemanlike attack, although he showed his good sense in treating it with the contempt it deserved. It was plaguy lucky for the doctor, I tell you, that he cut stick as he did, and made himself scarce, for Alden was an ugly customer; he'd a gin him a proper scalding – he'd a taken the bristles off his hide, as clean as the skin of a spring shote of a pig killed at Christmas. The Clockmaker was evidently excited by his own story, and to indemnify himself for these remarks on his countrymen, he indulged for some time in ridiculing the Nova Scotians.

Do you see that are flock of colts, said he, (as we passed one of those beautiful prairies that render the vallies of Nova

Scotia so verdant and so fertile,) well, I guess they keep too much of that are stock. I heerd an Indian one day ax a tavern keeper for some rum; why, Joe Spawdeeck, said he, I reckon you have got too much already. Too much of any thing, said Joe is not good, but too much rum is jist enough. I guess these Blue Noses think so bout their horses, they are fairly eat up by them, out of house and home, and they are no good neither. They beant good saddle horses, and they beant good draft beasts – they are jist neither one thing nor tother. They are like the drink of our Connecticut folks. At mowing time they use molasses and water, nasty stuff only fit to catch flies – it spiles good water and makes bad beer. No wonder the folks are poor. Look at them are great dykes; well, they all go to feed horses; and look at their grain fields on the upland; well, they are all sowed with oats to feed horses, and they buy their bread from us: so we feed the asses, and they feed the horses. If I had them critters on that are marsh, on a location of mine, I'd jist take my rifle and shoot every one on them; the nasty yo necked, cat hammed, heavy headed, flat eared, crooked shanked, long legged, narrow chested, good for nothin brutes; they aint worth their keep one winter. I vow, I wish one of these Blue Noses, with his go-to-meetin clothes on, coat tails pinned up behind like a leather blind of a Shay, an old spur on one heel, and a pipe stuck through his hat band, mounted on one of these limber timbered critters, that moves its hind legs like a hen scratchin gravel, was sot down in Broadway, in New York, for a sight. Lord! I think I hear the West Point cadets a larfin at him. Who brought that are scare-crow out of standin corn and stuck him here? I guess that are citizen came from away down east out of the Notch of the White Mountains. Here comes the Cholera doctor, from Canada – not from Canada, I guess, neither, for he don't *look as if he had ever been among the rapids.* If they would'nt poke fun at him its a pity. If they'd keep less horses, and more sheep, they'd have food and clothing, too, instead of buying both. I vow I've larfed afore now till I have fairly wet myself a cryin, to see one of these folks catch a horse: may be he has to go two or three miles of an arrand. Well, down he goes on the dyke with a bridle in one hand, and an old tin pan in another, full of oats, to catch his beast. First he goes to one flock of horses, and then to another, to see if he can find his own critter. At last he gets sight on him, and goes softly up to him, shakin of his oats, and a coaxin him, and jist as he goes to put his hand upon him, away he starts all head and tail, and the rest with him; that starts another flock, and they set a third off, and at last every troop on 'em goes, as if Old Nick was arter them, till they amount to two or three hundred in a drove. Well, he chases them clear across the Tantramer marsh, seven miles good, over ditches, creeks, mire holes, and flag ponds, and then they turn and take a fair chase for it back again seven miles more. By this time, I presume, they are all pretty considerably well tired, and Blue Nose, he goes and gets up all the men folks in the neighborhood, and catches his beast, as they do a moose arter he is fairly run down; so he runs fourteen miles, to ride two, because he is in a tarnation hurry. Its e'en a most equal to eatin soup with a fork, when you are short of time. It puts me in mind of catching birds by sprinkling salt on their tails; its only one horse a man can ride out of half a dozen, arter all. One has no shoes, tother has a colt, one arnt broke, another has a sore back, while a fifth is so etarnal cunnin, all Cumberland could'nt catch him, till winter drives him up to the barn for food.

Most of them are dyke marshes have what they call '*honey pots*' in 'em; that is a deep hole all full of squash, where you can't find no bottom. Well, every now and then, when a feller goes to look for his horse, he sees his tail a stickin right out an eend, from one of these honey pots, and wavin like a head of broom corn; and sometimes you see two or three trapped there, e'en a most smothered, everlastin' tired, half swimmin' half wadin, like rats in a molasses cask. When they find 'em in that are pickle, they go and get ropes, and tie 'em tight round their necks, and half hang 'em to make 'em float, and then haul 'em out. Awful looking critters they be, you may depend, when they do come out; for all the world like half drowned kittens – all slinkey – slimey – with their great long tails glued up like a swab of oakum dipped in tar. If they don't look foolish its a pity? Well, they have to nurse these critters all winter, with hot mashes, warm covering, and what not, and when spring comes, they mostly die, and if they don't they are never no good arter. I wish with all my heart half the horses in the country were barrelled up in these here 'honey pots,' and then there'd be near about one half too many left for profit. Jist look at one of these barn yards in the spring – half a dozen half starved colts, with their hair lookin a thousand ways for Sunday, and their coats hangin in tatters, and half a dozen good for nothin old horses, a crowdin out the cows and sheep.

Can you wonder that people who keep such an unprofitable stock, come out of the small eend of the horn in the long run?

THE ROAD TO A WOMAN'S HEART –
THE BROKEN HEART

As we approached the Inn at Amherst, the Clockmaker grew uneasy. Its pretty well on in the evening, I guess, said he, and Marm Pugwash is as onsartain in her temper as a mornin in April; its all sunshine or all clouds with her, and if she's in one of her tantrums, she'll stretch out her neck and hiss, like a goose with a flock of goslins. I wonder what on airth Pugwash was a thinkin on, when he signed articles of partnership with that are woman; she's not a bad lookin piece of furniture neither, and its a proper pity sich a clever woman should carry such a stiff upper lip – she reminds me of our old minister Joshua Hopewell's apple trees. The old minister had an orchard of most particular good fruit, for he was a great hand at buddin, graftin, and what not, and the orchard (it was on the south side of the house) stretched right up to the road. Well, there were some trees hung over the fence, I never seed such bearers, the apples hung in ropes, for all the world like strings of onions, and the fruit was beautiful. Nobody touched the minister's apples, and when other folks lost theirn from the boys, hisn always hung there like bait to a hook, but there never was so much as a nibble at em.

So I said to him one day, Minister, said I, how on airth do you manage to keep your fruit that's so exposed, when no one else cant do it nohow. Why, says he, they are dreadful pretty fruit, ant they? I guess, said I, there ant the like on em in all Connecticut. Well, says he, I'll tell you the secret, but you need'nt let on to no one about it. That are row next the fence, I grafted it myself, I took great pains to get the right kind, I sent clean up to Roxberry, and away down to Squaw-neck Creek, (I was afeared he was agoin to give me day and date for every graft, being a terrible long-winded man in his stories,) so says I, I know that, minister, but how do you preserve them? Why I was a goin to tell you, said he, when you stopped me. That are outward row I grafted myself with the choicest kind I could find, and I succeeded. They are beautiful, but so etarnal sour, no human soul can eat them. Well, the boys think the old minister's graften has all succeeded about as well as that row, and they sarch no farther. They snicker at my graften, and I laugh in my sleeve, I guess, at their penetration.

Now, Marm Pugwash is like the Minister's apples, very temptin fruit to look at, but desperate sour. If Pugwash had a watery mouth when he married, I guess its pretty puckery by this time. However, if she goes to act ugly, I'll give her a dose of 'soft sawder,' that will take the frown out of her frontispiece, and make her dial-plate as smooth as a lick of copal varnish. Its a pity she's such a kickin devil, too, for she has good points – good eye – good foot – neat pastern – fine chest – a clean set of limbs, and carries a good ————. But here we are, now you'll see what 'soft sawder' will do.

When we entered the house, the traveller's room was all in darkness, and on opening the opposite door into the sitting room, we found the female part of the family extinguishing the fire for the night. Mrs. Pugwash had a broom in her hand,

and was in the act (the last act of female housewifery) of sweeping the hearth. The strong flickering light of the fire, as it fell upon her tall fine figure and beautiful face, revealed a creature worthy of the Clockmaker's comments. Good evening, Marm, said Mr. Slick, how do you do, and how's Mr. Pugwash? He, said she, why he's been abed this hour, you don't expect to disturb him this time of night I hope. Oh no, said Mr. Slick, certainly not, and I am sorry to have disturbed you, but we got detained longer than we expected; I am sorry that ————. So am I, said she, but if Mr. Pugwash will keep an Inn when he has no occasion to, his family cant expect no rest. Here the Clockmaker, seeing the storm gathering, stooped down suddenly, and staring intently, held out his hand and exclaimed, well if that aint a beautiful child – come here, my little man and shake hands along with me – well I declare if that are little feller aint the finest child I ever seed – what, not abed yet? ah you rogue, where did you get them are pretty rosy cheeks; stole them from mamma, eh? Well, I wish my old mother could see that child, it is such a treat. In our country, said he, turning to me, the children are all as pale as chalk, or as yaller as an orange. Lord, that are little feller would be a show in our country – come to me my man. Here the soft sawder began to operate. Mrs. Pugwash said in a milder tone than we had yet heard, 'go my dear to the gentleman, go dear.' Mr. Slick kissed him, asked him if he would go to the States along with him, told him all the little girls there would fall in love with him, for they didn't see such a beautiful face once in a month of Sundays. Black eyes, let me see, ah mamma's eyes too, and black hair also; as I am alive, why you are mamma's own boy, the very image of mamma. Do be seated, gentlemen, said Mrs. Pugwash – Sally make a fire in the next room. She ought to be proud of you, he continued. Well, if I live to return here, I must paint your face, and have it put on my clocks, and our folks will buy the clocks for the sake of the face. Did you ever see, said he, again addressing me, such a likeness between one human and another, as between this beautiful little boy and his mother. I am sure you have had no supper, said Mrs. Pugwash to me; you must be hungry and weary, too – I will get you a cup of tea. I am sorry to give you so much trouble, said I. Not the least trouble in the world, she replied, on the contrary a pleasure. We were then shown into the next room, where the fire was now blazing up, but Mr. Slick protested he could not proceed without the little boy, and lingered behind me to ascertain his age, and concluded by asking the child if he had any aunts that looked like mamma.

As the door closed, Mr. Slick said, it's a pity she don't go well in gear. The difficulty with those critters is to get them to start, arter that there is no trouble with them if you don't check 'em too short. If you do, they'll stop again, run back and kick like mad, and then Old Nick himself would'nt start 'em. Pugwash, I guess, don't understand the natur of the critter; she'll never go kind in harness for him. *When I see a child, said the Clockmaker, I always feel safe with these women folk; for I have always found that the road to a woman's heart lies through her child.*

You seem, said I, to understand the female heart so well, I make no doubt you are a general favorite among the fair sex. Any man, he replied, that understands horses, has a pretty considerable fair knowledge of women, for they are jist alike in temper, and require the very identical same treatment. *Incourage the timid ones, be gentle and steady with the fractious, but lather the sulky ones like blazes.* People talk an everlastin sight of nonsense about wine, women and horses. I've bought and sold 'em all, I've traded in all of them, and I tell you, there aint one in a thousand that knows a grain about either on 'em.

You hear folks say, oh, such a man is an ugly grained critter – he'll break his wife's heart; jist as if a woman's heart was as brittle as a pipe stalk. The female heart, as far as my experience goes, is just like a new India Rubber Shoe; you may pull and pull at it, till it stretches out a yard long, and then let go, and it will fly right back to its old shape. Their hearts are made of stout leather, I tell you; there's a plaguy sight of wear in 'em, I never knowed but one case of a broken heart, and that was in tother sex, one Washington Banks. He was a sneezer. He was tall enough to spit down on the heads of your grenadiers, and near about high enough to wade across Charlestown River, and as strong as a tow boat. I guess he was somewhat less than a foot longer than the moral law and catechism too. He was a perfect pictur of a man; you could'nt falt him in no particular; he was so just a made critter; folks used to run to the winder when he passed, and say there goes Washington Banks, beant he lovely? I do believe there was'nt a gall in the Lowell factories, that warnt in love with him. Sometimes, at intermission, on Sabbath days, when they all came out together, (an amasin hansom sight too, near about a whole congregation of young galls) Banks used to say, 'I vow, young ladies, I wish I had five hundred arms to reciprocate one with each of you; but I reckon I have a heart big enough for you all; its a whapper, you may depend, and every mite and morsel of it at your service.' Well, how you do act, Mr. Banks, half a thousand little clipper clapper tongues would say, all at the same time, and their dear little eyes sparklin, like so many stars twinklin of a frosty night.

Well, when I last see'd him, he was all skin and bone, like a horse turned out to die. He was tetotally defleshed, a mere walkin skeleton. I am dreadful sorry, says I, to see you, Banks, lookin so peecked; why you look like a sick turkey hen, all legs;

what on airth ails you? I am dyin, says he, *of a broken heart.* What, says I, have the galls been jiltin you? No, no, says he, I beant such a fool as that neither. Well, says I, have you made a bad speculation? No, says he, shakin his head, I hope I have too much clear grit in me to take on so bad for that. What under the sun, is it, then? said I. Why, says he, I made a bet the fore part of summer with Leftenant Oby Knowles, that I could shoulder the best bower of the Constitution frigate. I won my bet, *but the Anchor was so etarnal heavy it broke my heart.* Sure enough he did die that very fall, and he was the only instance I ever heerd tell of *a broken heart.*

CUMBERLAND OYSTERS PRODUCE
MELANCHOLY FOREBODINGS

The '*soft sawder*' of the Clockmaker had operated effectually on the beauty of Amherst, our lovely hostess of Pugwash's Inn: indeed, I am inclined to think, with Mr. Slick, that 'the road to a woman's heart lies through her child,' from the effect produced upon her by the praises bestowed on her infant boy. I was musing on this feminine susceptibility to flattery, when the door opened, and Mrs. Pugwash entered, dressed in her sweetest smiles and her best cap, an auxiliary by no means required by her charms, which, like an Italian sky, when unclouded, are unrivalled in splendor. Approaching me, she said, with an irresistible smile, would you like Mr. ———, (here there was a pause, a hiatus, evidently intended for me to fill up with my name; but that no person knows, nor do I intend they shall; at Medley's Hotel, in Halifax, I was known as the stranger in No. 1. The attention that incognito procured for me, the importance it gave me in the eyes of the master of the house, its lodgers and servants, is indescribable. It is only great people who travel incog. State travelling is inconvenient and slow; the constant weight of form and etiquette oppresses at once the strength and the spirits. It is pleasant to travel unobserved, to stand at ease, or exchange the full suit for the undress coat and fatigue jacket. Wherever too there is mystery there is importance; there is no knowing for whom I may be mistaken – but let me once give my humble cognomen and occupation, and I sink immediately to my own level, to a plebeian station and a vulgar name: not even my beautiful hostess, nor my inquisitive friend, the Clockmaker, who calls me 'Squire,' shall extract that secret!) Would you like, Mr. ————. Indeed, I would, said I, Mrs. Pugwash; pray be seated, and tell me what it is. Would you like a dish of superior Shittyacks for supper? Indeed I would, said I, again laughing; but pray tell me what it is? Laws me! said she with a stare, where have you been all your days, that you never heerd of our Shittyack Oysters? I thought every body had heerd of them. I beg pardon, said I, but I understood at Halifax, that the only Oysters in this part of the world were found on the shores of Prince Edward Island. Oh! dear no, said our hostess, they are found all along the coast from Shittyack, through Bay of Vartes, away up to Ramshag. The latter we seldom get, though the best; there is no regular conveyance, and when they do come, they are generally shelled and in kegs, and never in good order. I have not had a real good Ramshag in my house these two years, since Governor Maitland was here; he was amazin fond of them, and Lawyer Talkemdeaf sent his carriage there on purpose to procure them fresh for him. Now we can't *get them*, but we have the Shittyacks in perfection; say the word, and they shall be served up immediately. A good dish and an unexpected dish is most acceptable, and certainly my American friend and myself did ample justice to the Oysters, which, if they have not so classical a name, have quite as good a flavor as their far famed brethren of Milton. Mr. Slick eat so heartily, that when

...med his conversation, he indulged in the most melan-
/ forebodings.

Did you see that are nigger, said he, that removed the
Oyster shells? well, he's one of our Chesapickers, one of
General Cuffy's slaves. I wish Admiral Cockburn had a taken
them all off our hands at the same rate. We made a pretty good
sale of them are black cattle, I guess, to the British; I wish we
were well rid of 'em all. *The Blacks and the Whites* in the States
show their teeth and snarl, they are jist ready to fall to. The
Protestants and Catholics begin to lay back their ears, and turn
tail for kickin. *The Abolitionists and Planters* are at it like two
bulls in a pastur. *Mob law and Lynch law* are working like yeast
in a barrell, and frothing at the bung hole. *Nullification and
Tariff* are like a charcoal pit, all covered up, but burning inside,
and sending out smoke at every crack, enough to stifle a horse.
General Government and State Government every now and then
square off and sparr, and the first blow given will bring a
genuine set-to. *Surplus Revenue* is another bone of contention;
like a shin of beef thrown among a pack of dogs, it will set the
whole on 'em by the ears. You have heerd tell of cotton rags
dipt in turpentine, hav'nt you, how they produce combustion?
Well, I guess we have the elements of spontaneous combustion among us in abundance; when it does break out, if you
don't see an eruption of human gore, worse than Etna lava,
then I'm mistaken. There'll be the very devil to pay, that's a
fact. I expect the blacks will butcher the Southern whites, and
the northerners will have to turn out and butcher them again;
and all this shoot, hang, cut, stab, and burn business, will
sweeten our folks' temper, as raw meat does that of a dog – it
fairly makes me sick to think on it. The explosion may clear
the air again, and all be tranquil once more, but its an even
chance if it dont leave us the three steam boat options; to be

blown sky high, to be scalded to death or drowned. If this sad picture you have drawn, be indeed true to nature, how does your country, said I, appear so attractive, as to draw to it so large a portion of our population? It tante its attraction, said the Clockmaker, its nothin but its power of suction; it is a great whirlpool – a great vortex – it drags all the straw, and chips and floatin sticks, drift wood and trash into it. The small crafts are sucked in, and whirl round and round like a squirrel in a cage – they'll never come out. Bigger ones pass through at certain times of tide, and can come in and out with good pilotage, as they do at *Hell Gate* up the Sound. You astonish me, said I, beyond measure; both your previous conversations with me, and the concurrent testimony of all my friends who have visited the States, give a different view of it. *Your friends!* said the Clockmaker, with such a tone of ineffable contempt, that I felt a strong inclination to knock him down for his insolence – your friends! Ensigns and leftenants, I guess, from the British marchin regiments in the Colonies, that run over five thousand miles of country in five weeks, on leave of absence, and then return, lookin as wise as the monkey that had seen the world. When they get back they are so chock full of knowledge of the Yankees, that it runs over of itself, like a hogshead of molasses rolled about in hot weather – a white froth and scum bubbles out of the bung; wishy washy trash they call tours, sketches, travels, letters, and what not; vapid stuff, jist sweet enough to catch flies, cockroaches, and half fledged galls. It puts me in mind of my French. I larnt French at night school one winter, of our minister, Joshua Hopewell (he was the most larned man of the age, for he taught himself een amost every language in Europe); well, next spring, when I went to Boston, I met a Frenchman, and I began to jabber away French to him: 'Polly woes a french say,' says I. I dont understand Yankee yet, says he. You dont understand! says I, why its French. I guess you didn't expect to hear such good French, did you, away down east here? but we speak it real well, and its generally allowed we speak English, too, better than the British. Oh, says he, you one very droll Yankee, dat very good joke, Sare; you talk Indian and call it French. But, says I, Mister Mount shear; it is French, I vow; real merchantable, without wainy edge or shakes – all clear stuff; it will pass survey in any market – its ready stuck and seasoned. Oh, very like, says he, bowin as polite as a black waiter at New Or*leens*, very like, only I never heerd it afore; oh, very good French dat – *clear stuff*, no doubt, but I no understand – its all my fault, I dare say, Sare.

Thinks I to myself a nod is as good as a wink to a blind horse, I see how the cat jumps – Minister knows so many languages he hant been particular enough to keep 'em in separate parcels and mark 'em on the back, and they've got mixed, and sure enough I found my French was so overrun with other sorts, that it was better to loose the whole crop than to go to weedin, for as fast as I pulled up any strange seedlin, it would grow right up agin as quick as wink, if there was the least bit of root in the world left in the ground, so I left it all rot on the field. There is no way so good to larn French as to live among 'em, and if you *want to understand us, you must live among us, too*; your Halls, Hamiltons, and De Rouses, and such critters, what *can* they know of us? Can a chap catch a likeness flying along a rail road? can he even see the featurs? Old Admiral Anson once axed one of our folks afore our glorious Revolution, (if the British had a known us a little grain better at that time, they would'nt have got whipped like a sack as they did then) where he came from. From the Chesapeeke, said he. Aye, aye, said the Admiral, from the West Indies. I guess, said the Southaner, you may have been clean *round the world*, Admiral, but you have been plaguy *little in it*, not to know better nor that. I shot a wild goose at River Philip last year, with the rice of Varginey fresh in his crop; he must have cracked on near about as fast as them other geese, the British travellers. Which know'd the most of the country they passed over, do you suppose? I guess it was much of a muchness – near about six of one and a half dozen of tother; two eyes aint much better than one, if they are both blind.

No, if you want to know all about us and the Blue Noses (a pretty considerable share of Yankee blood in them too, I tell you; the old stock comes from New England, and the breed is tolerable pure yet, near about one half apple sarce, and tother half molasses, all except to the Easterd, where there is a cross of the Scotch,) jist ax me and I'll tell you candidly. I'm not one of them that can't see no good points in my neighbor's critter, and no bad ones in my own; I've seen too much of the world for that, I guess. Indeed, in a general way, I praise other folks' beasts, and keep dark about my own. Says I, when I meet Blue Nose mounted, that's a real smart horse of yourn, put him out, I guess he'll trot like mad. Well, he lets him have the spur, and the critter does his best, and then I pass him like a streak of lightning with mine. The feller looks all taken aback at that. Why, says he, that's a real clipper of yourn, I vow. Middlin, says I, (quite cool, as if I had heard that are same thing a thousand times;) he's good enough for me, jist a fair trotter, and nothin to brag of. That goes near about as far agin in a general way, as a crackin and a boastin does. Never *tell* folks you can go a head on 'em, but *do* it; it spares a great deal of talk, and helps them to save their breath to cool their broth. No, if you want to know the inns and the outs of the Yankees – I've wintered them and summered them; I know all their points, shape, make and breed; I've tried 'em alongside of other folks, and I know where they fall short, where they mate 'em, and where they have the advantage, about as well as some who think they know a plaguy sight more. It tante them that stare the most, that see the best always, I guess. Our folks have their faults, and I know them, (I warnt born blind, I reckon,) but your friends, the tour writers, are a little grain too hard on us. Our old nigger wench had several dirty, ugly lookin children, and was proper cross to 'em. Mother used to say, *'Juno, its better never to wipe a child's nose at all, I guess, than to wring it off.'*

THE AMERICAN EAGLE

Jist look out of the door, said the Clockmaker, and see what a beautiful night it is, how calm, how still, how clear it is, beant it lovely? – I like to look up at them are stars, when I am away from home, they put me in mind of our national flag, and it is generally allowed to be the first flag in the univarse now. The British can whip all the world, and we can whip the British. Its near about the prettiest sight I know of, is one of our first class Frigates, manned with our free and enlightened citizens all ready for sea; it is like the great American Eagle, on its perch, balancing itself for a start on the broad expanse of blue sky, afeared of nothin of its kind, and president of all it surveys. It was a good emblem that we chose, warn't it? There was no evading so direct, and at the same time, so conceited an appeal as this. Certainly, said I, the emblem was well chosen. I was particularly struck with it on observing the device on your naval buttons during the last war – an eagle with an anchor in its claws. That was a natural idea, taken from an ordinary occurrence: a bird purloining the anchor of a frigate – an article so useful and necessary for the food of its young. It was well chosen, and exhibited great taste and judgment in the artist. The emblem is more appropriate than you are aware of – boasting of what you cannot perform – grasping at what you cannot attain – an emblem of arrogance and weakness – of ill-directed ambition and vulgar pretension. Its a common phrase, said he, (with great composure) among seamen, to say 'damn your buttons,' and I guess its natural for you to say so of the buttons of our navals; I guess you have a right to that are oath. Its a sore subject, that, I reckon, and I believe I hadn't ought to have spoken of it to you at all. Brag is a good dog, but hold fast is a better one. He was evidently annoyed, and with his usual dexterity gave vent to his feelings, by a sally upon the Blue Noses, who he says are a cross of English and Yankee, and therefore first cousins to us both. Perhaps, said he, that are Eagle might with more propriety have been taken off as perched on an anchor, instead of holding it in his claws, and I think it would have been more nateral; but I suppose it was some stupid foreign artist that made that are blunder, I never seed one yet that was equal to ourn. If that Eagle is represented as trying what *he cant do*, its an honorable ambition arter all, but these Blue Noses wont try what *they can do*. They put me in mind of a great big hulk of a horse in a cart, that wont put his shoulder to the collar at all for all the lambastin in the world, but turns his head round and looks at you, as much as to say, 'what an everlastin heavy thing an empty cart is, isnt it?' *An Owl should be their emblem, and the motto, 'He sleeps all the days of his life.'* The whole country is like this night; beautiful to look at, but silent as the grave – still as death, asleep, becalmed. If the sea was always calm, said he, it would pyson the univarse; no soul could breathe the air, it would be so uncommon bad. Stagnant water is always onpleasant, but salt water when it gets tainted beats all natur; motion keeps it sweet and wholesome, and that our minister used to say is one of the 'wonders of the great deep.' This province is stagnant; it tante deep like still water neither, for its shaller enough, gracious knows, but it is motionless, noiseless, lifeless. If you have ever been to sea, in a calm, you'd know what a plaguy tiresome thing it is for a man that's in a hurry. An everlastin flappin of the sails, and a creakin of the boombs, and an onsteady pitchin of the ship, and folks lyin about dozin away their time, and the sea a heavin a long heavy swell, like the breathin of the chist of some great monster asleep. A passenger wonders the sailors are so plaguy easy about it, and he goes a lookin out east, and a spyin out west, to see if there's any change of a breeze, and says to himself, 'Well, if this aint dull music its a pity.' Then how streaked he feels when he sees a steamboat a clippin it by him like mad, and the folks on board pokin fun at him, and askin him if he has any word to send to home. Well, he says, if any soul ever catches me on board a sail vessel again, when I can go by steam, I'll give him leave to tell me of it, that's a fact. That's partly the case here. They are becalmed, and they see us going a head on them, till we are een amost out of sight; yet they hant got a steamboat, and they hant got a rail road; indeed, I doubt if one half on em ever see'd or heerd tell of one or tother of them. I never see'd any folks like 'em except the Indians, and they wont even so much as look – they havn't the least morsel of curiosity in the world; from which one of our Unitarian preachers (they are dreadful hands at *doubtin* them. I dont *doubt* but some day or another, they will *doubt* whether every thing aint a *doubt*) in a very learned work, doubts whether they were ever descended from Eve at all. Old marm Eve's children, he says, are all lost, it is said, in consequence of *too much* curiosity, while these copper colored folks are lost from havin *too little*. How can they be the same? Thinks I, that may be logic, old Dubersome, but it ant sense, don't extremes meet? Now

63

these Blue Noses have no motion in 'em, no enterprise, no spirit, and if any critter shows any symptoms of activity, they say he is a man of no judgment, he's speculative, he's a schemer, in short he's mad. They vegitate like a lettuce plant in sarse garden, they grow tall and spindlin, run to seed right off, grow as bitter as gaul and die.

A gall once came to our minister to hire as a house help; says she, minister, I suppose you dont want a young lady to do chamber business and breed worms do you? For I've half a mind to take a spell of livin out (she meant, said the Clockmaker, house work and rearing silk worms.) My pretty maiden, says he, a pattin her on the cheek, (for I've often observed old men always talk kinder pleasant to young women,) my pretty maiden where was you brought up? why, says she, I guess I warnt brought up at all, I growed up; under what platform, says he, (for he was very particular that all his house helps should go to his meetin,) under what Church platform? Church platform, says she, with a toss of her head, like a young colt that's got a check of the curb, I guess I warnt raised under a platform at all, but in as good a house as yourn, grand as you be – you said well said the old minister, quite shocked when you said you growd up, dear, for you have grown up in great ignorance. Then I guess you had better get a lady that knows more than me, says she, that's flat. I reckon I am every bit and grain as good as you be – If I dont understand a bumbyx (silk worm) both feedin, breedin, and rearin, then I want to know who does, that's all; church platform indeed, says she, I guess you were raised under a glass frame in March, and transplanted on Independence day, warnt you? And off she sot, lookin as scorney as a London lady, and leavin the poor minister standin starin like a stuck pig. Well, well, says he, a liftin up both hands, and turnin up the whites of his eyes like a duck in thunder, if that dont bang the bush!! It fearly beats sheap shearin arter the blackberry bushes have got the wool. It does, I vow; them are the tares them Unitarians sow in our grain fields at night; I guess they'll ruinate the crops yet, and make the grounds so everlastin foul; we'll have to pare the sod and burn it, to kill the roots. Our fathers sowed the right seed here in the wilderness, and watered it with their tears, and watched over it with fastin and prayer, and now its fairly run out, that's a fact, I snore. Its got choaked up with all sorts of trash in natur, I declare. Dear, dear, I vow I never seed the beat o' that in all my born days.

Now the Blue Noses are like that are gall; they have grown up, and grown up in ignorance of many things they hadnt ought not to know; and its as hard to teach grown up folks as it is to break a six year old horse; and they do ryle one's temper so – they act so ugly that it tempts one sometimes to break their confounded necks – its near about as much trouble as its worth. What remedy is there for all this supineness, said I; how can these people be awakened out of their ignorant sloth-fulness, into active exertion? The remedy, said Mr. Slick, is at hand – it is already workin its own cure. They must recede before our free and enlightened citizens like the Indians; our folks will buy them out, and they must give place to a more intelligent and ac-*tive* people. They must go to the lands of Labrador, or be located back of Canada; they can hold on there a few years, until the wave of civilization reaches them, and then they must move again, as the savages do. It is decreed; I hear the bugle of destiny a soundin of their retreat, as plain as any thing. Congress will give them a concession of land, if they petition, away to Alleghany backside territory, and grant them relief for a few years; for we are out of debt, and dont know what to do with our surplus revenue. The only way to shame them, that I know, would be to sarve them as Uncle Enoch sarved a neighbor of his in Varginy.

There was a lady that had a plantation near hand to hisn, and there was only a small river atwixt the two houses, so that folks could hear each other talk across it. Well, she was a dreadful cross grained woman, a real catamount, as savage as a she bear that has cubs, an old farrow critter, as ugly as sin, and one that both hooked and kicked too – a most particular onmarciful she devil, that's a fact. She used to have some of her niggers tied up every day, and flogged uncommon severe, and their screams and screeches were horrid – no soul could stand it; nothin was heerd all day, but *oh Lord Missus! oh Lord Missus!* Enoch was fairly sick of the sound, for he was a tender hearted man, and says he to her one day, 'Now do marm find out some other place to give your cattle the cowskin, for it worries me to hear em take on so dreadful bad – I cant stand it, I vow; they are flesh and blood as well as we be, though the meat is a different color;' but it was no good – she jist up and told him to mind his own business, and she guessed she'd mind hern. He was determined to shame her out of it; so one mornin arter breakfast he goes into the cane field, and says he to Lavender, one of the black overseers, 'Muster up the whole gang of slaves, every soul, and bring 'em down to the whippin post, the whole stock of them, bulls, cows and calves. Well, away goes Lavender, and drives up all the niggers. Now you catch it, says he, you lazy villains; I tole you so many a time – I tole you Massa he lose all patience wid you, you good for nothin rascals. I grad, upon my soul, I werry grad; you mind now what old Lavender say anoder time. (The black overseers are always the most cruel, said the Clockmaker; they have no sort of feeling for their own people.)

Well, when they were gathered there according to orders, they looked streaked enough you may depend, thinkin they were going to get it all round, and the wenches they fell to a cryin, wringin their hands, and boo-hooing like mad. Lavender was there with his cowskin, grinnin like a chessy cat, and crackin it about, ready for business. Pick me out, says Enoch, four that have the loudest voices; hard matter dat, says Lavender, hard matter dat, Massa, dey all talk loud, dey all lub talk more better nor work – de idle villians; better gib 'em all a little tickle, jist to teach em larf on tother side of de mouth; dat side bran new, they never use it yet. Do as I order you, Sir, said Uncle, or I'll have you triced up, you cruel old rascal you. When they were picked out and sot by themselves, they hanged their heads, and looked like sheep goin to the shambles. Now, says Uncle Enoch, my Pickininnies, do you sing out as loud as Niagara, at the very tip eend of your voice –

> Dont kill a nigger, pray,
> Let him lib anoder day.
> > *Oh Lord Missus – oh Lord Missus.*
> My back be very sore,
> No stand it any more,
> > *Oh Lord Missus – oh Lord Missus.*

And all the rest of you join chorus, as loud as you can bawl, '*Oh Lord Missus.*' The black rascals understood the joke real well. They larfed ready to split their sides; they fairly lay down on the ground, and rolled over and over with lafter. Well, when they came to the chorus '*Oh Lord Missus,*' if they did'nt let go, its a pity. They made the river ring agin – they were heerd clean out to sea. All the folks ran out of the Lady's House, to see what on airth was the matter on Uncle Enoch's plantation – they thought there was actilly a rebellion there; but when they listened awhile, and heerd it over and over again, they took the hint, and returned a larfin in their sleeves. Says they, Master Enoch Slick, he upsides with Missus this hitch any how. Uncle never heerd any thing more of '*oh Lord Missus*' arter that. Yes, they ought to be shamed out of it, those Blue Noses. When reason fails to convince, there is nothin left but ridicule. If they have no ambition, apply to their feelings, clap a blister on their pride, and it will do the business. Its like a puttin ginger under a horse's tail; it makes him carry up real hand*sum*, I tell you. When I was a boy, I was always late to school: well father's preachin I didn't mind much, but I never could bear to hear mother say, 'Why Sam, are you actilly up for all day? Well, I hope your airly risin wont hurt you, I declare. What on airth is agoin to happen now? Well, wonders will never cease. It raised my dander; at last says I, 'Now, mother, dont say that are any more for gracious sake, for it makes me feel ugly, and I'll get up as airly as any on you'; and so I did, and I soon found what's worth knowin in this life, '*An airly start makes easy stages.*'

THE CLOCKMAKER'S
OPINION OF HALIFAX

The next morning was warmer than several that had preceded it. It was one of those uncommonly fine days that distinguish an American autumn. I guess, said Mr. Slick, the heat to-day is like a glass of Mint Julip, with a lump of ice in it, it tastes cool and feels warm – its real good, I tell you; I love such a day as this dearly. Its generally allowed the finest weather in the world is in America – there ant the beat of it to be found anywhere. He then lighted a cigar, and throwing himself back on his chair, put both feet out of the window, and sat with his arms folded, a perfect picture of happiness. You appear, said I, to have travelled over the whole of this Province, and to have observed the country and the people with much attention, pray what is your opinion of the present state and future prospects of Halifax? If you will tell me, said he, when the folks there will wake up, then I can answer you, but they are fast asleep; as to the Province, its a splendid province, and calculated to go ahead, it will grow as fast as a Varginy gall, and they grow so amazin fast, if you put your arm round one of their necks to kiss them, by the time you're done, they've grown up into women. It's a pretty Province I tell you, good above and better below; surface covered with pastures, meadows, woods, and a nation sight of water privileges, and under the ground full of mines – it puts me in mind of the soup at the *Tree*-mont House. One day I was a walkin in the Mall, and who should I meet but Major Bradford, a gentleman from Connecticut, that traded in calves and pumpkins for the Boston market. Says he, Slick, where do you get your grub to-day? At General Peep's tavern, says I; only fit for niggers, says he, why dont you come to the *Tree*-mont house, that's the most splendid thing its generally allowed in all the world. Why, says I, that's a notch above my mark, I guess it's too plaguy dear for me, I cant afford it no how. Well, says he, its dear in one sense, but its dog cheap in another – its a grand place for speculation – there's so many rich southerners and strangers there that have more money than wit, that you might do a pretty good business there, without goin out of the street door. I made two hundred dollars this mornin in little less than half no time. There's a Carolina Lawyer there, as rich as a bank, and says he to me arter breakfast, Major, says he, I wish I knew where to get a real slapping trotter of a horse, one that could trot with a flash of lightning for a mile, and beat it by a whole neck or so. Says I, my Lord, (for you must know, he says he's the nearest male heir to a Scotch dormant peerage,) my Lord, says I, I have one a proper sneezer, a chap that can go ahead of a rail road steamer, a real natural traveller, one that can trot with the ball out of the small eend of a rifle, and never break into a gallop. Says he, Major, I wish you wouldnt give me that are nickname, I dont like it, (though he looked as tickled all the time as possible,) I never knew says he a lord that warnt a fool, that's a fact, and that's the reason I don't go ahead and claim the title. Well, says I, my Lord I dont know, but somehow I cant help a thinkin, if you have a good claim, you'd be more like a fool not to go ahead with it. Well, says he, Lord or no Lord, let's look at your horse. So away I went to Joe Brown's livery stable, at tother eend of the city, and picked out the best trotter he had, and no great stick to brag on either; says I, Joe Brown what do you ax for that are horse? Two hundred dollars, says he; well, says I, I will take him out and try him, and if I like him I will keep him. So I shows our Carolina Lord the horse, and when he gets on him, says I, dont let him trot as fast as he can, resarve that for a heat; if folks find out how everlastin fast he is, they'd be afeared to stump you for a start. When he returned, he said he liked the horse amazinly, and axed the price; four hundred dollars, says I, you cant get nothin special without a good price, pewter cases never hold good watches; I know it, says he, the horse is mine. Thinks I to myself, that's more than ever I could say of him then any how.

Well, I was goin to tell you about the soup – says the Major, its near about dinner time, jist come and see how you like the location. There was a sight of folks there, gentlemen and ladies in the public room (I never seed so many afore except at commencement day,) all ready for a start, and when the gong sounded, off we sott like a flock of sheep. Well, if there warnt a jam you may depend – some one give me a pull, and I near abouts went heels up over head, so I reached out both hands, and caught hold of the first thing I could, and what should it be but a lady's dress – well, as I'm alive, rip went the frock, and tare goes the petticoat, and when I righted myself from my beam eends, away they all came home to me, and there she was, the pretty critter, with all her upper riggin standin as far as her waist, and nothin left below but a short linen under garment. If she didnt scream, its a pity, and the more she screamed the more folks larfed, for no soul could help larfin, till one of the waiters folded her up in a table cloth.

What an awkward devil you be, Slick, says the Major, now that comes of not falling in first, they should have formed four deep, rear rank in open order, and marched in to our splendid national air, and filed off to their seats right and left shoulders forward. I feel kinder sorry, too, says he, for that are young heifer, but she shewed a proper pretty leg tho' Slick, didnt she – I guess you dont often get such a chance as that are. Well I gets near the Major at table, and afore me stood a china utensil with two handles, full of soup, about the size of a foot tub, with a large silver scoop in it, near about as big as a ladle of a maple sugar kettle. I was jist about bailing out some soup into my dish, when the Major said fish it up from the bottom, Slick, – well, sure enough, I gives it a drag from the bottom, and up come the fat pieces of turtle, and the thick rich soup, and a sight of little forced meat balls of the size of sheep's dung. No soul could tell how good it was – it was near about as hand*sum* as father's old genuine particular cider, and that you could feel tingle clean away down to the tip eends of your toes. Now, says the Major, I'll give you, Slick, a new wrinkle on your horn. Folks aint thought nothin of unless they live at Treemont: its all the go. Do you dine at Peep's tavern every day, and then off hot foot to Treemont, and pick your teeth on the street steps there, and folks will think you dine there. I do it often, and it saves two dollars a day. Then he put his finger on his nose, and says he, "*Mum is the word.*" Now this Province is jist like that are soup, good enough at top, but dip down and you have the riches, the coal, the iron ore, the gypsum, and what not. As for Halifax, its well enough in itself, though no great shakes neither, a few sizeable houses, with a proper sight of small ones, like half a dozen old hens with their broods of young chickens; but the people, the strange critters, they are all asleep. They walk in their sleep, and talk in their sleep, and what they say one day they forget the next, they say they were dreaming. You know where Governor Campbell lives, dont you, in a large stone house with a great wall round it, that looks like a state prison; well, near hand there is a nasty dirty horrid lookin buryin ground there – its filled with large grave rats as big as kittens, and the springs of black water there, go through the chinks of the rocks and flow into all the wells, and fairly pyson the folks – its a dismal place, I tell you – I wonder the air from it dont turn all the silver in the Gineral's house of a brass color, (and folks say he has four cart loads of it) its so everlastin bad – its near about as nosey as a slave ship of niggers. Well you may go there and shake the folks to all etarnity and you wont wake em, I guess, and yet there ant much difference atween their sleep and the folks at Halifax, only they lie still there and are quiet, and don't walk and talk in their sleep like them above ground.

Halifax reminds me of a Russian officer I once seed at Warsaw; he had lost both arms in battle: but I guess I must tell you first why I went there, cause that will show you how we speculate. One Sabbath day, after bell ringin, when most of the women had gone to meetin (for they were great hands for pretty sarmons, and our Unitarian ministers all preach poetry, only they leave the ryme out, it sparkles like perry,) I goes down to East India wharf to see Captain Zeek Hancock, of Nantucket, to enquire how oil was, and if it would bear doing any thing in; when who should come along but Jabish Green. Slick, says he, how do you do; isn't this as pretty a day as you'll see between this and Norfolk; it whips English weather by a long chalk; and then he looked down at my watch seals, and looked and looked as if he thought I'd stole 'em. At last he looks up, and says he, Slick, I suppose you would'nt go to Warsaw, would you, if it was made worth your while? Which Warsaw? says I, for I believe in my heart we have a hundred of them. None of ourn at all, says he; Warsaw in Poland. Well, I don't know, says I; what do you call worth while? Six dollars a day, expenses paid, and a bonus of one thousand dollars, if speculation turns out well. I am off, says I, whenever you say go. Tuesday, says he, in the Hamburgh packet. Now, says he, I'm in a tarnation hurry; I'm goin a pleasurin to-day in the Custom House Boat, along with Josiah Bradford's galls down to Nahant. But I'll tell you what I am at: the Emperor of Russia has ordered the Poles to cut off their queues on the 1st of January; you must buy them all up, and ship them off to London for the wig makers. Human hair is scarce and risin. Lord a massy! says I, how queer they will look, wont they. Well, I vow, that's what the sea folks call sailing *under bare Poles*, come true, aint it? I guess it will turn out a good spec, says he; and a good one it did turn out – he cleared ten thousand dollars by it. When I was at Warsaw, as I was a sayin, there was a Russian officer there who had lost both his arms in battle; a good natured contented critter, as I een amost ever see'd, and he was fed with spoons by his neighbors, but arter a while they grew tired of it, and I guess he near about starved to death at last. Now Halifax is like that are *Spooney*, as I used to call him; it is fed by the outports, and they begin to have enough to do to feed themselves – it must larn to live without 'em. They have no river, and no country about them; let them make a rail road to Minas Basin, and they will have arms of their own to feed themselves with. If they don't do it, and do it soon, I guess they'll get into a decline that no human skill will cure. They are proper thin now; you can count their ribs een a most as far as you can see them. *The only thing that will either make or save Halifax, is a rail road across the country to Bay of Fundy.*

It will do to talk of, says one; you'll see it some day, says another; yes, says a third, it will come, but we are too young yet. Our old minister had a darter, a real clever lookin gall as you'd see in a day's ride, and she had two or three offers of marriage from sponsible men – most particular good specs – but minister always said 'Phœbe, you are too young – the day will come – but you are too young yet dear.' Well, Phœbe did'nt think so at all; she said she guessed she knew better nor that; so the next offer she had, she said she had no notion to lose another chance – off she sot to Rhode Island and got married; says she, father's too old, he don't know. That's jist the case at Halifax. The old folks say the country is too young – the time will come, and so on; and in the mean time the young folks won't wait, *and run off to the States, where the maxim is, 'youth is the time for improvement; a new country is never too young for exertion – push on – keep movin – go ahead.'* Darn it all, said the Clockmaker, rising with great animation, clinching his fist, and extending his arm – darn it all, it fairly makes my dander rise, to see the nasty idle loungin good for nothin do little critters – they aint fit to tend a bear trap, I vow. They ought to be quilted round and round a room, like a lady's lap dog, the matter of two hours a day, to keep them from dyin of apoplexy. Hush, hush, said I, Mr. Slick, you forget. Well, said he, resuming his usual composure – well, it's enough to make one vexed though, I declare – is'nt it?

Mr. Slick has often alluded to this subject, and always in a most decided manner; I am inclined to think he is right. Mr. Howe's papers on the rail road I read till I came to his calculations, but I never could read figures, 'I can't cypher,' and there I paused; it was a barrier: I retreated a few paces, took a running leap, and cleared the whole of them. Mr. Slick says he has *under* and not *over* rated its advantages. He appears to be such a shrewd, observing, intelligent man, and so perfectly at home on these subjects, that I confess I have more faith in this humble but eccentric Clockmaker, than in any other man I have met with in this Province. I therefore pronounce '*there will be a rail road.*'

SAYINGS AND DOINGS
IN CUMBERLAND

I reckon, said the Clockmaker, as we strolled through Amherst, you have read Hook's story of the boy that one day asked one of his father's guests who his next door neighbor was, and when he heerd his name, asked him if he warnt a fool. No, my little feller, said he, he beant a fool, he is a most particular sensible man; but why did you ax that are question? Why, said the little boy, mother said tother day you were next door to a fool, and I wanted to know who lived next door to you. His mother felt pretty ugly, I guess, when she heerd him run right slap on that are breaker. Now these Cumberland folks have curious next door neighbors, too; they are placed by their location right atwixt fire and water; they have New Brunswick politics on one side, and Nova Scotia politics on tother side of them, and Bay Fundy and Bay Varte on tother two sides; they are actilly in hot water; they are up to their croopers in politics, and great hands for talking of House of Assembly, political Unions, and what not. Like all folks who wade so deep, they can't always tell the natur of the ford. Sometimes they strike their shins agin a snag of a rock; at other times they go whap into a quicksand, and if they don't take special care they are apt to go souse over head and ears into deep water. I guess if they'd talk more of *Rotations*, and less of *elections*, more of them are *Dykes* and less of *Banks*, and attend more to *top-dressing*, and less to *re-dressing*, it ed be better for 'em. Now you mention the subject, I think I have observed, said I, that there is a great change in your countrymen in that respect. Formerly, whenever you met an American, you had a dish of politics set before you, whether you had an appetite for it or not; but lately I have remarked they seldom allude to it. Pray to what is this attributable? I guess, said he, they have enough of it to home, and are sick of the subject. They are cured the way our pastry cooks cure their prentices of stealing sweet notions out of their shops. When they get a new prentice they tell him he must never so much as look at all them are nice things; and if he dares to lay the weight of his finger upon one of them, they'll have him up for it before a justice; they tell him its every bit and grain as bad as stealing from a till. Well, that's sure to set him at it, just as a high fence does a breachy ox, first to look over it, and then to push it down with his rump; its human natur. Well, the boy eats and eats till he cant eat no longer, and then he gets sick at his stomach, and hates the very sight of sweetmeats arterwards. We've had politics with us, till we're dog sick of 'em, I tell you. Besides, I guess we are as far from perfection as when we set out a roin for it. You may get *purity of election*, but how are you to get *purity of Members?* It would take a great deal of cyphering to tell that. I never see'd it yet, and never heerd tell of one who had see'd it. The best member I een amost ever seed was John Adams. Well, John Adams could no more plough a straight furrow in politics than he could haul the plough himself. He might set out straight at beginnin for a little way, but he was sure to get crooked afore he got to the eend of the ridge – and sometimes he would have two or three crooks in it. I used to say to him, how on airth is it, Mr. Adams, (for he was no way proud like, though he was president of our great nation – and it is allowed to be the greatest nation in the world, too – for you might see him sometimes of an arternoon, a swimmin along with the boys in the Potomac; I do believe that's the way he larned to give the folks the dodge so spry;) well, I used to say to him, how on airth is it, Mr. Adams, you can't make straight work on it? He was a grand hand at an excuse, (though minister used to say that folks that were good at an excuse, were seldom good for nothin else); sometimes, he said, the ground was so tarnation stony, it throwed the plough out; at other times, he said, the off ox was such an ugly wilful tempered critter, there was no doin nothin with him; or that there was so much machinery about the plough, it made it plaguy hard to steer; or may be it was the fault of them that went afore him, that they laid it down so bad; unless he was hired for another term of four years, the work would'nt look well; and if all them are excuses would'nt do, why he would take to scolding the nigger that drove the team – throw all the blame on him, and order him to have an everlastin lacin with the cowskin. You might as well catch a weazel asleep as catch him. He had somethin the matter with one eye – well, he knew I know'd that when I was a boy; so one day, a feller presented a petition to him, and he told him it was very affectin. Says he, it fairly draws tears from me, and his weak eye took to lettin off its water like statiee; so as soon as the chap went, he winks to me with tother one, quite knowin, as much as to say, you *see its all in my eye*, Slick, but don't let on to any one about it, that I said so. That eye was a regular cheat, a complete New England wooden nutmeg. Folks said Mr. Adams was a very tender hearted man. Perhaps he was, but I guess that eye didn't pump its water out o' that place.

Members in general aint to be depended on, I tell you. Politics makes a man as crooked as a pack does a pedlar; not that they are so awful heavy, neither, but it *teaches a man to stoop in the long run.* Arter all, there's not that difference in 'em (at least there aint in Congress) one would think; for if one of them is clear of one vice, why, as like as not, he has another fault just as bad. An honest farmer, like one of these Cumberland folks, when he goes to choose atwixt two that offers for votes, is jist like the flying fish. That are little critter is not content to stay to home in the water, and mind its business, but he must try his hand at flyin, and he is no great dab at flyin, neither. Well, the moment he's out of water, and takes to flyin, the sea fowl are arter him, and let him have it; and if he has the good luck to escape them, and makes a dive into the sea, the dolphin, as like as not, has a dig at him, that knocks more wind out of him than he got while aping the birds, a plaguy sight. I guess the Blue Noses know just about as much about politics as this foolish fish knows about flyin. *All critters in natur are better in their own element.*

It beats cock fightin, I tell you, to hear the Blue Noses, when they get together, talk politics. They have got three or four evil spirits, like the Irish Banshees, that they say cause all the mischief in the Province – the Council, the Banks, the House of Assembly and the Lawyers. If a man places a higher valiation on himself than his neighbors do, and wants to be a magistrate before he is fit to carry the ink horn for one, and finds himself safely delivered of a mistake, he says it is all owing to the Council. The members are cunnin critters, too; they know this feelin, and when they come home from Assembly, and people ax 'em "where are all them are fine things you promised us?" why, they say, we'd a had 'em all for you, but for that etarnal Council, they nullified all we did. The country will come to no good till them chaps show their respect for it, by covering their bottoms with homespun. If a man is so tarnation lazy he wont work, and in course has no money, why he says its all owin to the banks, they wont discount, there's no money, they've ruined the Province. If there beant a road made up to every citizen's door, away back to the woods (who as like as not has squatted there) why he says the House of Assembly have voted all the money to pay great men's salaries, and there's nothin left for poor settlers, and cross roads. Well, the lawyers come in for their share of cake and ale, too; if they don't catch it, its a pity.

There was one Jim Munroe of Onion County, Connecticut, a desperate idle fellow, a great hand at singin songs, a skatin, drivin about with the galls, and so on. Well, if any body's windows were broke, it was Jim Munroe – and if there were any youngsters in want of a father, they were sure to be poor Jim's. Jist so it is with the lawyers here; they stand Godfathers for every misfortune that happens in the country. When there is a mad dog a goin about, every dog that barks is said to be bit by the mad one, so he gets credit for all the mischief that every dog does for three months to come. So every feller that goes yelpin home from a court house, smartin from the law, swears he is bit by a lawyer. Now there may be something wrong in all these things, (and it cant be otherwise in nature) in Council, Banks, House of Assembly, and Lawyers: but change them all, and its an even chance if you dont get worse ones in their room. It is in politics as in horses; when a man has a beast that's near about up to the notch, he'd better not swap him; if he does, he's een amost sure to get one not so good as his own. *My rule is, I'd rather keep a critter whose faults I do know, than change him for a beast whose faults I dont know.*

THE DANCING MASTER ABROAD

I wish that are black heifer in the kitchen would give over singing that are everlastin dismal tune, said the Clockmaker, it makes my head ache. You've heerd a song afore now, said he, hav'nt you, till you was fairly sick of it? for I have, I vow. The last time I was in Rhode Island, (all the galls sing there, and its generally allowed there's no such singers any where; they beat the *Eye*-talians a long chalk – they sing so high some on 'em, they go clear out o' hearin sometimes, like a lark) well, you heerd nothin but 'Oh no, we never mention her;' well, I grew so plaguy tired of it, I used to say to myself, I'd sooner see it, than heer tell of it, I vow; I wish to gracious you 'would never mention her,' for it makes me feel ugly to hear that same thing for ever and ever and amen that way. Well, they've got a cant phrase here, 'the schoolmaster is abroad,' and every feller tells you that fifty times a day. There was a chap said to me not long ago, at Truro, Mr. Slick, this Country is rapidly improving, 'the schoolmaster is abroad now,' and he looked as knowin as though he had found a mare's nest. So I should think, said I, and it would jist be about as well, I guess, if he'd stay to home and mind his business, for your folks are so consoomedly ignorant, I reckon he's abroad een amost all his time. I hope when he returns, he'll be the better of his travels, and that's more nor many of our young folks are who go 'abroad,' for they import more airs and nonsense, than they dispose of one while, I tell you – some of the stock remains on hand all the rest of their lives. There's nothin I hate so much as cant, of all kinds; its a sure sign of a tricky disposition. If you see a feller cant in religion, clap your hand into your pocket, and lay right hold of your puss, or he'll steal it as sure as you're alive; and if a man cant in politics, he'll sell you if he gets a chance, you may depend. Law and physic are jist the same, and every mite and morsel as bad. If a lawyer takes to cantin, its like the fox preachin to the geese, he'll eat up his whole congregation; and if a doctor takes to it, he's a quack as sure as rates. The Lord have massy on you, for he wont. I'd sooner trust my chance with a naked hook any time, than one that's half covered with bad bait. The fish will sometimes swaller the one, without thinkin, but they get frightened at tother, turn tail and off like a shot. Now, to change the tune, I'll give the Blue Noses a new phrase. They'll have an election most likely next year, and then '*the dancin master will be abroad.*' A candidate is a most purticular polite man, a noddin here, and a bowin there, and a shakin hands all round. Nothin improves a man's manners like an election. '*The Dancin Master's abroad then;*' nothin gives the paces equal to that, it makes them as squirmy as an eel, they cross hands and back agin, set to their partners and right and left in great style, and slick it off at the eend, with a real complete bow, and a smile for all the world as sweet as a cat makes at a pan of new milk. Then they get as full of compliments as a dog is full of fleas – enquirin how the old lady is to home, and the little boy that made such a wonderful smart answer, they never can forget it till next time; a praisin a man's farm to the nines, and a tellin of him, how scandalous the road that leads to his location has been neglected, and how much he wants to find a real complete hand that can build a bridge over his brook, and axin him if *he* ever built one. When he gets the hook baited with the right fly, and the simple critter begins to jump out of water arter it, all mouth and gills, he winds up the reel, and takes leave, a thinkin to himself, 'now you see what's to the eend of my line, I guess I'll know where to find you when I want you.'

There's no sort of fishin requires so much practice as this. When bait is scarce one worm must answer for several fish. A handful of oats in a pan, arter it brings one horse up in a pastur for the bridle, serves for another, a shakin of it, is better than a givin of it, it saves the grain for another time. It's a poor business arter all is electioneering, and when '*the Dancin Master is abroad*,' he's as apt to teach a man to cut capers and get larfed at as any thing else. It tante every one that's soople enough to dance real complete. Politics take a great deal of time, and grinds away a man's honesty near about as fast as cleaning a knife with brick dust, '*it takes its steel out.*' What does a critter get arter all for it in this country, why nothin but expense and disappointment. As King Solomon says, (and that are man was up to a thing or two, you may depend, tho' our professor did say he warn't so knowin as Uncle Sam,) it's all vanity and vexation of spirit.

I raised a four year old colt once, half blood, a perfect pictur of a horse, and a genuine clipper, could gallop like the wind; a real daisy, a perfect doll, had an eye like a weasel, and nostril like Commodore Rodgers's speakin trumpet. Well, I took it down to the races at New York, and father he went along with me; for says he, Sam, you don't know every thing, I guess, you hant cut your wisdom teeth yet, and you are goin among them that's had 'em through their gums this while past. Well, when we gets to the races, father he gets colt and puts him in an old waggon, with a worn out Dutch harness, and breast band; he looked like Old Nick, that's a fact. Then he fastened a head martingale on, and buckled it to the girths atwixt his fore legs. Says I, father, what on airth are you at? I vow I feel ashamed to be seen with such a catamaran as that, and colt looks like old Saytan himself – no soul would know him. I guess I warn't born yesterday, says he, let me be, I know what I am at. I guess I'll slip it into 'em afore I've done as slick as a whistle. I guess I can see as far into a mill stone as the best on 'em. Well, father never entered the horse at all, but stood by and see'd the races, and the winnin horse was followed about by the matter of two or three thousand people, a praisin of him and admirin him. They seemed as if they never had see'd a horse afore. The owner of him was all up on eend a boastin of him, and a stumpin the course to produce a horse to run agin him for four hundred dollars. Father goes up to him, lookin as soft as dough, and as meechin as you please, and says he, friend, it tante every one that has four hundred dollars – its a plaguy sight of money, I tell you; would you run for one hundred dollars, and give me a little start? if you would, I'd try my colt out of my old waggon agin you, I vow. Let's look at your horse, says he; so away they went, and a proper sight of people arter them to look at colt, and when they see'd him they sot up such a larf, I felt een a most ready to cry for spite. Says I to myself, what can possess the old man to act arter that fashion, I do believe he has taken leave of his senses. You need'nt larf, says father, he's smarter than he looks; our Minister's old horse, Captain Jack, is reckoned as quick a beast of his age as any in our location, and that are colt can beat him for a lick of a quarter of a mile quite easy – I see'd it myself.

Well, they larfed agin louder than before, and says father, if you dispute my word, try me; what odds will you give? Two to one, says the owner – 800 to 400 dollars. Well, that's a great deal of money, aint it, says father, if I was to lose it I'd look pretty foolish, would'nt I. How folks would pass their jokes at me when I went home again. You would'nt take that are waggon and harness for fifty dollars of it, would you? says he. Well, says the other, sooner than disappoint you, as you seem to have set your mind on losing your money, I don't care if I do.

As soon as it was settled, father drives off to the stables, and then returns mounted, with a red silk pocket handkerchief tied round his head, and colt a looking like himself, as proud as a nabob, chock full of spring like the wire eend of a bran new pair of trowser galluses – one said, that's a plaguy nice lookin colt that old feller has arter all, that horse will show play for it yet, says a third; and I heard one feller say, I guess that's a regular Yankee trick, a complete take in. They had a fair start for it, and off they sot, father took the lead and kept it, and won the race, tho' it was a pretty tight scratch, for father was too old to ride colt, he was near about the matter of seventy years old. Well when the colt was walked round after the race, there was an amazin crowd arter him, and several wanted to buy him; but, says father, how am I to get home without him, and what shall I do with that are waggon and harness so far as I be from Slickville. So he kept them in talk, till he felt their pulses pretty well, and at last he closed with a Southerner for 700 dollars, and we returned, having made a considerable good spec of colt. Says father to me, Sam, says he, you seed the crowd a follerin the winnin horse, when we came there, did'nt you? yes Sir, said I, I did. Well, when colt beat him, no one follered him at all, but come a crowded about *him*. That's popularity, said he, soon won, soon lost – cried up sky high one minute, and deserted the next or run down; colt will share the same fate. He'll get beat afore long, and then he's done for. The multitude are always fickle minded. Our great Washington found that out, and the British officer that beat Bounaparte, the bread they gave him turned sour afore he got half through the loaf. His soap had hardly stiffened afore it ran right back to lye and grease agin. I was sarved the same way, I liked to have missed my pension, the Committee said I warn't at Bunker's Hill at all, the villans. That was a Glo———, (thinks I, old boy, if you once get into that are field, you'll race longer than colt, a plaguy sight; you'll run clear away to the fence to the far eend afore you stop, so I jist cut in and took a hand myself,) yes, says I, you did 'em father, properly, that old waggon was a bright scheme, it led 'em on till you got 'em on the right spot, did'nt it? Says father, *there's a moral Sam, in every thing in natur.* Never have nothin to do with elections, you see the valy of popularity in the case of that are horse – sarve the public 999 times, and the 1000th, if they don't agree with you, they desart and abuse you – see how they sarved old John Adams, see how they let Jefferson starve in his old age, see how good old Munroe like to have got right into Jail, after his term of President was up. They may talk of independence, says father, but Sam, I'll tell you what independence is, and he gave his hands a slap agin his trowses pocket, and made the gold eagles he won at the race all jingle agin; *that,* says he, giving them another wipe with his fist, (and winkin as much as to say do you hear that my boy) *that I call independence.* He was in great spirits, the old man, he was so proud of winnin the race, and puttin the leake into the New Yorkers – he looked all dander. Let them great hungry, ill favored, long legged bitterns, says he, (only he called them by another name that don't sound quite pretty) from the outlandish states to Congress, *talk about* independence; but Sam, said he, (hitting the Shiners agin till he made them dance right up an eend in his pocket) *I like to feel it.*

No Sam, said he, line the pocket well first, make that independent, and then the spirit will be like a horse turned out to grass in the spring, for the first time, he's all head and tail, a snortin and kickin and racin and carryin on like mad – it soon gets independent too. While it's in the stall it may hold up, and paw, and whiner, and feel as spry as any thing, but the leather strap keeps it to the manger, and the lead weight to the eend of it makes it hold down its head at last. No, says he, here's independence, and he gave the eagles such a drive with his fist, he bust his pocket and sent a whole raft of them a spinnin down his leg to the ground – says I, father, (and I swear I could hardly keep from larfin, he looked so peskily vexed) father, says I, I guess there's a moral in that are too – *Extremes nary way are none o' the best.* Well, well, says he, (kinder snappishly) I suppose you're half right, Sam, but weve said enough about it, let's drop the subject, and see if I have picked em all up, for my eyes are none of the best now, I'm near hand to seventy.

MR. SLICK'S OPINION
OF THE BRITISH

What success had you, said I, in the sale of your clocks among the Scotch in the eastern part of the Province? do you find them as gullible as the Blue Noses? Well, said he, you have heerd tell that a Yankee never answers one question, without axing another, havent you? Did you ever see an English Stage Driver make a bow? because if you hante obsarved it, I have, and a queer one it is, I swan. He brings his right arm up, jist across his face, and passes on, with a knowin nod of his head, as much as to say, how do you do? but keep clear o' my wheels, or I'll fetch your horses a lick in the mouth as sure as youre born; jist as a bear puts up his paw to fend off the blow of a stick from his nose. Well, that's the way I pass them are bare breeched Scotchmen. Lord, if they were located down in these here Cumberland mashes, how the musquitoes would tickle them up, would'nt they? They'd set 'em scratching thereabouts, as an Irishman does his head, when he's in sarch of a lie. Them are fellers cut their eye teeth afore they ever sot foot in this country, I expect. When they get a bawbee, they know what to do with it, that's a fact; they open their pouch and drop it in, and its got a spring like a fox trap – it holds fast to all it gets, like grim death to a dead nigger. They are proper skin flints, you may depend. Oatmeal is no great shakes at best; it tante even as good for a horse as real yaller Varginy corn, but I guess I warnt long in finding out that the grits hardly pay for the riddlin. No, a Yankee has as little chance among them as a Jew has in New England; the sooner he clears out, the better. You can no more put a leake into them, than you can send a chisel into Teake wood – it turns the edge of the tool the first drive. If the Blue Noses knew the value of money as well as they do, they'd have more cash, and fewer clocks and tin reflectors, I reckon. Now, its different with the Irish; they never carry a puss, for they never have a cent to put in it. They are always in love or in liquor, or else in a row; they are the merriest shavers I ever seed. Judge Beeler, I dare say you have heerd tell of him – he's a funny feller – he put a notice over his factory gate at Lowell, 'no cigars or Irishmen admitted within these walls;' for, said he, the one will set a flame agoin among my cottons, and t'other among my galls. I wont have no such inflammable and dangerous things about me on no account. When the British wanted our folks to join in the treaty to chock the wheels of the slave trade, I recollect hearin old John Adams say, we had ought to humor them; for, says he, they supply us with labor on easier terms, by shippin out the Irish. Says he, they work better, and they work cheaper, and they dont live so long. The blacks, when they are past work hang on for ever, and a proper bill of expence they be; but hot weather and new rum rub out the poor rates for tother ones. The English are the boys for tradin with; they shell out their cash like a sheaf of wheat in frosty weather – it flies all over the thrashin floor; but then they are a cross grained, ungainly, kicken breed of cattle, as I een a most ever see'd. Whoever gave them the name of John Bull, knew what he was about, I tell you; for they are bull-necked, bull-headed folks, I vow; sulky, ugly tempered, vicious critters, a pawin and a roarin the whole time, and plaguy onsafe unless well watched. They are as headstrong as mules, and as conceited as peacocks.

The astonishment with which I heard this tirade against my countrymen, absorbed every feeling of resentment. I listened with amazement at the perfect composure with which he uttered it. He treated it as one of those self evident truths, that need neither proof nor apology, but as a thing well known and admitted by all mankind. There's no richer sight that I know of, said he, than to see one on 'em when he first lands in one of our great cities. He swells out as big as a balloon, his skin is ready to bust with wind – a regular walking bag of gas; and he prances over the pavement like a bear over hot iron – a great awkward hulk of a feller, (for they aint to be compared to the French in manners) a smirkin at you, as much as to say, 'look here, Jonathan, here's an Englishman; here's a boy that's got blood as pure as a Norman pirate, and lots of the blunt of both kinds, a pocket full of one, and a mouthfull of tother; beant he lovely?' and then he looks as fierce as a tiger, as much as to say, 'say boo *to a goose*, if you dare.' No, I believe we may stump the Univarse; we improve on every thing, and we have improved on our own species. You'll sarch one while, I tell you, afore you'll find a man that, take him by and large, is equal to one of our free and enlightened citizens. He's the chap that has both speed, wind and bottom; he's clear grit – ginger to the back bone, you may depend. Its generally allowed there aint the beat of them to be found any where. Spry as a fox, supple as an eel, and cute as a weasel. Though I say it that should'nt say it, they fairly take the shine off creation – they are actilly equal to cash.

He looked like a man who felt that he had expressed himself so aptly and so well, that any thing additional would only weaken its effect; he therefore changed the conversation immediately, by pointing to a tree at some little distance from the house, and remarking that it was the rock maple or sugar tree. Its a pretty tree, said he, and a profitable one too to raise. It will bear tapping for many years, tho' it gets exhausted at last. This Province is like that are tree, it is tapped till it begins to die at the top, and if they dont drive in a spile and stop the everlastin flow of the sap, it will perish altogether. All the money that's made here, all the interest that's paid in it, and a pretty considerable portion of rent too, all goes abroad for investment, and the rest is sent to us to buy bread. Its drained like a bog, it has opened and covered trenches all through it, and then there's others to the foot of the upland to cut off the springs. Now you may make even a bog too dry; you may take the moisture out to that degree, that the very sile becomes dust and blows away. The English funds, and our banks, rail roads, and canals, are all absorbing your capital like a spunge, and will lick it up as fast as you can make it. That very Bridge we heerd of at Windsor, is owned in New Brunswick, and will pay tole to that province. The capitalists of Nova Scotia treat it like a hired house, they wont keep it in repair; they neither paint it to presarve the boards, nor stop a leak to keep the frame from rottin; but let it go to wrack sooner than drive a nail or put in a pane of glass. It will sarve our turn out they say. There's neither spirit, enterprise, nor patriotism here; but the whole country is as inactive as a bear in winter, that does nothin but scrouch up in his den, a thinkin to himself, "well if I ant an unfortunate divil, it's a pity; I have a most splendid warm coat as are a gentleman in these here woods, let him be who he will; but I got no socks to my feet, and have to sit for everlastingly a suckin of my paws to keep 'em warm; if it warn't for that, I guess, I'd make some o' them chaps that have hoofs to their feet and horns to their heads, look about them pretty sharp, I know." It's dismal now, aint it? If I had the framin of the Governor's message, if I would'nt shew 'em how to put timber together you may depend, I'd make them scratch their heads and stare, I know. I went down to Matanzas in the Fulton Steam Boat once – well, it was the first of the kind they ever see'd, and proper scared they were to see a vessel, without sails or oars, goin right straight a head, nine knots an hour, in the very wind's eye, and a great streak of smoke arter her as long as the tail of a Comet. I believe they thought it was Old Nick alive, a treatin himself to a swim. You could see the niggers a clippin it away from the shore, for dear life, and the soldiers a movin about as if they thought that we were a goin to take the whole country. Presently a little half starved orange-coloured looking Spanish officer, all dressed off in his livery, as fine as a fiddle, came off with two men in a boat to board us. Well, we yawed once or twice, and motioned to him to keep off for fear he should get hurt; but he came right on afore the wheel, and I hope I may be shot if the paddle did'nt strike the bow of the boat with that force, it knocked up the starn like a plank tilt, when one of the boys playing on it is heavier than t'other; and chucked him right atop of the wheel house – you never see'd a feller in such a dunderment in your life. He had picked up a little English from seein our folks there so much, and when he got up, the first thing he said was, 'Damn all sheenery, I say, where's my boat?' and he looked round as if he thought it had jumped on board too. Your boat, said the Captain, why I expect it's gone to the bottom, and your men have gone down to look arter it, for we never see'd or heerd tell of one or t'other of them arter the boat was struck. Yes, I'd make 'em stare like that are Spanish officer, as if they had see'd out of their eyes for the first time. Governor Campbell did'nt expect to see such a country as this, when he came here, I reckon; I know he did'nt. When I was a little boy, about knee high or so, and lived down Connecticut River, mother used to say, Sam, if you don't give over acting so like old Scratch, I'll send you off to Nova Scotia as sure as you are born; I will, I vow. Well, Lord, how that are used to frighten me; it made my hair stand right up an eend, like a cat's back when she is wrathy; it made me drop it as quick as wink – like a tin night cap put on a dipt candle agoin to bed, it put the fun right out. Neighbor Dearborn's darter married a gentleman to Yarmouth, that speculates in the smugglin line; well, when she went on board to sail down to Nova Scotia, all her folks took on as if it was a funeral; they said she was goin to be buried alive like the nuns in Portengale that get a frolickin, break out of the pastur, and race off, and get catched and brought back agin. Says the old Colonel, her father, Deliverance, my dear, I would sooner foller you to your grave, for that would be an eend to your troubles, than to see you go off to that dismal country, that's nothin but an iceberg aground; and he howled as loud as an Irishman that tries to wake his wife when she is dead. Awful accounts we have of the country, that's a fact; but if the Province is not so bad as they make it out, the folks are a thousand times worse. You've seen a flock of partridges of a frosty mornin in the fall, a crowdin out of the shade to a sunny spot, and huddlin up there in the warmth – well, the Blue Noses have nothin else to do half the time but sun themselves. Whose fault is that? Why it's the fault of the legislature; *they don't encourage internal improvement, nor the investment of capital in the country; and the result is apathy, inaction and poverty.* They spend three months in Halifax, and what do they do? Father gave me a dollar once, to go to the fair at Hartford, and when I came back, says he, Sam, what have you got to show for it? Now I ax what have they to show for their three months' setting? They mislead folks; they make 'em believe all the use of the Assembly is to bark at Councillors, Judges, Bankers, and such cattle, to keep 'em from eatin up the crops; and it actilly costs more to feed them when they are watchin, than all the others could eat if they did break a fence and get in. Indeed some folks say they are the most breachy of the two, and ought to go to pound themselves. If their fences are good them hungry cattle could'nt break through; and if they aint, they ought to stake 'em up, and with them well; *but it's no use to make fences unless the land is cultivated.* If I see a farm all gone to wrack, I say here's bad husbandry and bad management; and if I see a Province like this, of great capacity, and great natural resources, poverty-stricken, I say there's bad legislation. No, said he, (with an air of more seriousness than I had yet observed,) *how much it is to be regretted, that, laying aside personal attacks and petty jealousies, they would not unite as one man, and with one mind and one heart apply themselves sedulously to the internal improvement and developement of this beautiful Province. Its value is utterly unknown, either to the general or local Government, and the only persons who duly appreciate it, are the Yankees.*

A YANKEE HANDLE
FOR A HALIFAX BLADE

I met a man this mornin, said the Clockmaker, from Halifax, a real conceited lookin critter as you een a most ever seed, all shines and didos. He looked as if he had picked up his airs, arter some officer of the regilars had worn 'em out and cast 'em off. They sot on him like second hand clothes, as if they had'nt been made for him and did'nt exactly fit. He looked fine, but awkward, like a captain of militia, when he gets his uniform on, to play sodger; a thinkin himself mighty hand*sum*, and that all the world is a lookin at him. He marched up and down afore the street door like a peacock, as large as life and twice as natural; he had a riding whip in his hand and every now and then struck it agin his thigh, as much as to say, aint that a splendid leg for a boot, now? Wont I astonish the Amherst folks, that's all? thinks I you are a pretty blade, aint you? I'd like to fit a Yankee handle on to you, that's a fact. When I came up, he held up his head near about as high as a Shot factory, and stood with his fists on his hips, and eyed me from head to foot, as a shakin quaker does a town lady: as much as to say what a queer critter you be, that's toggery I never seed afore, you'r some carnal minded maiden, that's sartain.

Well, says he to me, with the air of a man that chucks a cent into a beggar's hat, "a fine day this, Sir;" do you actilly think so, said I? and I gave it the real Connecticut drawl. Why, said he, quite short, if I did'nt think so, I would'nt say so. Well, says I, I don't know, but if I did think so, I guess I would'nt say so; why not? says he – because, I expect, says I, any fool could see that as well as me; and then I stared at him, as much as to say, now if you like that are swap, I am ready to trade with you agin as soon as you like. Well he turned right round on his heel and walked off, a whistlin Yankee Doodle to himself. He looked jist like a man that finds whistlin a plaguy sight easier than thinkin. Presently, I heard him ax the groom who that are Yankee lookin feller was. That, said the groom, why, I guess its Mr. Slick. Sho!! said he, how you talk. What, Slick the Clockmaker, why it ant possible; I wish I had a known that are afore, I declare, for I have a great curiosity to see *him*, folks say he is an amazin clever feller that, and he turned and stared, as if it was old Hickory himself. Then he walked round and about like a pig, round the fence of a potatoe field, a watchin for a chance to cut in; so, thinks I, I'll jist give him something to talk about, when he gets back to the city, I'll fix a Yankee handle on to him in no time. How's times to Halifax, Sir, said I – better, says he, much better, business is done on a surer bottom than it was, and things look bright agin; so does a candle, says I, jist afore it goes out; it burns up ever so high and then sinks right down, and leaves nothin behind but grease, and an everlastin bad smell. I guess they don't know how to feed their lamp, and it can't burn long on nothin. No, Sir, the jig is up with Halifax, and it's all their own fault. If a man sits at his door, and sees stray cattle in his field, a eatin up of his crop, and his neighbors a cartin off his grain, and won't so much as go and drive 'em out, why I should say it sarves him right. I don't exactly understand, Sir, said he – thinks I, it would be strange if you did, for I never see one of your folks yet that could understand a hawk from a handsaw. Well, says I, I will tell you what I mean – draw a line from Cape Sable to Cape Cansoo, right thro' the Province, and it will split it into two, this way, and I cut an apple into two halves; now, says I, the worst half, like the rotten half of the apple, belongs to Halifax, and the other and sound half belongs to St. John. Your side of the province on the sea coast is all stone – I never seed such a proper sight of rocks in my life, it's enough to starve a rabbit. Well, tother side on the Bay of Fundy is a super-fine country, there aint the beat of it to be found any where. Now, would'nt the folks living away up to the Bay, be pretty fools to go to Halifax, when they can go to St. John with half the trouble. St. John is the natural capital of the Bay of Fundy, it will be the largest city in America next to New York. It has an immense back country as big as Great Britain, a first chop river, and amazin sharp folks, most as cute as the Yankees – it's a splendid location for business. Well, they draw all the produce of the Bay shores, and where the produce goes, the supplies return – it will take the whole trade of the Province; I guess your rich folks will find they've burnt their fingers, they've put their foot in it, that's a fact. Houses without tenants – wharves without shipping, a town without people – what a grand invest-ment!! If you have any loose dollars, let 'em out on mortgage in Halifax, that's the security – keep clear of the country for your life – the people may run, but the town can't. No, take away the troops, and you're done – you'll sing the dead march folks did at Louisburg and Shelburne. Why you hant got a single thing worth havin, but a good harbor, and as for that the coast is full on 'em. You hav'nt a pine log, a spruce board or a refuse shingle; you neither raise wheat, oats, or hay, nor never can; you have no staples on airth, unless it be them iron ones for the padlocks, in Bridewell – you've sowed pride and reaped poverty, take care of your crop, for it's worth harvestin – you have no River and no Country, what in the name of fortin have you to trade on? But, said he, (and he shewed the whites of his eyes like a wall eyed horse) but, said he, Mr. Slick, how is it then, Halifax ever grew at all, has'nt it got what it always had; it's no worse than it was. I guess, said I, that pole aint strong enough to bear you, neither; if you trust to that you'll be into the brook, as sure as you are born; you once had the trade of the whole Province, but St. John has run off with that now – you've lost all but your trade in blue berries and rabbits with the niggers at Hammond Plains. *You've lost your customers, your rivals have a better stand for business – they've got the corner store – four great streets meet there, and its near the market slip.*

Well he stared; says he, I believe you're right, but I never thought of that afore; (thinks I, nobody ever suspect you of the trick of thinkin that ever I heer'd tell of) some of our great men, said he, laid it all to your folks selling so many Clocks and Polyglot Bibles, they say you have taken off a horrid sight of money; did they, indeed, said I; well, I guess it tante pins and needles that's the expense of house-keepin, it is something more costly than that. Well, some folks say its the Banks, says he; better still, says I, perhaps you've hearn tell too that greasing the axle, makes a gig harder to draw, for there's jist about as much sense in that. Well then, says he, others say its smugglin has made us so poor. That guess, said I, is most as good as tother one, whoever found out that secret ought to get a patent for it, for its worth knowin. Then the country has grown poorer, has'nt it, because it has bought cheaper this year, than it did the year before? Why, your folks are cute chaps, I vow; they'd puzzle a Philadelphia Lawyer, they are so amazin knowin. Ah, said he, and he rubb'd his hands and smiled like a young doctor, when he gets his first patient; ah, said he, if the timber duties are altered, down comes St. John, body and breeches, it's built on a poor foundation – its all show – they are speculatin like mad – they'll ruin themselves. Says I, if you wait till they're dead, for your fortin, it will be one while, I tell you, afore you pocket the shiners. Its no joke waitin for a dead man's shoes. Suppose an old feller of 80 was to say when that are young feller dies, I'm to inherit his property, what would you think? Why, I guess you'd think he was an old fool. *No Sir, if the English don't want their timber we do want it all, we have used ourn up, we hant got a stick even to whittle.* If the British dont offer we will, and St. John, like a dear little weeping widow, will dry up her tears, and take to frolickin agin and accept it right off. There is'nt at this moment such a location hardly in America, as St. John; for beside all its other advantages, it has this great one, its only rival, Halifax, has got a dose of opium that will send it snoring out of the world, like a feller who falls asleep on the ice of a winter's night. It has been asleep so long, I actilly think it never will wake. Its an easy death too, you may rouse them up if you like, but I vow I wont. I once brought a feller too that was drowned, and one night he got drunk and quilted me, I could'nt walk for a week; says I, your the last chap I'll ever save from drowning in all my born days, if that's all the thanks I get for it. No Sir, Halifax has lost the run of its custom. Who does Yarmouth trade with? St. John. Who does Annapolis County trade with? St. John. Who do all the folks on the Basin of Mines, and Bay shore, trade with? St. John. Who does Cumberland trade with? St. John. Well Pictou, Lunenburg and Liverpool, supply themselves, and the rest that aint worth havin, trade with Halifax. They take down a few half starved pigs, old viteran geese, and long legged fowls, some ram mutton and tuf beef, and swap them for tea, sugar, and such little notions for their old women to home; while the rail roads and canals of St. John are goin to cut off your Gulf Shore trade to Miramichi, and along there. Flies live in the summer and die in winter, you're jist as noisy in war as those little critters, but you sing small in peace.

No, your done for, you are up a tree, you may depend; pride must fall. Your town is like a ball room arter a dance. The folks have eat, drank, and frolicked, and left an empty house; the lamps and hangings are left, but the people are gone. Is there no remedy for this? said he, and he looked as wild as a Cherokee Indian. Thinks I, the handle is fitten on proper tight now. Well, says I, when a man has a cold, he had ought to look out pretty sharp, afore it gets seated on his lungs; if he don't, he gets into a gallopin consumption, and it's gone goose with him. There is a remedy, if applied in time: *make a rail road to Minas Basin, and you have a way for your customers to get to you, and a conveyance for your goods to them.* When I was in New York last, a cousin of mine, Hezekiah Slick, said to me, I do believe Sam, I shall be ruined; I've lost all my custom, they are widening and improving the streets, and there's so many carts and people to work in it, folks can't come to my shop to trade, what on airth shall I do, and I'm payin a dreadful high rent too? Stop Ki, says I, when the street is all finished off and slicked up, they'll all come back agin, and a whole raft more on 'em too, you'll sell twice as much as ever you did, you'll put off a proper swad of goods next year, you may depend; and so he did, he made money, hand over hand. A rail road will bring back your customers, if done right off; but wait till trade has made new channels, and fairly gets settled in them, and you'll never divart it agin to all eternity. When a feller waits till a gall gets married, I guess it will be too late to pop the question then. St. John *must* go ahead, at any rate; you *may*, if you choose, but you must exert yourselves I tell you. If a man has only one leg, and wants to walk, he must get an artificial one. If you have no river, make a rail road, and that will supply its place. But, says he, Mr. Slick, people say it never will pay in the world; they say its as mad a scheme as the canal. Do they indeed, says I, send them to me then, and I'll fit the handle on to them in tu tu's. I say it will pay, and the best proof is, our folks will take tu thirds of the stock. Did you ever hear any one else but your folks, ax whether a dose of medicine would pay when it was given to save life? If that ever-lastin long Erie canal can secure to New York the supply of that far off country, most tother side of creation, surely a rail road of 45 miles can give you the trade of the Bay of Fundy. A rail road will go from Halifax to Windsor and make them one town, easier to send goods from one tother, than from Governor Campbell's House to Admiral Cockburn's. A bridge makes a town, a river makes a town, a canal makes a town, but a rail road is bridge, river, thoroughfare, canal, all in one; what a wappin large place that would make, would'nt it? It would be the dandy, that's a fact. No, when you go back, take a piece of chalk, and the first dark night, write on every door in Halifax, in large letters – *a rail road* – and if they dont know the meanin of it, says you its a Yankee word; if you'll go to Sam Slick, the Clockmaker, (the chap that fixed a Yankee handle on to a Halifax blade, and I made him a scrape of my leg, as much as to say, that's you,) every man that buys a Clock shall hear all about a *Rail Road*.

THE GRAHAMITE AND THE
IRISH PILOT

I think, said I, this is a happy country, Mr. Slick. The people are fortunately all of one origin, there are no national jealousies to divide and no very violent politics to agitate them. They appear to be cheerful and contented, and are a civil, good natured, hospitable race. Considering the unsettled state of almost every part of the world, I think I would as soon cast my lot in Nova Scotia as in any part I know of. Its a clever country, you may depend, said he, a very clever country; full of mineral wealth, aboundin in superior water privileges and noble harbors, a large part of it prime land, and it is in the very heart of the fisheries. But the folks put me in mind of a sect in our country they call the Grahamites – they eat no meat and no exciting food, and drink nothin stronger than water. They call it Philosophy (and that is such a pretty word it has made fools of more folks than them afore now,) but I call it tarnation nonsense. I once travelled all through the State of Maine with one of them are chaps. He was as thin as a whippin post. His skin looked like a blown bladder arter some of the air had leaked out, kinder wrinkled and rumpled like, and his eye as dim as a lamp that's livin on a short allowance of ile. He put me in mind of a pair of kitchen tongs, all legs, shaft and head, and no belly; a real gander gutted lookin critter, as holler as a bamboo walkin cane, and twice as yaller. He actilly looked as if he had been picked off a rack at sea, and dragged through a gimlet hole. He was a lawyer. Thinks I, the Lord a massy on your clients, you hungry half starved lookin critter, you, you'll eat em up alive as sure as the Lord made Moses. You are just the chap to strain at a gnat and swallow a camel, tank, shank and flank, all at a gulp. Well, when we came to an inn, and a beef steak was sot afore us for dinner, he'd say: oh that is too good for me, its too exciting, all fat meat is diseased meat, give me some bread and cheese. Well, I'd say, I dont know what you call too good, but it tante good enough for me, for I call it as tuf as laushong, and that will bear chawing all day. When I liquidate for my dinner, I like to get about the best that's goin, and I ant a bit too well pleased if I dont. Exciting indeed!! thinks I. Lord, I should like to see you excited, if it was only for the fun of the thing. What a temptin lookin critter you'd be among the galls, would'nt you? Why, you look like a subject the doctor boys had dropped on the road arter they had dug you up, and had cut stick and run for it. Well, when tea came, he said the same thing, it's too exciting, give me some water, do; that's follorin the law of natur. Well, says I, if that's the case, you ought to eat beef; why, says he, how do you make out that are proposition? Why, says I, if drinking water instead of tea is natur, so is eatin grass accordin to natur; now all flesh is grass, we are told, so you had better eat that and call it vegetable; like a man I once seed who fasted on fish on a Friday, and when he had none, whipped a leg o' mutton into the oven, and took it out fish, says he it's "changed *plaice*," that's all, and "*plaice*" aint a bad fish. The Catholics fast enough, gracious knows, but then they fast on a great rousin big splendid salmon at two dollars and forty cents a pound, and lots of old Madeira to make it float light on the stomach; there's some sense in mortifying the appetite arter that fashion, but plaguy little in your way. No, says I, friend, you may talk about natur as you please, I've studied natur all my life, and I vow if your natur could speak out, it would tell you, it dont over half like to be starved arter that plan. If you know'd as much about the marks of the mouth as I do, you'd know that you have carniverous as well as graniverous teeth, and that natur meant by that, you should eat most any thing that are door-keeper, your nose, would give a ticket to, to pass into your mouth. Father rode a race at New York course, when he was near hand to seventy, and that's more nor you'll do, I guess, and he eats as hearty as a turkey cock, and he never confined himself to water neither, when he could get anything convened him better. Says he, Sam, grandfather Slick used to say there was an old proverb in Yorkshire "a full belly makes a strong back," and I guess if you try it, natur will tell you so too. If ever you go to Connecticut, jist call into father's, and he'll give you a real right down genuine New England breakfast, and if that dont happify your heart, then my name's not Sam Slick. It will make you feel about among the stiffest, I tell you. It will blow your jacket out like a pig at sea. You'll have to shake a reef or two out of your waistbans and make good stowage, I guess, to carry it all under hatches. There's nothin like a good pasture to cover the ribs, and make the hide shine, depend on't.

Now this Province is like that are Grahamite lawyer's beef, its too good for the folks that's in it; they either dont avail its value or wont use it, because work ant arter their "law of nature." As you say they are quiet enough (there's worse folks than the Blue Noses, too, if you come to that,) and so they had ought to be quiet for they have nothin to fight about. As for politics, they have nothin to desarve the name, but they talk enough about it, and a plaguy sight of nonsense they do talk too. Now with us the country is divided into two parties, of the mammouth breed, the *ins* and the *outs*, the *administration* and the *opposition*. But where's the administration here? Where's the war office, the Foreign Office and the Home Office? Where's the Secretary of the Navy? Where's the State Bank? Where's the Ambassadors and Diplomatists (them are the boys to wind off a snarl of ravellins as slick as if it were on a reel) and where's that Ship of State, fitted up all the way from the forecastle clean up to the starn post, chock full of good snug berths, handsumly found and furnished, tier over tier, one above another, as thick as it can hold? That's a helm worth handlen, I tell you; I dont wonder that folks mutiny below and fight on the decks above for it – it makes a plaguy uproar the whole time, and keeps the passengers for everlastinly in a state of alarm for fear they'd do mischif by bustin the byler, a runnin aground, or gettin foul of some other craft. This Province is better as it is, quieter and happier far; they have berths enough and big enough, they should be careful not to increase 'em; and if they were to do it over agin, perhaps they'd be as well with fewer. They have two parties here, the Tory party and the Opposition party, and both on em run to extremes. Them radicals, says one, are for levelin all down to their own level, tho' not a peg lower; that's their gage, jist down to their own notch and no further; and they'd agitate the whole country to obtain that object, for if a man can't grow to be as tall as his neighbor, if he cuts a few inches off him why then they are both of one heighth. They are a most dangerous, disaffected people – they are etarnally appealin to the worst passions of the mob. Well, says tother, them aristocrats, they'll ruinate the country, they spend the whole revenu on themselves. What with Bankers, Councillors,

Judges, Bishops and Public Officers, and a whole tribe of Lawyers as hungry as hawks, and jist about as marciful, the country is devoured as if there was a flock of locusts a feedin on it. There's nothin left for roads and bridges. When a chap sets out to canvass, he's got to antagonise one side or tother. If he hangs on to the powers that be, then he's a Council man, he's for votin large salaries, for doin as the great people at Halifax tell him. *He is a fool.* If he is on tother side, a railin at Banks, Judges, Lawyers and such cattle, and baulin for what he knows he can't get, then *he is a rogue.* So that, if you were to listen to the weak and noisy critters on both sides, you'd believe the House of Assembly was *one half rogues and tother half fools.* All this arises from ignorance. *If they knew more of each other, I guess they'd lay aside one half their fears and all their abuse. The upper classes don't know one half the virtue that's in the middlin and lower classes; and they don't know one half the integrity and good feelin that's in the others, and both are fooled and gulled by their own noisy and designin champions.* Take any two men that are by the ears, they opinionate all they hear of each other, impute all sorts of onworthy motives, and misconstrue every act; let them see more of each other, and they'll find out to their surprise, that they have not only been lookin thro' a magnifyin glass, that warnt very true, but a coloured one also, that changed the complexion and distorted the featurs, and each one will think tother a very good kind of chap; and like as not a plaguy pleasant one too.

If I was axed which side was farthest from the mark in this Province, I vow I should be puzzled to say. As I dont belong to the country, and dont care a snap of my finger for either of 'em, I suppose I can judge better than any man in it, but I snore I dont think there's much difference. The popular side (I wont say patriotic, for we find in our steam boats a man who has a plaguy sight of property in his portmanter, is quite as anxious for its safety, as him that's only one pair of yarn stockings and a clean shirt, is for hisn) the popular side are not so well informed as tother, and they have the misfortin of havin their passions addressed more than their reason, therefore they are often out of the way, or rather led out of it and put astray by bad guides; well, tother side have the prejudices of birth and education to dim their vision, and are alarmed to undertake a thing from the dread of ambush or open foes, that their guides are etarnally descryin in the mist – *and beside, power has a nateral tendency to corpulency.* As for them guides, I'd make short work of 'em if it was me. In the last war with Britain, the Constitution frigate was close in once on the shores of Ireland, a lookin arter some marchant ships, and she took on board a pilot; well, he was a deep, sly, twistical lookin chap, as you een amost ever seed. He had a sort of dark down look about him, and a lear out of the corner of one eye, like a horse that's goin to kick. The captain guessed he read in his face "well now, if I was to run this here Yankee right slap on a rock and bilge her, the King would make a man of me forever." So, says he to the first leftenant, reeve a rope thro' that are block at the tip eend of the fore yard, and clap a runnin nuse in it. The leftenant did it as quick as wink, and came back, and says he, I guess it's done. Now says the captain, look here, pilot, here's a rope you hant seed yet, I'll jist explain the use of it to you in case you want the loan of it. If this here frigate, manned with our free and enlightened citizens, gets aground, I'll give you a ride on the slack of that are rope, right up to that yard by the neck, by Gum. Well, it rub'd all the writin out of his face, as quick as spittin on a slate takes a sum out, you may depend. Now, they should rig up a crane over the street door of the State house at Halifax, and when any of the pilots at either eend of the buildin, run 'em on the breakers on purpose, string em up like an onsafe dog. A sign of that are kind, with "a house of public entertainment," painted under it, would do the business in less than no time. If it would'nt keep the hawks out of the poultry yard, it's a pity – it would scare them out of a year's growth, that's a fact – if they used it once, I guess they would'nt have occasion for it agin in a hurry – it would be like the Aloe tree, and that bears fruit only once in a hundred years. If you want to know how to act any time, squire, never go to books, leave them to galls and school boys; but go right off and cypher it out of natur, that's a sure guide, it will never deceive you, you may depend. For instance, "*what's that to me,*" is a phrase so common that it shows it's a natural one, when people have no particular interest in a thing. Well, when a feller gets so warm on either side as never to use that phrase at all, watch him, that's all! keep your eye on him, or he'll walk right into you afore you know where you be. If a man runs to me and says, "your fence is down," thank you, says I, that's kind – if he comes agin and says, "I guess some stray cattle have broke into your short sarce garden," I thank him again; says I, come now, this is neighborly; but when he keeps etarnally tellin me this thing of one sarvant, and that thing of another sarvant, hints that my friends ant true, that my neighbors are inclined to take advantage of me, and that suspicious folks are seen about my place, I say to myself, what on airth makes this critter take such a wonderful interest in my affairs? I dont like to hear such tales – he's arter somethin as sure as the world, if he war'nt he'd say, "*what's that to me.*" I never believe much what I hear said by a man's *violent friend,* or *violent enemy,* I want to hear what a disinterested man has to say – now, *as a disinterested man, I say if the members of the House of Assembly, instead of raisin up ghosts and hobgoblins to frighten folks with, and to shew what swordsmen they be, a cuttin and a thrustin at phantoms that only exist in their own brains, would turn to, heart and hand, and develope the resources of this fine country, facilitate the means of transport – promote its internal improvement, and encourage its foreign trade, they would make it the richest and greatest, as it now is one of the happiest sections of all America – I hope I may be skinned if they would'nt – they would I swan.*

THE CLOCKMAKER QUILTS
A BLUE NOSE

The descendants of Eve have profited little by her example. The curiosity of the fair sex is still insatiable, and, as it is often ill directed, it frequently terminates in error. In the country this feminine propensity is troublesome to a traveller, and he who would avoid importunities, would do well to announce at once, on his arrival at a Cumberland Inn, his name and his business, the place of his abode and the length of his visit. Our beautiful hostess, Mrs. Pugwash, as she took her seat at the breakfast table this morning, exhibited the example that suggested these reflections. She was struck with horror at our conversation, the latter part only of which she heard, and of course misapplied and misunderstood. She was run down by the President, said I, and has been laid up for some time. Gulard's people have stripped her, in consequence of her making water so fast. Stripped whom? said Mrs. Pugwash, as she suddenly dropped the teapot from her hand; stripped whom, – for heaven's sake tell me who it is? The Lady Ogle, said I. Lady Ogle, said she, how horrid! Two of her ribs were so broken as to require to be replaced with new ones. Two new ribs, said she, well I never heer'd the beat of that in all my born days; poor critter, how she must have suffered. On examining her below the waist they found – Examining her still lower, said she (all the pride of her sex revolting at the idea of such an indecent exhibition,) you don't pretend to say they stripped her below the waist; what did the Admiral say? Did he stand by and see her handled in that way? The Admiral, madam, said I, did not trouble his head about it. They found her extremely unsound there, and much worm eaten. Worm eaten, she continued, how awful! it must have been them nasty jiggers, that got in there; they tell me they are dreadful thick in the West Indies; Joe Crow had them in his feet, and lost two of his toes. Worm eaten, dear, dear!! but still that aint so bad as having them great he fellows strip one. I promise you if them Gulards had undertaken to strip me, I'd a taught them different guess manners; I'd a died first before I'd a submitted to it. I always heerd tell the English quality ladies were awful bold, but I never heerd the like o' that.

What on airth are you drivin at? said Mr. Slick. I never seed you so much out in your latitude afore, marm, I vow. We were talking of reparin a vessel, not strippin' a woman, what under the sun could have put that are crotchet into your head? She looked mortified and humbled at the result of her own absurd curiosity, and soon quitted the room. I thought I should have snorted right out two or three times, said the Clockmaker; I had to pucker up my mouth like the upper eend of a silk puss, to keep from yawhawin in her face, to hear the critter let her clapper run that fashion. She is not the first hand that has caught a lobster, by puttin in her oar afore her turn, I guess. She'll mind her stops next hitch, I reckon. This was our last breakfast at Amherst.

An early frost that smote the potatoe fields, and changed the beautiful green color of the Indian corn into shades of light yellow, and dark brown, reminded me of the presence of autumn – of the season of short days and bad roads, I determined to proceed at once to Parrsboro, and thence by the Windsor and Kentville route to Annapolis, Yarmouth, and Shelburne, and to return by the shore road, through Liverpool and Lunenburg to Halifax. I therefore took leave, (though not without much reluctance) of the Clockmaker, whose intention had been to go to Fort Lawrence. Well, said he, I vow I am sorry to part company along with you; a considerable long journey like ourn, is like sitting up late with the galls, a body knows its getting on pretty well towards mornin, and yet feels loth to go to bed, for its just the time folks grow sociable.

I got a scheme in my head, said he, that I think will answer both on us; I got debts due to me in all them are places for Clocks sold by the concarn, now suppose you leave your horse on these mashes this fall, he'll get as fat as a fool, he wont be able to see out of his eyes in a month, and I'll put "*Old Clay*," (I call him Clay arter our senator, who is a prime bit of stuff) into a Yankee waggon I have here, and drive you all round the coast. This was too good an offer to be declined. A run at grass for my horse, an easy and comfortable waggon, and a guide so original and amusing as Mr. Slick, were either of them enough to induce my acquiescence.

As soon as we had taken our seats in the waggon, he observed, we shall progress real handsum now; that are horse goes etarnal fast, he near about set my axle on fire twice. He's a spanker you may depend. I had him when he was a two year old, all legs and tail, like a devil's darnin needle, and had him broke on purpose by father's old nigger, January Snow. He knows English real well, and can do near about any thing but speak it. He helped me once to ginn a Blue Nose a proper handsum quiltin. He must have stood a poor chance indeed, said I, a horse kickin, and a man striking him at the same time. Oh! not arter that pattern at all, said he, Lord if "Old Clay" had a kicked him, he'd a smashed him like that are sarcer you broke at Pugnose's inn, into ten hundred thousand million flinders. Oh! no, if I did'nt fix his flint for him in fair play it's a pity. I'll tell you how it was. I was up to Truro, at Ezra Whitter's Inn. There was an arbitration there atween Deacon Text and Deacon Faithful. Well, there was a nation sight of folks there, for they said it was a biter bit, and they came to witness the sport, and to see which critter would get the ear mark.

Well, I'd been doin a little business there among the folks, and had jist sot off for the river, mounted on "Old Clay," arter takin a glass of Ezra's most particular handsum Jamaiky, and was trottin off pretty slick, when who should I run agin but Tim Bradley. He is a dreadful ugly cross grained critter, as you een amost ever seed, when he is about half shaved. Well, I stopped short, and says I, Mr. Bradley, I hope you beant hurt; I'm proper sorry I run agin you, you cant feel uglier than I do about it, I do assure you. He called me a Yankee pedlar, a cheatin vagabond, a wooden nutmeg, and threw a good deal of assorted hardware of that kind at me; and the crowd of folks cried out, down with the Yankee, let him have it Tim, teach him better manners; and they carried on pretty high, I tell you. Well, I got my dander up too, I felt all up on eend like; and, thinks I to myself, my lad if I get a clever chance, I'll give you such a quiltin as you never had since you were raised from a seedlin, I vow. So, says I, Mr. Bradley, I guess you had better let me be; you know I cant fight no more than a cow – I never was brought up to wranglin, and I don't like it. Haul off the cowardly rascal, they all bawled out, haul him off, and lay it into him. So he lays right hold of me by the collar, and gives me a pull, and I lets on as if I'd lost my balance and falls right down. Then I jumps up on eend, and says I "go ahead Clay," and the old horse he sets off a head, so I knew I had him when I wanted him. Then, says I, I hope you are satisfied now, Mr. Bradley, with that are ungenteel fall you ginn me. Well, he makes a blow at me, and I dodged it; now, says I, you'll be sorry for this, I tell you; I wont be treated this way for nothin, I'll go right off and swear my life agin you, I'm most afeerd you'll murder me. Well, he strikes at me agin, (thinkin he has a genuine soft horn to deal with,) and hits me in the shoulder. Now, says I, I wont stand here to be lathered like a dog all day long this fashion, it tante pretty at all, I guess I'll give you a chase for it. Off I sets arter my horse like mad, and he arter me, (I did that to get clear of the crowd, so that I might have fair play at him.) Well, I soon found I had the heels of him, and could play him as I liked. Then I slackened up a little, and when he came close up to me, so as nearly to lay his hand upon me, I squatted right whap down, all short, and he pitched over me near about a rod or so, I guess, on his head, and plowed up the ground with his nose, the matter of a foot or two. If he didn't polish up the coulter, and both mould boards of his face, its a pity. Now, says I, you had better lay where you be and let me go, for I am proper tired; I blow like a horse that's got the heaves; and besides, says I, I guess you had better wash your face, for I am most a feard you hurt yourself. That ryled him properly; I meant that it should; so he ups and at me awful spiteful like a bull; then I lets him have it, right, left, right, jist three corkers, beginning with the right hand, shift-ing to the left, and then with the right hand agin. This way I did it, said the Clockmaker, (and he showed me the manner in which it was done) its a beautiful way of hitting, and always does the business – a blow for each eye and one for the mouth. It sounds like ten pounds ten on a blacksmith's anvil; I bunged up both eyes for him, and put in the dead lights in two tu's, and drew three of his teeth, quicker a plaguy sight than the Truro doctor could, to save his soul alive. Now, says I, my friend, when you recover your eye-sight I guess you'll see your mistake – I warnt born in the woods to be scared by an owl. The next time you feel in a most particular elegant good humour, come to me and I'll play you the second part of that identical same tune; that's a fact. With that, I whistled for Old Clay, and back he comes, and I mounted and off, jist as the crowd came up. The folks looked staggered, and wondered a little grain how it was done so cleverly in short metre. If I did'nt quilt him in no time, you may depend; I went right slap into him, like a flash of lightning into a gooseberry bush. He found his suit ready made and fitted afore he thought he was half measured. Thinks I, friend Bradley, I hope you know yourself now, for I vow no livin soul would; your swallowed your soup without singin out scaldins, and your near about a pint and a half nearer cryin than larfin.

Yes, as I was sayin, this "Old Clay" is a real knowin one, he's as spry as a colt yet, clear grit, ginger to the back bone; I cant help a thinkin sometimes the breed must have come from old Kentucky, half horse, half alligator, with a cross of the airth-quake.

I hope I may be tetotally ruinated, if I'd take eight hundred dollars for him. Go ahead, you old clinker built villain, said he, and show the gentleman how wonderful hand*sum* you can travel. Give him the real Connecticut quick step. That's it – that's the way to carry the President's message to Congress, from Washington to New York, in no time – that's the go to carry a gall from Boston to Rhode Island, and trice her up to a Justice to be married, afore her father's out of bed of a summer's mornin. Aint he a beauty? a real doll? none of your Cumberland critters, that the more you quilt them, the more they wont go; but a proper one, that will go free gratis for nothin, all out of his own head volunt*errily*. Yes, a horse like "Old Clay," is worth the whole seed, breed and generation, of them Amherst beasts put together. He's a horse, every inch of him, stock, lock, and barrel, is *Old Clay*.

There goes one of them are everlastin rottin poles in that bridge; they are no better than a trap for a critter's leg, said the Clockmaker. They remind me of a trap Jim Munroe put his foot in one night, that near about made one leg half a yard longer than tother. I believe I told you of him, what a desperate idle feller he was – he came from Onion County in Connecticut. Well, he was courtin Sister Sall – she was a real handsum lookin gall; you scarce ever seed a more out and out complete critter than she was – a fine figur head, and a beautiful model of a craft as any in the state: a real clipper, and as full of fun and frolick as a kitten. Well he fairly turned Sall's head; the more we wanted her to give him up the more she would'nt, and we got plaguy oneasy about it, for his character was none of the best. He was a univarsal favorite with the galls, and tho' he did'nt behave very pretty neither, forgetting to marry where he promised, and where he had'nt ought to have forgot too; yet, so it was, he had such an un-common winnin way with him, he could talk them over in no time – Sall was fairly bewitched. At last, father said to him one evening when he came a courtin, Jim, says he, you'll never come to no good, if you act like old Scratch as you do; you aint fit to come into no decent man's house at all, and your absence would be ten times more agreeable than your company, I tell you. I won't consent to Sall's goin to them are huskin parties and quiltin frolics along with you no more, on no account, for you know how Polly Brown and Nancy White ———. Now don't says he, now don't, Uncle Sam; say no more about that; if you knowed all you would'nt say it was my fault; and besides, I have turned right about, I am on tother tack now, and the long leg, too; I am as steady as a pump bolt now. I intend to settle myself and take a farm – yes yes, and you could stock it, too, by all accounts, pretty well, unless you are much misreported, says father, but it won't do. I knew your father; he was our Sargeant, a proper clever and brave man he was too; he was one of the heroes of our glorious revolution. I had a great respect for him, and I am sorry for his sake you will act as you do; but I tell you once for all you must give up all thoughts of Sall, now and for everlastin. When Sall heerd this, she began to nit away like mad in a desperate hurry – she looked foolish enough, that's a fact. First she tried to bite in her breath, and look as if there was nothin particular in the wind, then she blushed all over like scarlet fever, but she recovered that pretty soon, and then her colour went and came, and came and went, till at last she grew as white as chalk, and down she fell slap off her seat on the floor, in a faintin fit. I see, says father, I see it now, you etarnal villain, and he made a pull at the old fashioned sword, that always hung over the fire place, (we used to call it old Bunker, for his stories always begun, "when I was at Bunker's Hill,") and drawing it out, he made a clip at him as wicked as if he was stabbing at a rat with a hay fork; but Jim he outs of the door like a shot, and draws it too arter him, and father sends old Bunker right through the panel. I'll chop you up as fine as mince meat, you villain, said he, if ever I catch you inside my door agin; mind what I tell you, *"you'll swing for it yet."* Well, he made himself considerable scarce arter that, he never sot foot inside the door agin, and I thought he had ginn up all hopes of Sall, and she of him; when one night, a most particular uncommon dark night, as I was a comin home from neighbor Dearborne's, I heerd some one a talkin under Sall's window. Well, I stops and listens, and who should be near the ash saplin, but Jim Munroe, a tryin to persuade Sall to run off with him to Rhode Island to be married. It was all settled, he should come with a horse and shay to the gate, and then help her out of the window, jist at nine o'clock, about the time she commonly went to bed. Then he axes her to reach down her hand for him to kiss, (for he was proper clever at soft sawder) and she stretches it down and he kisses it; and, says he, I believe I must have the whole of you out arter all, and gives her a jirk that kinder startled her; it came so sudden like it made her scream; so off he sot hot foot, and over the gate in no time.

Well, I cyphered over this all night, a calculatin how I should reciprocate that trick with him, and at last I hit on a scheme. I recollected father's words at partin, *"mind what I tell you, you'll swing for it yet;"* and thinks I, friend Jim, I'll make that prophecy come true yet, I guess. So the next night, jist at dark, I gives January Snow, the old nigger, a nidge with my elbow, and as soon as he looks up, I winks and walks out and he arter me – says I, January can you keep your tongue within your teeth, you old nigger you? Why massa, why you ax that are question? my Gor Ormity, you tink old Snow he dont know dat are yet; my tongue he got plenty room now, debil a tooth left, he can stretch out ever so far; like a little leg in a big bed, he lay quiet enough, Massa, neber fear. Well, then, says

I, bend down that are ash saplin softly, you old Snowball, and make no noise. The saplin was no sooner bent than secured to the ground by a notched peg and a noose, and a slip knot was suspended from the tree, jist over the track that led from the pathway to the house. Why, my Gor, massa, that's a ———.
Hold your mug, you old nigger, says I, or I'll send your tongue a sarchin arter your teeth; keep quiet, and follow me in presently. Well, jist as it struck nine o'clock, says I, Sally, hold this here hank of twine for a minute, till I wind a trifle on it off; that's a dear critter. She sot down her candle, and I put the twine on her hands, and then I begins to wind and wind away ever so slow, and drops the ball every now and then, so as to keep her down stairs. Sam, says she, I do believe you won't wind that are twine off all night, do give it to January, I won't stay no longer, I'm een a most dead asleep. The old feller's arm is so plaguy onsteady, says I, it won't do; but hark, what's that, I'm sure I heerd something in the ash saplin, did'nt you Sall? I heerd the geese there, that's all, says she, they always come under the windows at night; but she looked scared enough, and says she, I vow I'm tired a holdin out of arms, this way, and I won't do it no longer; and down she throw'd the hank on the floor. Well, says I, stop one minute, dear, till I send old January out to see of any body is there; perhaps some o' neighbor Dearborne's cattle have broke into the sarce garden. January went out, tho' Sall say'd it was no use, for she knew the noise of the geese, they always kept close to the house at night, for fear of the varmin. Presently in runs old Snow, with his hair standin up an eend, and the whites of his eyes lookin as big as the rims of a soup plate; oh! Gor Ormity, said he, oh massa, oh Miss Sally, oh!! What on airth is the matter with you, said Sally, how you do frighten me, I vow I believe you'r mad – oh my Gor said he, oh!! massa Jim Munroe he hang himself, on the ash saplin

under Miss Sally's window – oh my Gor!!! That shot was a settler, it struck poor Sall right atwixt wind and water; she gave a lurch ahead, then healed over and sunk right down in another faintin fit; and Juno, old Snow's wife, carried her off and laid her down on the bed – poor thing, she felt ugly enough, I do suppose.

Well, father, I thought he'd a fainted too, he was so struck up all of a heap, he was completely bung fungered; dear, dear, said he, I did'nt think it would come to pass so soon, but I knew it would come; I foretold it; says I, the last time I seed him, Jim, says I, mind what I say, *you'll swing for it yet.* Give me the sword I wore when I was at Bunker's Hill, may be there is life yet, I'll cut him down. The lantern was soon made ready, and out we went to the ash saplin. Cut me down, Sam, that's a good fellow, said Jim, all the blood in my body has swashed into my head, and's a runnin out o' my nose, I'm een a most smothered, be quick for heaven's sake. The Lord be praised, said father, the poor sinner is not quite dead yet. Why, as I'm alive – well if that don't beat all natur, why he has hanged himself by one leg, and's a swingin like a rabbit upside down, that's a fact. Why, if he aint snared, Sam; he is properly wired I declare – I vow this is some o' your doins, Sam – well it was a clever scheme too, but a little grain too dangerous, I guess. Don't stand staring and jawin there all night, said Jim, cut me down, I tell you – or cut my throat and be damned to you, for I am choakin with blood. Roll over that are hogshead, old Snow, said I, till I get a top on it and cut him down; so I soon released him but he could'nt walk a bit. His ankle was swelled and sprained like vengeance, and he swore one leg was near about six inches longer than tother. Jim Munroe, says father, little did I think I should ever see you inside my door agin, but I bid you enter now, we owe you that kindness, any how. Well, to make a long story short, Jim was so chap fallen, and so down in the mouth, he begged for heaven's sake it might be kept a secret; he said he would *run* the state, if ever it got wind, he was sure he could'nt *stand* it. It will be one while, I guess, said father, afore you are able to run or stand either; but if you will give me your hand, Jim, and promise to give over your evil ways, I will not only keep it secret, but you shall be a welcome guest at old Sam Slick's once more, for the sake of your father – he was a brave man, one of the heroes of Bunker's Hill, he was our Sergeant and ————. He promises, says I, father, (for the old man had stuck his right foot out, the way he always stood when he told about the old war; and as Jim could'nt stir a peg, it was a grand chance, and he was a goin to give him the whole revolution from General Gage up to Independence,) he promises, says I, father. Well it was all settled, and things soon grew as calm as a pan of milk two days old; and afore a year was over, Jim was as steady a goin man as Minister Joshua Hopewell, and was married to our Sall. Nothin was ever said about the snare till arter the weddin. When the Minister had finished axin a blessin, father goes up to Jim, and says he, Jim Munroe, my boy, givin him a rousin slap on the shoulder that sot him a coughin for the matter of five minutes, (for he was a mortal powerful man, was father) Jim Munroe, my boy, says he, you've got the snare round your neck, I guess now, instead of your leg; the saplin has been a father to you, may you be the father of many saplins.

We had a most special time of it, you may depend, all except the minister; father got him into a corner, and gave him chapter and verse for the whole war. Every now and then as I come near them, I heard "Bunker's Hill, Brandywine, Clinton,

Gates," and so on. It was broad day when we parted, and the last that went was poor minister. Father followed him clean down to the gate, and says he, "minister, we had'nt time this hitch, or I'd a told you all about the *'Evakyation'* of New York, but I'll tell you that the next time we meet."

SETTING UP FOR GOVERNOR

I never see one of them queer little old fashioned tea pots, like that are in the cupboard of Marm Pugwash, said the Clockmaker, that I dont think of Lawyer Crowningshield and his wife. When I was down to Rhode Island last, I spent an evening with them. Arter I had been there a while, the black House help brought in a little home made dipt candle, stuck in a turnip sliced in two, to make it stand straight, and sot it down on the table. Why, says the Lawyer to his wife, Increase my dear, what on earth is the meanin o' that? what does little Viney mean by bringin in such a light as this, that aint fit for even a log hut of one of our free and enlightened citizens away down east; where's the lamp? My dear, says she, I ordered it – you know they are agoin to set you up for Governor next year, and I allot we must economise or we will be ruined – the salary is only four hundred dollars a year, you know, and you'll have to give up your practice – we can't afford nothin now. Well, when tea was brought in, there was a little wee china tea pot, that held about the matter of half a pint or so, and cups and sarcers about the bigness of children's toys. When he seed that, he grew most peskily ryled, his under lip curled down like a peach leaf that's got a worm in it, and he stripped his teeth, and showed his grinders, like a bull dog; what foolery is this, said he? My dear, said she, its the foolery of being Governor; if you choose to sacrifice all your comfort to being the first rung in the ladder, dont blame me for it. I did'nt nominate you – I had not art nor part in it. It was cooked up at that are Convention, at Town Hall. Well, he sot for some time without sayin a word, lookin as black as a thunder cloud, just ready to make all natur crack agin. At last he gets up, and walks round behind his wife's chair, and takin her face between his two hands, he turns it up and gives her a buss that went off like a pistol – it fairly made my mouth water to see him; thinks I, them lips aint a bad bank to deposit one's spare kisses in, neither. Increase, my dear, said he, I believe you are half right, I'll decline to-morrow, I'll have nothin to do with it – *I wont be a Governor, on no account.*

Well, she had to haw and gee like, both a little, afore she could get her head out of his hands; and then she said, Zachariah, says she, how you do act, aint you ashamed? Do for gracious sake behave yourself: (and she colored up all over like a crimson piany; if you hav'nt foozled all my hair too, that's a fact, says she; and she put her curls to rights, and looked as pleased as fun, though poutin all the time, and walked right out of the room. Presently in come two well dressed House Helps, one with a splendid gilt lamp, a real London touch, and another with a tea tray, with a large solid silver coffee pot, and tea pot, and a cream jug, and sugar boul, of the same genuine metal, and a most an elegant sett of real gilt china. Then in came Marm Crowningshield herself, lookin as proud as if she would not call the President her cousin; and she gave the Lawyer a look, as much as to say, I guess when Mr. Slick is gone, I'll pay you off that are kiss with interest, you dear you – I'll answer a bill at sight for it, I will, you may depend. I believe, said he agin, you are right Increase, my dear, its an expensive kind of honor that bein Governor, and no great thanks neither; great little cry and little wool, all talk and no cider – its enough I guess for a man to govern his own family, aint it, dear? Sartin, my love, said she, sartin, a man is never so much in his own proper sphere as there; and beside, said she, his will is supreme to home, there is no danger of any one non-concurring him there: and she gave me a sly look, as much as to say, I let him think he is master in his own house, *for when ladies wear the breeches, their petticoats ought to be long enough to hide them*; but I allot, Mr. Slick, you can see with half an eye that the "grey mare is the better horse here."

What a pity it is, continued the Clockmaker, that the Blue Noses would not take a leaf out of Marm Crowningshield's book – talk more of their own affairs and less of politics. I'm sick of the everlastin sound of "House of Assembly," and "Council," and "great folks." They never alleviate talking about them from July to eternity. I had a curious conversation about politics once, away up to the right here. Do you see that are house, said he, in the field, that's got a lurch to leeward, like a north river sloop, struck with a squall, off West Point, lopsided like? It looks like Seth Pine, a tailor down to Hartford, that had one leg shorter than tother, when he stood at ease at militia trainin, a restin on the littlest one. Well, I had a special frolic there the last time I passed this way. I lost the linch pin out of my forred axle, and I turned up there to get it sot to rights. Just as I drove through the gate, I saw the eldest gall a makin for the house for dear life – she had a short petticoat on that looked like a kilt, and her bare legs put me in mind of the long shanks of a bittern down in a rush swamp, a drivin away like mad full chizel arter a frog. I could not think what on airth was the matter. Thinks I, she wants to make herself look decent like afore I get in, she dont like to pull her stockings on afore me; so I pulls up the old horse and let her have a fair start. Well, when I came to the door, I heard a proper scuddin; there was a regular flight into Egypt, jist such a noise as little children make when the mistress comes suddenly into school, all a huddlin and scroudgin into their seats, as quick as wink. Dear me, says the old woman, as she put her head out of a broken window to avail who it was, is it you, Mr. Slick? I sniggers, if you did not frighten us properly, we actilly thought it was the Sheriff; do come in. Poor thing, she looked half starved and half savage, hunger and temper had made proper strong lines in her face, like water furrows in a ploughed field; she looked bony and thin, like a horse, that has had more work than oats, and had a wicked expression, as though it warnt over safe to come too near her heels – an everlastin kicker. You may come out, John, said she to her husband, its only Mr. Slick; and out came John from under the bed backwards, on all fours, like an ox out of the shoein frame, or a lobster skullin wrong eend foremost – he looked as wild as a hawk. Well, I swan I thought I should have split, I could hardly keep from bustin right out with larfter – he was all covered with feathers, lint and dust, the savins of all the sweepins since the house was built, shoved under there for tidiness. He actilly sneezed for the matter of ten minutes – he seemed half choked with the flaff and stuff, that came out with him like a cloud. Lord, he looked like a goose half picked, as if all the quills were gone, but the pen feathers and down were left, jist ready for singin and stuffin. He put me in mind of a sick Adjutant, a great tall hulkin bird, that comes from the East Indgies, a most as high as a man, and most as knowin as a Blue Nose. I'd a ginn a hundred dollars to have had that chap as a show at a fair – tar and feathers war'nt half as nateral. You've seen a gall both larf and cry at the same time, hante you? well, I hope I may be shot if I could'nt have done the same. To see that critter come like a turkey out of a bag at Christmas, to be fired at for ten cents a shot, was as good as a play; but to look round and see the poverty – the half naked children – the old pine stumps for chairs – a small bin of poor watery yaller potatoes in the corner – day light through the sides and roof of the house, lookin like the tarred seams of a ship, all black where the smoak got out – no utensils for cookin or eatin – and starvation wrote as plain as a handbill on their holler cheeks, skinney fingers, and sunk eyes, went right straight to the heart. I do declare I believe I should have cried, only they did'nt seem to mind it themselves. They had been used to it, like a man that's married to a thunderin ugly wife, he gets so accustomed to the look of her everlastin dismal mug, that he don't think her ugly at all. Well, there was another chap a settin by the fire, and he *did* look as if he saw it and felt it too, he did'nt seem over half pleased, you may depend. He was the District Schoolmaster, and he told me he was takin a spell at boardin there, for it was their turn to keep him. Thinks I to myself, poor devil, you've brought your pigs to a pretty market, that's a fact. I see how it is, the Blue Noses can't "cypher." The cat's out of the bag now – its no wonder they don't go ahead, for they dont know nothin – the "Schoolmaster is *abroad*," with the devil to it, for he has *no home* at all. Why, Squire, you might jist as well expect a horse to go right off in gear, before he is halter broke, as a Blue Nose to get on in the world, when he has got no schoolin. But to get back to my story. Well, say's I, how's times with you, Mrs. Spry? Dull, says she, very dull, there's no markets now, things don't fetch nothin. Thinks I, some folks had'nt ought to complain of markets, for they don't raise nothin to sell, but I did'nt say so; *for poverty is keen enough, without sharpening its edge by pokin fun at it.* Potatoes, says I, will fetch a good price this fall, for it's a short crop in a general way; how's yourn? Grand, says she, as complete as ever you seed; our tops were small and did'nt look well; but we have the handsomest bottoms, its generally allowed, in all our place; you never seed the beat of them, they are actilly worth lookin at. I vow I had to take a chaw of tobacky to keep from snorting right out, it sounded so queer like. Thinks I to myself, old lady, its a pity you could'nt be changed eend for eend then, as some folks do their stockings; it would improve the look of your dial plate amazinly then, that's a fact.

Now there was human natur, Squire, said the Clockmaker, there was pride even in that hovel. It is found in rags as well as King's robes, where butter is spread with the thumb as well as the silver knife, *natur is natur wherever you find it.* Jist then, in came one or two neighbors to see the sport, for they took me for a Sheriff or Constable, or something of that breed, and when they saw it was me they sot down to hear the news; they fell right too at politics as keen as any thing, and if it had been a dish of real Connecticut Slap Jacks, or Hominy; or what is better still, a glass of real genuine splendid mint julep, *whe-eu-up*, it fairly makes my mouth water to think of it. I wonder, says one, what they will do for us this winter in the House of Assembly? Nothin, says the other, they never do nothin but what the great people at Halifax tell 'em. Squire Yeoman is the man, he'll pay up the great folks this hitch, he'll let 'em have their own, he's jist the boy that can do it. Says I, I wish I could say all men were as honest then, for I am afeard there are a great many wont pay me up this winter; I should like to trade with your friend, who is he? Why, says he, he is the member for Isle Sable County, and if he dont let the great folks have it, its a pity. Who do you call great folks, said I, for I vow I hav'nt see'd one since I came here. The only one that I know that comes near hand to one is Nicholas Overknocker, that lives all along shore, about Margaret's Bay, and *he is* a great man, it takes a yoke of oxen to drag him. When I first see'd him, says I, what on airth is the matter o' that man, has he the dropsy, for he is actilly the greatest man I ever see'd; he must weigh the matter of five hundred weight; he'd cut three inches on the rib – he must have a proper sight of lard, that chap? No, says I, dont call 'em great men, for there aint a great man in the country, that's a fact; there aint one that desarves the name; folks will only larf at you if you talk that way. There may be some rich men, and I believe there be, and its a pity there warn't more on 'em, and a still greater pity they have so little spirit or enterprise among 'em, but a country is none the worse of having rich men in it, you may depend. Great folks, well come, that's a good joke – that bangs the bush. No, my friend, says I, the meat that's *at the top of the barrel, is sometimes not so good as that that's a little grain lower down; the upper and lower eends are plaguy apt to have a little taint in 'em, but the middle is always good.*

Well, says the Blue Nose, perhaps they beant great men, exactly in that sense, but they are great men compared to us poor folks; and they eat up all the revenue, there's nothin left for roads and bridges, they want to ruin the country, that's a fact. Want to ruin your granny, says I, (for it raised my dander to hear the critter talk such nonsense.) I did hear of one chap, says I, that sot fire to his own house once, up to Squantum, but the cunnin rascal insured it first; now how can your great folks ruin the country without ruinin themselves, unless they have insured the Province? Our folks will insure all creation for half nothin, but I never heerd tell of a country being insured agin rich men. Now if you ever go to Wall Street to get such a policy, leave the door open behind you, that's all; or they'll grab right hold of you, shave your head and blister it, clap a straight jacket on you, and whip you right into a mad house, afore you can say Jack Robinson. No, your great men are nothin but rich men, and I can tell you for your comfort, there's nothin to hinder you from bein rich too, if you will take the same means as they did. They were once all as poor folks as you be, or their fathers afore them; for I know their whole breed, seed and generation, and they would'nt thank you to tell them that you knew their fathers and grand fathers, I tell you. If ever you want the loan of a hundred pounds from any of them, keep dark about that – see as far ahead as you please, but it tante always pleasant to have folks see too far back. Perhaps they be a little proud or so, but that's nateral; all folks that grow up right off, like a mushroom in one night, are apt to think no small beer of themselves. A cabbage has plaguy large leaves to the bottom, and spreads them out as wide as an old woman's petticoats, to hide the ground it sprung from, and conceal its extraction, but what's that to you? If they get too large salaries, dock 'em down at once, but dont keep talkin about it for everlastinly. If you have too many sarvents, pay some on 'em off, or when they quit your sarvice dont hire others in their room, that's all; but you miss your mark when you keep firin away the whole blessed time that way.

I went out a gunnin when I was a boy, and father went with me to teach me. Well, the first flock of plover I seed I let slip at them and missed them. Says father, says he, what a blockhead you be, Sam, that's your own fault, they were too far off, you had'nt ought to have fired so soon. At Bunker's Hill we let the British come right on till we seed the whites of their eyes, and then we let them have it slap bang. Well, I felt kinder grigged at missin my shot, and I did'nt over half like to be scolded too; so, says I yes, father, but recollect you had a mud bank to hide behind, where you were proper safe, and you had a rest for your guns too; but as soon as you seed a little more than the whites of their eyes, you run for dear life, full split, and so I dont see much to brag on in that arter all, so come now. I'll teach you to talk that way, you puppy you, said he, of that glorious day; and he fetched me a wipe that I do believe if I had'nt a dodged, would have spoiled my gunnin for that hitch; so I gave him a wide birth arter that all day. Well, the next time I missed, says I, she hung fire so ever-lastinly, its no wonder – and the next miss, says I, the powder is no good, I vow. Well, I missed every shot, and I had an excuse for every one on 'em – the flint was bad, or she flashed in the pan, or the shot scalded, or something or another; and when all would'nt do, I swore the gun was no good at all. Now, says father, (and he edged up all the time, to pay me off for that hit at his Bunker Hill story, which was the only shot I did'nt miss,) you han't got the right reason arter all. It was your own fault, Sam. Now that's jist the case with you; you may blame Banks and Council, and House of Assembly, and "the great men," till you are tired, but its all your own fault – *you've no spirit and no enterprise, you want industry and economy; use them, and you'll soon be as rich as the people at Halifax you call great folks* – they did'nt grow rich by talking, but by working; instead of lookin after other folks' business, they looked about the keenest arter their own. You are like the machinery of one of our boats, good enough, and strong enough, but of no airthly use till you get the steam up; you want to be set in motion, and then you'll go ahead like any thing, you may depend. *Give up politics – its a barren field, and well watched too; where one critter jumps a fence into a good field and gets fat, more nor twenty are chased round and round, by a whole pack of yelpin curs, till they are fairly beat out, and eend by bein half starved, and are at the liftin at last. Look to your farms – your water powers – your fisheries, and factories. In short, says I, puttin on my hat and startin, look to yourselves, and don't look to others.*

A CURE FOR CONCEIT

I ts a most curious unaccountable thing, but its a fact, said the Clockmaker, the Blue Noses are so conceited, they think they know everything; and yet there aint a livin soul in Nova Scotia knows his own business real complete, farmer or fisherman, lawyer or doctor, or any other folk. A farmer said to me one day, up to Pugnose's Inn at River Philip, Mr. Slick, says he, I allot this aint "*a bread country*;" I intend to sell off the house I improve, and go to the States. If it aint a bread country, said I, I never see'd one that was. There is more bread used here, made of best superfine flour, and No. 1. Genesssee, than in any other place of the same population in the univarse. You might as well say it aint a Clock Country, when, to my sartin knowledge, there are more clocks than bibles in it. I guess you expect to raise your bread ready made, dont you? Well there's only one class of our free and enlightened citizens that can do that, and that's them that are born with silver spoons in their mouths. It's a pity you was'nt availed of this truth, afore you up killoch and off – take my advice and bide where you be. Well the fishermen are jist as bad. The next time you go into the fish market at Halifax, stump some of the old hands; says you "how many fins has a cod at a word," and I'll liquidate the bet if you lose it. When I've been along-shore afore now, a vendin of my clocks, and they began to raise my dander, by belittleing the Yankees, I always brought them up by a round turn by that requirement, "how many fins has a cod at a word." Well they never could answer it; and then, says I, when you larn your own business, I guess it will be time enough to teach other folks theirn. How different it is with our men folk, if they cant get thro' a question, how beautifully they can go round it, can't they? Nothin never stops them. I had two brothers, Josiah and Eldad, one was a lawyer, and the other a doctor. They were a talkin about their examinations one night, at a huskin frolic, up to Governor Ball's big stone barn at Slickville. Says Josy, when I was examined, the Judge axed me all about real estate; and, says he, Josiah, says he, what's a fee? Why, says I, Judge, it depends on the natur of the case. In a common one, says I, I call six dollars a pretty fair one; but lawyer Webster has got afore now, I've heerd tell, 1000 dollars, and that *I do call* a fee. Well, the Judge he larfed ready to split his sides; (thinks I, old chap, you'll bust like a steam byler, if you hant got a safety valve somewhere or another,) and, says he, I vow that's superfine; I'll indorse your certificate for you, young man; there's no fear of you, you'll pass the inspection brand any how.

Well, says Eldad, I hope I may be skinned if the same thing did'nt een amost happen to me at my examination. They axed me a nation sight of questions, some on 'em I could answer, and some on 'em no soul could, right off the reel at a word, without a little cypherin; at last they axed me, "How would you calculate to put a patient into a sweat, when common modes would'nt work no how?" Why, says I, I'd do as Dr. Comfort Payne sarved father; and how was that, said they.

Why, says I, he put him into such a sweat as I never seed him in afore, in all my born days, since I was raised, by sending him in his bill, and if that did'nt sweat him it's a pity; it was an *active* dose you may depend. I guess that are chap has cut his eye teeth, said the President, let him pass as approbated.

They both knowed well enough, they only made as if they did'nt, to poke a little fun at them, for the Slick family were counted in a general way to be pretty considerable cute.

They reckon themselves here, a chalk above us Yankees, but I guess they have a wrinkle or two to grow afore they progress ahead on us yet. If they hant got a full cargo of conceit here, then I never seed a load, that's all. They have the hold chock full, deck piled up to the pump handles, and scuppers under water. They larnt that of the British, who are actilly so full of it, they remind me of Commodore Trip. When he was about half shaved he thought every body drunk but himself. I never liked the last war, I thought it unnateral, and that we hadnt ought to have taken hold of it at all, and so most of our New England folks thought; and I wasn't sorry to hear Gineral Dearborne was beat, seeing we had no call to go into Canada. But when the Guerriere was captivated by our old Ironsides, the Constitution, I did feel lifted up amost as high as a stalk of Varginy corn among Connecticut middlins; I grew two inches taller I vow, the night I heerd that news. Brag, says I, is a good dog, but hold fast is better. The British navals had been a braggin and a hectorin so long, that when they landed in our cities, they swaggered een amost as much as Uncle Peleg (big Peleg as he was called), and when he walked up the centre of one of our narrow Boston streets, he used to swing his arms on each side of him, so that folks had to clear out of both foot paths; he's cut, afore now, the fingers of both hands agin the shop windows on each side of the street. Many the poor feller's cruper bone he's smashed, with his great thick boots, a throwin out his feet afore him een amost out of sight, when he was in full rig a swigglin away at the top of his gait. Well they cut as many shines as Uncle Peleg. One frigate they guessed would captivate, sink, or burn our whole navy. Says a naval one day, to the skipper of a fishing boat that he took, says he, is it true Commodore Decatur's sword is made of an old iron hoop? Well, says the skipper, I'm not quite certified as to that, seein as I never sot eyes on it; but I guess if he gets a chance he'll shew you the temper of it some of these days, any how.

I mind once a British man-o'-war took one of our Boston vessels, and ordered all hands on board, and sent a party to skuttle her; well, they skuttled the fowls and the old particular genuine rum, but they obliviated their arrand and left her. Well, the next day another frigate (for they were as thick as toads arter a rain) comes near her, and fires a shot for her to bring to. No answer was made, there bein no livin soul on board, and another shot fired, still no answer. Why what on airth is the meanin of this, said the Captain, why dont they haul down that damn goose and gridiron (thats what he called our eagle and stars on the flag.) Why, says the first leftenant, I guess they are all dead men, that shot frightened them to death. They are afeared to show their noses says another, lest they should be shaved off by our shots. They are all down below a "*calculatin*" their loss I guess, says a third. I'll take my davy says the Captain, its some Yankee trick, a torpedo in her bottom or some such trap – we'll let her be, and sure enough, next day, back she came to shore of herself. I'll give you a quarter of an hour, says the Captain of the Guerriere to his men, to take that are Yankee frigate the Constitution. I guess he found his mistake where he didn't expect it, without any great sarch for it either. Yes, (to eventuate my story) it did me good, I felt dreadful nice, I promise you. It was as lovely as bitters of a cold mornin. Our folks beat 'em arter that so often, they got a little grain too much conceit also. They got their heels too high for their boots, and began to walk like Uncle Peleg too, so that when the Chesapeake got whipped I warnt sorry. We could spare that one, and it made our navals look round, like a feller who gets a hoist, to see who's a larfin at him. It made 'em brush the dust off, and walk on rather sheepish. It cut their combs that's a fact. The war did us a plaguy sight of good in more ways than one, and it did the British some good too. It taught 'em not to carry their chins too high, for fear they should'nt see the gutters – a mistake that's spoiled many a bran new coat and trowsers afore now.

Well, these Blue Noses have caught this disease, as folks do the Scotch fiddle, by shakin hands along with the British. Conceit has become here, as Doctor Rush says, (you have heerd tell of him, he's the first man of the age, and its generally allowed our doctors take the shine off of all the world) acclimated, it is citizenised among 'em, and the only cure is a real good quiltin. I met a first chop Colchester Gag this summer a goin to the races to Halifax, and he knowed as much about racin, I do suppose, as a Chictaw Ingian does of a rail road. Well, he was a praisin of his horse, and runnin on like Statiee. He was begot, he said, by Roncesvalles, which was better than any horse that ever was seen, because he was once in a duke's stable in England. It was only a man that had blood like a lord, said he, that knew what blood in a horse was. Capt. Currycomb, an officer at Halifax, had seen his horse and praised him, and that was enough – that stamped him – that fixed his value. It was like the President's name to a bank note, it makes it pass current. Well, says I, I hant got a drop of blood in me nothin stronger than molasses and water, I vow, but I guess I know a horse when I see him for all that, and I dont think any great shakes of your beast, any how; what start will you give me, says I, and I will run "Old Clay" agin you, for a mile lick right an eend. Ten rods, said he, for twenty dollars. Well, we run, and I made "Old Clay" bite in his breath and only beat him by half a neck. A tight scratch says I, that, and it would have sarved me right if I had been beat. I had no business to run an old roadster so everlastin fast, it aint fair on him, is it? Says he, I will double the bet and start even, and run you agin if you dare. Well, says I, since I won the last it would'nt be pretty not to give you a chance; I do suppose I oughtn't to refuse, but I dont love to abuse my beast by knockin him about this way.

As soon as the money was staked, I said, had'nt we better, says I, draw stakes, that are blood horse of yourn has such uncommon particular bottom, he'll perhaps leave me clean out of sight. No fear of that, said he, larfin, but he'll beat you easy, any how. No flinchin, says he, I'll not let you go back of the bargain. Its run or forfeit. Well, says I, friend, there is fear of it; your horse will leave me out of sight, to a sartainty, thats a fact, for he *cant keep up to me no time.* I'll drop him, hull down, in tu twos. If Old Clay did'nt make a fool of him; its a pity. Did'nt he gallop pretty, that's all? He walked away from him, jist as the Chancellor Livingston steam boat passes a sloop at anchor in the north river. Says I, I told you your horse would beat me clean out of sight, but you would'nt believe me; now, says I, I will tell you something else. That are horse will help you to lose more money to Halifax than you are a thinkin on; for there aint a beast gone down there that wont beat him. He cant run a bit, and you may tell the British Captain I say so. *Take him home and sell him, buy a good yoke of oxen; they are fast enough for a farmer, and give up blood horses to them that can afford to keep stable helps to tend 'em, and leave bettin alone to them, as has more money nor wit, and can afford to lose their cash, without thankin agin of their loss.* When *I want* your advice, said he, I will *ask it*, most peskily sulky. You might have got it before you *axed* for it, said I, but not afore you *wanted* it, you may depend on it. But stop, said I, let's see that all's right afore we part; so I counts over the fifteen pounds I won of him, note by note, as slow as any thing, on purpose to ryle him, then I mounts "Old Clay" agin, and says I, friend, you have considerably the advantage of me this hitch, any how. Possible! says he, how's that? Why, says I, I guess you'll return rather lighter than you came – and that's more nor I can say, any how, and then I gave him a wink and a jupe of the head, as much as to say, "do you take?" and rode on and left him starin and scratchin his head like a feller who's lost his road. If that citizen aint a born fool, or too far gone in the disease, depend on't, he found "*a cure for conceit.*"

THE BLOWIN TIME

The long rambling dissertation on conceit to which I had just listened, from the Clockmaker, forcibly reminded me of the celebrated aphorism "gnothi seauton," know thyself, which, both from its great antiquity and wisdom, has been by many attributed to an oracle.

With all his shrewdness to discover, and his humor to ridicule the foibles of others, Mr. Slick was blind to the many defects of his own character; and, while prescribing "a cure for conceit," exhibited in all he said, and all he did, the most overweening conceit himself. He never spoke of his own countrymen, without calling them "the most free and enlightened citizens on the face of the airth," or as "takin the shine off of all creation." His country he boasted to be the "best atween the poles," "the greatest glory under heaven." The Yankees he considered (to use his expression) as "actilly the class-leaders in knowledge among all the Americans," and boasted that they have not only "gone ahead of all others," but had lately arrived at that most enviable ne plus ultra point "of goin ahead of themselves." In short, he entertained no doubt that Slickville was the finest place in the greatest nation in the world, and the Slick family the wisest family in it. I was about calling his attention to this national trait, when I saw him draw his reins under his foot, (a mode of driving peculiar to himself, when he wish'd to economise the time that would otherwise be lost by an unnecessary delay,) and taking off his hat, (which, like a pedlar's pack, contained a general assortment,) select from a number of loose cigars one that appeared likely to "go," as he called it. Having lighted it by a lucifer, and ascertained that it was "true in draft," he resumed his reins and remarked, "This must be an everlastin fine country beyond all doubt, for the folks have nothin to do but to ride about and talk politics. In winter, when the ground is covered with snow, what grand times they have a slayin over these here mashes with the galls, or playin ball on the ice, or goin to quiltin frolics of nice long winter evenings, and then a drivin home like mad, by moonlight. Natur meant that season on purpose for courtin. A little tidy scrumptious lookin slay, a real clipper of a horse, a string of bells as long as a string of inions round his neck, and a sprig on his back, lookin for all the world like a bunch of apples broke off at gatherin time, and a sweetheart alongside, all muffled up but her eyes and lips – the one lookin right into you, and the other talkin right at you – is een a most enough to drive one ravin tarin distracted mad with pleasure, aint it? And then the dear critters say the bells make such a din there's no hearin one's self speak; so they put their pretty little mugs close up to your face, and talk, talk, talk, till one can't help lookin right at them instead of the horse, and then whap you both go capsized into a snow drift together, skins, cushions and all. And then to see the little critter shake herself when she gets up, like a duck landin from a pond, a chatterin away all the time like a Canary bird, and you a haw-hawin with pleasure, is fun alive, you may depend. In this way Blue Nose gets led on to offer himself as a lovier, afore he knows where he bees. But when he gets married, he recovers his eyesight in little less than half no time. He soon finds he's treed; his flint is fixed then, you may depend. She larns him how vinegar is made: *Put plenty of sugar into the water aforehand, my dear, says she, if you want to make it real sharp.* The larf is on the other side of his mouth then. If his slay gets upsot, its no longer a funny matter, I tell you; he catches it right and left. Her eyes don't look right up to hisn any more, nor her little tongue ring, ring, ring, like a bell any longer, but a great big hood covers her head, and a whappin great muff covers her face, and she looks like a bag of soiled clothes agoin to the brook to be washed. When they get out, she don't wait any more for him to walk lock and lock with her, but they march like a horse and a cow to water, one in each gutter. If there aint a transmogrification its a pity. The difference atween a wife and a sweetheart is near about as great as there is between new and hard cider – a man never tires of puttin one to his lips, but makes plaguy wry faces at tother. It makes me so kinder wamblecropt when I think on it, that I'm afeared to venture on matrimony at all. I have seen some Blue Noses most properly bit you may depend. You've seen a boy a slidin on a most beautiful smooth bit of ice, ha'nt you, larfin, and hoopin, and hallooin like one possessed, when presently sowse he goes in over head and ears? How he out fins and flops about, and blows like a porpoise properly frightened, don't he? and when he gets out there he stands, all shiverin and shakin, and the water a squish-squashin in his shoes, and his trowsers all stickin slimsey like to his legs. Well, he sneaks off home, lookin like a fool, and thinkin every body he meets is a larfin at him – many folks here are like that are boy, afore they have been six months married. They'd be proper glad to get out of the scrape too, and sneak off if they could, that's a fact. The marriage yoke is plaguy apt to gall the neck, as the ash bow does the ox in rainy weather, unless it be most particularly well fitted. You've seen a yoke of cattle that warn't properly mated, they spend more strength in pullin agin each other, than in pullin the load. Well that's apt to be the case with them as choose their wives in sleighin parties, quiltin frolics, and so on; instead of the dairies, looms, and cheese house. Now the Blue Noses are all a stirrin in winter. The young folks drive out the galls, and talk love and all sorts of things as sweet as dough-nuts. The old folks find it near about as well to leave the old women to home, for fear they should'nt keep tune together; so they drive out alone to chat about House of Assembly with their neighbors, while the boys and hired helps do the chores. When the spring comes, and the fields are dry enough to be sowed, they all have to be plowed, *cause fall rains wash the lands too much for fall ploughin.* Well the ploughs have to be mended and sharpened, *cause what's the use of doin that afore its wanted.* Well the wheat gets in too late, and then comes rust, but whose fault is that? *Why the climate to be sure, for Nova Scotia aint a bread country.*

When a man has to run ever so far as fast as he can clip, he has to stop and take breath; you must do that or choke. So it is with a horse; run him a mile, and his flanks will heave like a Blacksmith's bellows; you must slack up the rein and give him a little wind, or he'll fall right down with you. It stands to reason, don't it? Atwixt spring and fall work is "*Blowin time.*" Then Courts come on, and Grand Jury business, and Militia trainin, and Race trainin, and what not; and a fine spell of ridin about and doin nothin, a real "*Blowin time.*" Then comes harvest, and that is proper hard work, mowin and pitchin hay, and reapin and bindin grain, and potatoe diggin. That's as hard as sole leather, afore its hammered on the lap stone – it's most next to any thing. It takes a feller as tuff as Old Hickory (General Jackson) to stand that.

Ohio is most the only country I know of where folks are saved that trouble; and there the freshets come jist in the nick of time for 'em, and sweep all the crops right up in a heap for 'em, and they have nothin to do but take it home and house it, and sometimes a man gets more than his own crop, and finds a proper swad of it all ready piled up, only a little wet or so; but all countries aint like Ohio. Well, arter harvest comes fall, and then there's a grand "blowin time" till spring. Now, how the Lord the Blue Noses can complain of their country, when its only one-third work and two-thirds "blowin time," no soul can tell. Father used to say, when I lived on the farm along with him – Sam, says he, I vow I wish there was jist four hundred days in the year, for its a plaguy sight too short for me. I can find as much work as all hands on us can do for 365 days, and jist 35 days more, if we had 'em. We han't got a minit to spare; you must shell the corn and winner the grain at night, and clean up slick, or I guess we'll fall astarn as sure as the Lord made Moses. If he didn't keep us all at it, a drivin away full chisel, the whole blessed time, its a pity. There was no "blowin time" there, you may depend. We plowed all the fall for dear life; in winter we thrashed, made and mended tools, went to market and mill, and got out our firewood and rails. As soon as frost was gone, came sowin and plantin, weedin and hoein – then harvest and spreadin compost – then gatherin manure, fencin and ditchin – and then turn tu and fall plowin agin. It all went round like a wheel without stoppin, and so fast, I guess you couldn't see the spokes, just one long everlastin stroke from July to etarnity, without time to look back on the tracks. Instead of racin over the country like a young doctor, to show how busy a man is that has nothin to do, as Blue Nose does, and then take a "blowin time," we kept a rale travellin gate, an eight-mile-an-hour pace, the whole year round. *They buy more nor they sell, and eat more than they raise*, in this country. What a pretty way that is, is'nt it? If the critters knew how to cypher, they would soon find out that a sum stated that way always eends in a naught. I never knew it to fail, and I defy any soul to cypher it so, as to make it come out any other way, either by Schoolmaster's Assistant or Algebra. When I was a boy, the Slickville bank broke, and an awful disorderment it made, that's a fact; nothin else was talked of. Well, I studied it over a long time, but I could'nt make it out: so says I, father, how came that are bank to break? Warn't it well built? I thought that are Quincy granite was so amazin strong all natur would'nt break it. Why you foolish critter, says he, it tante the buildin that's broke, its the consarn that's smashed. Well, says I, I know folks are plaguilly consarned about it, but what do you call "folks smashin their consarns?" Father he larfed out like any thing; I thought he never would stop – and sister Sall got right up and walked out of the room, as mad as a hatter. Says she, Sam, I do believe you are a born fool, I vow. When father had done larfin, says he, I'll tell you, Sam, how it was. They cyphered it so that they brought out nothin for a remainder. Possible! says I; I thought there was no eend to their puss. I thought it was like Uncle Peleg's musquash hole, and that no soul could ever find the bottom of. My!! says I. Yes, says he, that are bank spent and lost more money than it made, and when folks do that, they must smash at last, if their puss be as long as the national one of Uncle Sam. This Province is like that are Bank of ourn, it's goin the same road, and they'll find the little eend of the horn afore they think they are half way down to it.

If folks would only give over talkin about that everlastin House of Assembly and Council, and see to their farms, it would be better for 'em, I guess; for arter all, what is it? Why it's only a sort of first chop Grand Jury, and nothin else. It's no more like Congress or Parliament, than Marm Pugwash's keepin room is like our State hall. It's jist nothin – Congress makes war and peace, has a say in all treaties, confarms all great nominations of the President, regilates the army and navy, governs twenty-four independent States, and snaps its fingers in the face of all the nations of Europe, as much as to say, who be you? I allot I am as big as you be. If you are six foot high, I am six foot six in my stockin feet, by gum, and can lambaste any two on you in no time. The British can whip all the world, and we can whip the British. But this little House of Assembly that folks make such a touss about, what is it? Why jist a decent Grand Jury. They make their present-ments of little money votes, to mend these everlastin rottin little wooden bridges, to throw a poultice of mud once a year on the roads, and then take a "blowin time" of three months and go home. The littler folks be, the bigger they talk. You never seed a small man that did'nt wear high heel boots, and a high crowned hat, and that war'nt ready to fight most any one, to show he was a man every inch of him. I met a member the other day, who swaggered near about as large as Uncle Peleg. He looked as if he thought you could'nt find his "ditto" any where. He used some most particular educational words, genuine jaw-breakers. He put me in mind of a squirrel I once shot in our wood location. The little critter got a hickory nut in his mouth; well, he found it too hard to crack, and too big to swaller, and for the life and soul of him, he could'nt spit it out agin. If he did'nt look like a proper fool, you may depend. We had a pond back of our barn about the bigness of a good sizeable wash-tub, and it was chock full of frogs. Well, one of these little critters fancied himself a bull-frog, and he puffed out his cheeks, and took a real "blowin time" of it; he roared away like thunder; at last he puffed and puffed out till he bust like a byler. If I see the Speaker this winter, (and I shall see him to a sartainty if they don't send for him to London, to teach their new Speaker) and he's up to snuff, that are man; he knows how to cypher – I'll jist say to him, Speaker, says I, if any of your folks in the House go to swell out like dropsy, give 'em a hint in time. Says you, if you have are a little safety valve about you, let off a little steam now and then, or you'll go for it; recollect the Clockmaker's story of the "Blowin time."

FATHER JOHN O'SHAUGHNESSY

To-morrow will be Sabbath day, said the Clockmaker; I guess we'll bide where we be till Monday. I like a Sabbath in the country – all natur seems at rest. There's a cheerfulness in the day here, you don't find in towns. You have natur before you here, and nothin but art there. The deathy stillness of a town, and the barred windows, and shut shops, and empty streets, and great long lines of big brick buildins, look melancholy. It seems as if life had ceased tickin, but there had'nt been time for decay to take hold on there; as if day had broke, but man slept. I can't describe exactly what I mean, but I always feel kinder gloomy and whamblecropt there. Now in the country its jist what it ought to be – a day of rest for man and beast from labor. When a man rises on the Sabbath, and looks out on the sunny fields and wavin crops, his heart feels proper grateful, and he says, come, this is a splendid day, aint it? let's get ready and put on our bettermost close, and go to meetin. His first thought is prayerfully to render thanks; and then when he goes to worship he meets all his neighbors, and he knows them all, and they are glad to see each other, and if any two on 'em hant exactly gee'd together durin the week, why they meet on kind of neutral ground, and the minister or neighbors make peace atween them. But it tante so in towns. You don't know no one you meet there. Its the worship of neighbors, but its the worship of strangers, too, for neighbors don't know nor care about each other. Yes, I love a Sabbath in the country. While uttering this soliloquy, he took up a pamphlet from the table, and turning to the title page, said, have you ever seen this here book on the "Elder Controversy."[*] This author's friends say its a clincher; they say he has sealed up Elder's mouth as tight as a bottle. No, said I, I have not; I have heard of it, but never read it. In my opinion the subject has been exhausted already, and admits of nothing new bein said upon it. These religious controversies are a serious injury to the cause of true religion; they are deeply deplored by the good and moderate men of all parties. It has already embraced several denominations in the dispute in this Province, and I hear the agitation has extended to New Brunswick, where it will doubtless be renewed with equal zeal. I am told all the pamphlets are exceptionable in point of temper, and this one in particular, which not only ascribes the most unworthy motives to its antagonist, but contains some very unjustifiable and gratuitous attacks, upon other sects unconnected with the dispute. The author has injured his own cause, for an *intemperate advocate is more dangerous than an open foe.* There is no doubt on it, said the Clockmaker, it is as clear as mud, and you are not the only one that thinks so, I tell you. About the hottest time of the dispute, I was to Halifax, and who should I meet but Father John O'Shaughnessy, a Catholic Priest. I had met him afore in Cape Breton, and had sold him a clock. Well, he was a leggin it off hot foot. Possible! says I, Father

---

[*] *A Controversy on the subject of Infant Baptism.*

John, is that you? Why, what on airth is the matter of you – what makes you in such an everlastin hurry, driven away like one ravin distracted mad? A sick visit, says he; poor Pat Lanigan, him that you mind to Bradore Lake, well he's near about at the pint of death. I guess not, said I, for I jist heerd tell he was dead. Well, that brought him up all standin, and he bouts ship in a jiffy, and walks a little way with me, and we got a talkin about this very subject. Says he, what are you, Mr. Slick? Well, I looks up to him and winks, a Clockmaker, says I; well he smiled, and says he, I see; as much as to say I had'nt ought to have axed that are question at all, I guess, for every man's religion is his own, and nobody else's business. Then, says he, you know all about this country, who do folks say has the best of the dispute. Says I, Father John, its like the battles up the Canada lines last war, each side claims victory; I guess there aint much to brag on nary way, damage done on both sides, and nothin gained, as far as I can learn. He stopt short, and looked me in the face, and says he, Mr. Slick you are a man that has seed a good deal of the world, and a considerable of an understandin man, and I guess I *can* talk to *you*. Now, says he, for gracious sake do jist look here, and see how you heretics (protestants I mean, says he, for I guess that are word slipt out without leave,) are by the ears, a driven away at each other, the whole blessed time tooth and nail, hip and thigh, hammer and tongs, disputin, revilin, wranglin, and beloutin each other, with all sorts of ugly names that they can lay their tongues to. Is that the way you love your neighbor as yourself? *We say this is a practical comment on schism*, and by the powers of Moll Kelly, said he, but they all ought to be well lambasted together, the whole batch on 'em entirely. Says I, Father John, give me your hand; there are some things, I guess, you and I don't agree on, and most likely never will, seein that you are a

Popish priest; but in that idee I do opinionate with you, and I wish with all my heart all the world thought with us. I guess he didn't half like that are word Popish priest; it seemed to grig him like; his face looked kinder ryled, like well water arter a heavy rain; and said he, Mr. Slick, says he, your country is a free country, aint it? The freest, says I, on the face of the airth – you can't "ditto" it nowhere. We are as free as the air, and when our dander's up, stronger than any hurricane you ever seed – tear up all creation most; there aint the beat of it to be found any where. Do you call this a free country? said he. Pretty considerable middlin, says I, seein that they are under a king. Well, says he, if you were seen in Connecticut a shakin hands along with a Popish priest, as you are pleased to call me, (and he made me a bow, as much as to say mind your trumps the next deal) as you now are in the streets of Halifax along with me, with all your crackin and boastin of your freedom, I guess you wouldn't sell a clock agin in that State for one while, I tell you, and he bid me good mornin and turned away. Father John! says I. I can't stop, says he; I must see that poor critter's family; they must be in great trouble, and a sick visit is afore controvarsy in my creed. Well, says I, one word with you afore you go; if that are name Popish priest was an on-genteel one, I ax your pardon; I didn't mean no offence, I do assure you, and I'll say this for your satisfaction, tu, you're the first man in this Province that ever gave me a real right down complete checkmate since I first sot foot in it, I'll be skinned if you aint. Yes, said Mr. Slick, Father John was right; these antagonizing chaps ought to be well quilted, the whole raft of 'em. It fairly makes me sick to see the folks, each on 'em a backin up of their own man. At it agin, says one; fair play, says another; stick it into him, says a third; and that's your sort, says a fourth. Them are the folks who do mischief. They show such clear grit it fairly frightens me. It makes my hair stand right up an eend to see ministers do that are. *It appears to me that I could write a book in favor of myself and my notions, without writin agin any one, and if I couldn't I would'nt write at all, I snore.* Our old minister, Mr. Hopewell, (a real good man, and a larned man too that,) they sent to him once to write agin the Unitarians, for they are a goin ahead like statiee in New England, but he refused. Said he, Sam, says he, when I first went to Cambridge, there was a boxer and wrastler came there, and he beat every one wherever he went. Well, old Mr. Possit was the Church of England parson at Charlestown, at the time, and a terrible powerful man he was – a rael sneezer, and as *active* as a weasel. Well, the boxer met him one day, a little way out of town, a takin of his evenin walk, and said he, Parson, says he, they say you are a most a plaguy strong man and uncommon stiff too. Now, says he, I never seed a man yet that was a match for me; would you have any objection jist to let me be availed of your strength here in a friendly way, by ourselves, where no soul would be the wiser; if you will I'll keep dark about it, I swan. Go your way, said the Parson, and tempt me not; you are a carnal minded wicked man, and I take no pleasure in such vain idle sports. Very well, said the boxer; now here I stand, says he, in the path, right slap afore you; if you pass round me, then I take it as a sign that you are afeard on me, and if you keep the path, why then you must first put me out – that's a fact. The Parson jist made a spring forrard, and kitched him up as quick as wink, and throwed him right over the fence whap on the broad of his back, and then walked on as if nothin had happened – as demure as you please, and lookin as meek as if butter would'nt melt in his mouth. Stop, said the boxer, as soon as he picked himself up, stop Parson, said he, that's a good man, and jist chuck over my horse too, will you, for I swan I believe you could do one near about as easy as tother. My! said he, if that don't bang the bush; you are another guess chap from what I took you to be, any how. Now, said Mr. Hopewell, says he, I won't write, but if are a Unitarian crosses my path, I'll just over the fence with him in no time, as the parson did the boxer; *for writin only aggravates your opponents, and never convinces them. I never seed a convart made by that way yet, but I'll tell you what I have seed, a man set his own flock a doubtin by his own writin. You may happify your enemies, cantankerate your opponents, and injure your own cause by it, but I defy you to sarve it.* These writers, said he, put me in mind of that are boxer's pupils. He would sometimes set two on 'em to spar; well, they'd put on their gloves and begin, larfin and jokin all in good humor. Presently one on 'em would put in a pretty hard blow; well, tother would return it in airnest. Oh, says the other, if that's your play, off gloves and at it; and sure enough, away would fly their gloves, and at it they'd go tooth and nail.

No, Sam, the misfortin is, we are all apt to think Scriptur intended for our neighbors, and not for ourselves. The poor all think it made for the rich. Look at that are Dives, they say, what an all fired scrape he got into by his avarice, with Lazarus; and aint it writ as plain as any thing, that them folks will find it as easy to go to heaven, as for a camel to go through the eye of a needle. Well, then, the rich think it all made for the poor – that they sharnt steal nor bear false witness, but shall be obedient to them that's in authority. And as for them are Unitarians, and he always got his dander up when he spoke of them, why there's no doin nothin with them, says he. When they get fairly stumped, and you produce a text that they can't get over, nor get round, why they say it tante in our varsion at all – that's an interpolation, its an invention of them are everlastin monks; there's nothin left for you to do with them, but to sarve them as Parson Possit detailed the boxer – lay right hold of 'em, and chuck 'em over the fence, even if they were as big as all out doors. That's what our folks ought to have done with 'em at first, pitched 'em clean out of the state, and let 'em go down to Nova Scotia, or some such outlandish place, for they aint fit to live in no christian country at all.

Fightin is no way to make convarts; *the true way is to win 'em.* You may stop a man's mouth, Sam, says he, by a crammin a book down his throat, but you won't convince him. Its a fine thing to write a book all covered over with Latin, and Greek, and Hebrew, like a bridle that's real jam, all spangled with brass nails, but who knows whether its right or wrong? why not one in ten thousand. If I had my religion to choose, and warn't able to judge for myself, I'll tell you what I'd do: I'd jist ask myself *who leads the best lives?* Now, says he, Sam, I won't say who do, because it would look like vanity to say it was the folks who hold to our platform, but I'll tell you who don't. *It aint them that makes the greatest professions always*; and mind what I tell you, Sam, when you go a tradin with your clocks away down east to Nova Scotia, and them wild provinces, keep a bright look out on them as cant too much, *for a long face* is a plaguy apt to *cover a long conscience* – that's a fact.

TAMING A SHREW

The road from Amherst to Parrsboro is tedious and uninteresting. In places it is made so straight, that you can see several miles of it before you, which produces an appearance of interminable length, while the stunted growth of the spruce and birch trees bespeaks a cold thin soil, and invests the scene with a melancholy and sterile aspect. Here and there occurs a little valley with its meandering stream, and verdant and fertile intervale, which, though possessing nothing peculiar to distinguish it from many other of the same kind, strikes the traveller as superior to them all, from the contrast to the surrounding country. One of these secluded spots attracted my attention, from the number and neatness of the buildings, which its proprietor, a tanner and currier, had erected for the purposes of his trade. Mr. Slick said he knew him, and he guessed it was a pity he couldn't keep his wife in as good order as he did his factory. They don't hitch their horses together well at all. He is properly hen-pecked, said he; he is afeerd to call his soul his own, and he leads the life of a dog; you never seed the beat of it, I vow. Did you ever see a rooster hatch a brood of chickens? No, said I, not that I can recollect. Well then I have, said he, and if he don't look like a fool all the time he is a settin on the eggs, its a pity; no soul could help larfin to see him. Our old nigger, January Snow, had a spite agin one of father's roosters, seein that he was a coward, and would'nt fight. He used to call him Dearborne, arter our General that behaved so ugly to Canada; and, says he one day, I guess you are no better than a hen, you everlastin old chicken-hearted villain, and I'll make you a larfin stock to all the poultry. I'll put a trick on you you'll bear in mind all your born days. So he catches old Dearborne, and pulls all the feathers off his breast, and strips him as naked as when he was born, from his throat clean down to his tail, and then takes a bundle of nettles and gives him a proper switchin that stung him, and made him smart like mad; then he warms some eggs and puts them in a nest, and sets the old cock right a top of 'em. Well, the warmth of the eggs felt good to the poor critter's naked belly, and kinder kept the itchin of the nettles down, and he was glad to bide where he was, and whenever he was tired and got off, his skin felt so cold, he'd run right back and squat down agin, and when his feathers began to grow, and he got obstropolous, he got another ticklin with the nettles, that made him return double quick to his location. In a little time he larnt the trade real complete.

Now, this John Porter, (and there he is on the bridge I vow, I never seed the beat o' that, speak of old Saytin and he's sure to appear;) well, he's jist like old Dearborne, only fit to hatch eggs. When we came to the Bridge, Mr. Slick stopped his horse, to shake hands with Porter, whom he recognized as an old acquaintance and customer. He enquired after a bark mill he had smuggled from the States for him, and enlarged on the value of such a machine, and the cleverness of his countrymen who invented such useful and profitable articles; and was recommending a new process of tanning, when a female voice from the house was heard vociferating, "John Porter, come here this minute." Coming, my dear, said the husband. "Come here, I say, directly, why do you stand talking to that Yankee villain there." The poor husband hung his head, looked silly, and bidding us good bye, returned slowly to the house. As we drove on, Mr. Slick said, that was me – I did that. Did what? said I. That was me that sent him back, I called him and not his wife. I had that are bestowment ever since I was knee high or so; I'm a real complete hand at Ventriloquism; I can take off any man's voice I ever heerd to the very nines. If there was a law agin forgin that as there is for handwritin, I guess I should have been hanged long ago. I've had high goes with it many a time, but its plaguy dangersome, and I dont prac*tise* it now but seldom. I had a real bout with that are citizen's wife once, and completely broke her in for him; she went as gentle as a circus horse for a space, but he let her have her head agin, and she's as bad as ever now. I'll tell you how it was. I was down to the Island a sellin clocks, and who should I meet but John Porter; well, I traded with him for one, part cash, part truck and pro*duce*, and also put off on him that are bark mill you heerd me axin about, and it was pretty considerable on in the evenin afore we finished our trade. I came home along with him, and had the clock in the waggon to fix it up for him, and to shew him how to regilate it. Well, as we neared his house, he began to fret and take on dreadful oneasy; says he, I hope Jane wont be abed, cause if she is she'll act ugly, I do suppose. I had heerd tell of her afore; how she used to carry a stiff upper lip, and make him and the broomstick well acquainted together; and, says I, why do you put up with her tantrums, I'd make a fair division of the house with her, if it was me, I'd take the inside and allocate her the outside of it pretty quick that's a fact. Well, when we came to the house, there was no light in it, and the poor critter looked so streaked and down in the mouth, I felt proper sorry for him. When he rapped at the door, she called out, who's there? Its me, dear, says Porter. You, is it, said she, then you may stay where you be, them as gave you your supper, may give you your bed, instead of sendin you sneakin home at night like a thief. Said I, in a whisper, says I, leave her to me, John Porter – jist take the horses up to the barn, and see after them, and I'll manage her for you, I'll make her as sweet as sugary candy, never fear. The barn you see is a good piece off to the eastward of the house; and, as soon as he was cleverly out of hearin, says I, a imitatin of his voice to the life, do let me in, Jane, says I, that's a dear critter, I've brought you home some things you'll like, I know. Well, she was an awful jealous critter; says she, take 'em to her you spent the evenin with, I don't want you nor your presents neither. Arter a good deal of coaxin I stood on tother tack, and began to threaten to break the door down; says I, you old unhansum lookin sinner, you vinerger cruet you, open the door this minit or I'll smash it right in. That grigged her properly, it made her very wrathy, (for nothin sets up a woman's spunk like callin her ugly, she gets her back right up like a cat when a strange dog comes near her; she's all eyes, claws and bristles.)

I heerd her bounce right out of bed, and she came to the door as she was, ondressed, and onbolted it; and, as I entered it, she fetched me a box right across my cheek with the flat of her hand, that made it tingle agin. I'll teach you to call names agin, says she, you varmint. It was jist what I wanted; I pushed the door tu with my foot, and seizing her by the arm with one hand, I quilted her with the horsewhip real handsum, with the other. At first she roared like mad; I'll give you the ten commandments, says she, (meaning her ten claws,) I'll pay you for this, you cowardly villain, to strike a woman. How dare you lift your hand, John Porter, to your lawful wife, and so on; all the time runnin round and round, like a colt that's a breakin, with the mouthin bit, rarein, kickin, and plungin like statiee. Then she began to give in. Says she, I beg pardon, on my knees I beg pardon – don't murder me, for Heaven's sake – don't, dear John, don't murder your poor wife, that's a dear. I'll do as you bid me, I promise to behave well, upon my honor I do – oh! dear John, do forgive me, do dear. When I had her properly brought too, for havin nothin on but a thin undergarment, every crack of the whip told like a notch on a baker's tally, says I, take that as a taste of what you'll catch, when you act that way like old Scratch. Now go and dress yourself, and get supper for me and a stranger I have brought home along with me, and be quick, for I vow I'll be master in my own house. She moaned like a dog hit with a stone, half whine, half yelp; dear, dear, says she, if I aint all covered over with welts as big as my finger, I do believe I'm flayed alive; and she boohood right out like any thing. I guess, said I, you've got 'em where folks wont see 'em, any how, and I calculate you won't be over forrard to show 'em where they be. But come, says I, be a stirrin, or I'll quilt you agin as sure as you're alive – I'll tan your hide for you, you may depend, you old ungainly tempered heifer you.

When I went to the barn, says I, John Porter, your wife made right at me, like one ravin distracted mad, when I opened the door, thinkin it was you; and I was obliged to give her a crack or two of the cowskin to get clear of her. It has effectuated a cure completely; now foller it up, and don't let on for your life, it warn't you that did it, and you'll be master once more in your own house. She's all docity jist now, keep her so. As we returned we saw a light in the keepin room, the fire was blazin up cheerfulsome, and Marm Porter moved about as brisk as a parched pea, though as silent as dumb, and our supper was ready in no time. As soon as she took her seat and sot down, she sprung right up on eend, as if she had sot on a pan of hot coals, and colored all over; and then tears started in her eyes. Thinks I to myself, I calculate I wrote that are lesson in large letters any how, I can read that writin without spellin, and no mistake; I guess you've got pretty well warmed thereabouts this hitch. Then she tried it agin, first she sot on one leg then on tother, quite oneasy, and then right atwixt both, a fidgettin about dreadfully; like a man that's rode all day on a bad saddle, and lost a little leather on the way. If you had seed how she stared at Porter, it would have made you snicker. She could'nt credit her eyes. He warn't drunk, and he warn't crazy, but there he sot as peeked and as meechin as you please. She seemed all struck up of a heap at his rebellion. The next day when I was about startin, I advised him to act like a man, and keep the weather gage now he had it, and all would be well; but the poor critter only held on a day or two, she soon got the upper hand of him, and made him confess all, and by all accounts he leads a worse life now than ever. I put that are trick on him jist now to try him, and I see it's gone goose with him; the jig is up with him, she'll soon call him with a whistle like a dog. I often think of the hornpipe she danced there in the dark along with me, to the music of my whip – she touched it off in great style, that's a fact. I shall mind that go one while, I promise you. It was actilly equal to a play at old Bowry. You may depend, Squire, the only way to tame a shrew, is by the cowskin. Grandfather Slick was raised all along the coast of Kent in Old England, and he used to say there was an old saying there, which, I expect, is not far off the mark:

A woman, a dog, and a walnut tree,
The more you lick 'em, the better they be.

THE MINISTER'S HORN MUG

This country, said Mr. Slick, abounds in superior mill privileges, and one would naterally calculate that such a sight of water power, would have led to a knowledge of machinery. I guess if a Blue Nose was to go to one of our free and enlightened citizens, and tell him Nova Scotia was intersected with rivers and brooks in all directions, and nearly one quarter of it covered with water, he'd say, well I'll start right off and see it, I vow, for I guess I'll larn somethin. I allot I'll get another wrinkle away down east there. With such splendid chances for experimentin, what first-chop mills they must have, to a sartainty. I'll see such new combinations, and such new applications of the force of water to motion, that I'll make my fortin, for we can improve on any thing amost. Well, he'd find his mistake out I guess, as I did once, when I took passage in the night at New York for Providence, and found myself the next mornin clean out to sea, steerin away for Cape Hatteras, in the Charleston steamer. He'd find he'd gone to the wrong place, I reckon; there aint a mill of any kind in the Province fit to be seen. If we had 'em, we'd sarve 'em as we do the gamblin houses down south, pull 'em right down, there would'nt be one on 'em left in eight and forty hours.

Some domestic factories they ought to have here; its an essential part of the social system. Now we've run to the other extreme, its got to be too big an interest with us, and aint suited to the political institutions of our great country. Natur designed us for an agricultural people, and our government was predicated on the supposition that we would be so. Mr. Hopewell was of the same opinion. He was a great hand at gardenin, orchadin, farming, and what not. One evenin I was up to his house, and says he, Sam, what do you say to a bottle of my old genu*ine* cider? I guess I got some that will take the shine off of your father's, by a long chalk, much as the old gentleman brags of his'n – I never bring it out afore him. He thinks he has the best in all Connecticut. Its an innocent ambition that; and Sam, it would be but a poor thing for me to gratify my pride, at the expense of humblin his'n. So I never lets on that I have any better, but keep dark about this superfine particular article of mine, for I'd as lives he'd think so as not. He was a real prim*itive* good man was minister. I got some, said he, that was bottled that very year, that glorious action was fought atween the Constitution and the Guerriere. Perhaps the whole world could'nt shew such a brilliant whippin as that was. It was a splendid deed, that's a fact. The British can whip the whole airth, and we can whip the British. It was a bright promise for our young eagle; a noble bird that, too; great strength, great courage, and surpassing sagacity.

Well, he went down to the cellar, and brought up a bottle, with a stick tied to its neck, and day and date to it, like the lye-bills on the trees in Squire Hendrick's garden. I like to see them are cobwebs, says he, as he brushed 'em off, they are like grey hairs in an old man's head, they indicate venerable old age. As he uncorked it, says he, I guess Sam, this will warm your gizzard, my boy; I guess our great nation may be stumped to produce more eleganter liquor than this here. Its the dandy, that's a fact. That, said he, a smackin his lips, and lookin at its sparklin top, and layin back his head, and tippin off a horn mug brim full of it – that, said he, and his eyes twinkled agin, for it was plaguy strong, that is the produce of my own orchard. Well, I said, minister, says I, I never see you a swiggin it out of that are horn mug, that I dont think of one of your texts. What's that, Sam, says he? for you always had a most a special memory when you was a boy; why says I, "that the horn of the righteous man shall be exalted," I guess that's what they mean by "exalten the horn," aint it? Lord if ever you was to New Orleens, and seed a black thunder cloud rise right up and cover the whole sky in a minit, you'd a thought of it if you had seed his face. It looked as dark as Egypt. For shame, says he, Sam, that's ondecent; and let me tell you that a man that jokes on such subjects, shews both a lack of wit and sense too. I like mirth, you know I do, for its only the Pharisees and hypocrites that wear long faces, but then mirth must be inno-cent to please me; and when I see a man make merry with serious things, I set him down as a lost sheep. That comes of your speculatin to Lowell: and, I vow, them factorin towns will corrupt our youth of both sexes, and become hotbeds of iniq-uity. Evil communications endamnify good manners, as sure as rates; one scabby sheep will infect a whole flock – vice is as catchin as that nasty disease the Scotch have, it's got by shakin hands, and both eend in the same way – in brimstone. I appro-bate domestic factories, but nothin further for us. It don't suit us or our institutions. A republic is only calculated for an enlightened and vartuous people, and folks chiefly in the farmin line. That is an innocent and a happy vocation. Agriculture was ordained by Him as made us, for our chief occupation.

Thinks I, here's a pretty how do you do: I'm in for it now, that's a fact; he'll jist fall to and read a regular sarmon, and he knows so many by heart he'll never stop. It would take a Philadelphia lawyer to answer him. So, says I, minister, I ax your pardon, I feel very ugly at havin given you offence, but I did'nt mean it, I do assure you. It jist popt out unexpectedly, like a cork out of one of them are cider bottles, I'll do my possibles that the like don't happen agin, you may depend; so 'spose we drink a glass to our reconciliation. That I will, said he, and we will have another bottle too, but I must put a little water into *my glass*, (and he dwelt on that word, and looked at me, quite feelin, as much as to say, don't for goodness sake make use of that are word *horn* agin, for it's a joke I don't like,) for my head hante quite the strength my cider has. Taste this, Sam, said he, (openin of another bottle,) it's of the same age as the last, but made of different apples, and I am fairly stumped sometimes to say which is best.

These are the pleasures, says he, of a country life. A man's own labor provides him with food, and an appetite to enjoy it. Let him look which way he will, and he sees the goodness and bounty of his Creator, his wisdom, his power, and his majesty. There never was any thing so true, as that are old sayin, "man made the town, but God made the country," and both bespeak their different architects in terms too plain to be misunderstood. The one is filled with virtue and the other with vice. One is the abode of plenty, and the other of want; one is a ware-duck of nice pure water – and tother one a cesspool. Our towns are gettin so commercial and factoring, that they will soon generate mobs, Sam, (how true that are has turned out, haint it? He could see near about as far into a mill-stone, as them that picks the hole into it,) and mobs will introduce disobedience and defiance to laws, and that must eend in anarchy and bloodshed. No, said the old man, raising his voice, and giving the table a wipe with his fist that made the glasses all jingle agin, give me the country; that country to which he that made it said, "Bring forth grass, the herb yieldin seed, and the tree yieldin fruit," *and who saw that it was good.* Let me jine with the feathered tribe in the mornin, (I hope you get up airly now, Sam; when you was a boy there was no gitten you out of bed at no rate,) and at sunset, in the hymns which they utter in full tide of song to their Creator. Let me pour out the thankfulness of my heart to the Giver of all good things, for the numerous blessings I enjoy, and intreat him to bless my increase, that I may have wherewithal to relieve the wants of others, as he prevents and relieves mine. No! give me the country. Its —————— Minister was jist like a horse that has the spavin; he sot off considerable stiff at first, but when he once got under way, he got on like a house a fire. He went like the wind, full split.

He was jist beginnin to warm on the subject, and I knew if he did, what wonderful bottom he had; how he would hang on for ever amost; so, says I, I think so too, Minister, I like the country, I always sleep better there than in towns; it tante so plaguy hot, nor so noisy neither, and then its a pleasant thing to set out on the stoop and smoke in the cool, aint it? I think, says I, too, Minister, that that are uncommon handsum cider of yourn desarves a pipe, what do you think? Well, says he, I think myself a pipe would'nt be amiss, and I got some rael good Varginy, as you een amost ever seed, a present from Rowland Randolph, an old college chum; and none the worse to my palate, Sam, for bringin bye gone recollections with it.

Phœbe, my dear, said he to his darter, bring the pipes and tobacco. As soon as the old gentleman fairly got a pipe in his mouth, I gave Phœbe a wink, as much as to say, warnt that well done. That's what I call a most particular handsum fix. He can *talk* now, (and that *I do like* to hear him do,) but he can't make a speech, or preach a sarmon, and that *I don't like* to hear him do, except on Sabbath day, or up to Town Hall, on oration times.

Minister was an uncommon pleasant man, (for there was nothin amost he did'nt know,) except when he got his dander up, and then he did spin out his yarns for everlastinly.

But I'm of his opinion. If the folks here want their country to go ahead, they must honor the plough, and General Campbell ought to hammer that are into their noddles, full chisell, as hard as he can drive. I could larn him somethin, I guess, about hammerin he aint up to. It tante every one that knows how to beat a thing into a man's head. How could I have sold so many thousand clocks, if I had'nt had that nack. Why, I would'nt have sold half a dozen, you may depend.

Agriculture is not only neglected but degraded here. What a number of young folks there seem to be in these parts, a ridin about, titivated out real jam, in their go-to-meetin clothes, a doin nothin. It's melancholy to think on it. That's the effect of the last war. The idleness and extravagance of those times took root, and bore fruit abundantly, and now the young people are above their business. They are too high in the instep, that's a fact. Old Drivvle, down here to Maccan, said to me one day, for gracious sake, says he, Mr. Slick, do tell me what I shall do with Johnny. His mother sets great store by him, and thinks he's the makins of a considerable smart man – he's growin up fast now, and I am pretty well to do in the world, and reasonable forehanded, but I dont know what the dogs to put him to. The Lawyers are like spiders, they've eat up all the flies, and I guess they'll have to eat each other soon, for there's more on 'em than causes now every court. The Doctors' trade is a poor one, too, they don't get barely cash enough to pay for their medicines; I never seed a country practitioner yet that made any thing worth speakin of. Then, as for preachin, why church and dissenters are pretty much tarred with the same stick, they live in the same pastur with their flocks; and, between 'em, its fed down pretty close I tell you. What would you advise me to do with him? Well, says I, I'll tell you if you won't be miffy with me. Miffy with you indeed, said he, I guess I'll be very much obliged to you; it tante every day one gets a chance to consult with a person of your experience – I count it quite a privilege to have the opinion of such an understandin man as you be. Well, says I, take a stick and give him a rael good quiltin, jist tantune him like blazes, and set him to work. – What does the critter want? you have a good farm for him, let him go and airn his bread; and when he can raise that, let him get a wife to make butter for it; and when he has more of both than he wants, let him sell em and lay up his money, and he will soon have his bread buttered on both sides – put him to, eh! why put him to the PLOUGH, *the most nateral, the most happy, the most innocent, and the most healthy employment in the world.* But, said the old man (and he did not look over half pleased) markets are so confounded dull, labor so high, and the banks and great folks a swallerin all up so, there dont seem much encouragement for farmers, its hard rubbin, now-a-days, to live by the plough – he'll be a hard workin poor man all his days. Oh! says I, if he wants to get rich by farmin, he can do that, too. Let him sell his wheat, and eat his oatmeal and rye; send his beef, mutton and poultry to market, and eat his pork and potatoes; make his own cloth, weave his own linen, and keep out of shops, and he'll soon grow rich – there are more fortins got by savin than by makin, I guess, a plaguy sight – he cant eat his cake and have it too, that's a fact. *No, make a farmer of him, and you will have the satisfaction of seeing him an honest, an independent, and a respectable member of society – more honest than traders, more independent than professional men, and more respectable than either.*

Ahem! says Marm Drivvle, and she began to clear her throat for action; she slumped down her nittin, and clawed off her spectacles, and looked right straight at me, so as to take good aim. I seed a regular norwester a bruin, I knew it would bust somewhere sartan, and make all smoke agin, so I cleared out and left old Drivvle to stand the squall. I conceit he must have had a tempestical time of it, for she had got her Ebenezer up, and looked like a proper sneezer. Make her Johnny a farmer, eh! I guess that was too much for the like o' her to stomach.

Pride, Squire, continued the Clockmaker, (with such an air of concern, that, I verily believe, the man feels an interest in the welfare of a Province, in which he has spent so long a time,) *Pride, Squire, and a false pride, too, is the ruin of this country, I hope I may be skinned if it tante.*

THE WHITE NIGGER

One of the most amiable, and at the same time most amusing traits, in the Clockmaker's character, was the attachment and kindness with which he regarded his horse. He considered "Old Clay" as far above a Provincial Horse, as he did one of his "free and enlightened citizens" superior to a Blue Nose. He treated him as a travelling companion, and when conversation flagged between us, would often soliloquize to him, a habit contracted from pursuing his journeys alone. Well now, he would say, "Old Clay," I guess you took your time a goin up that are hill, 'spose we progress now. Go along you old sculpin, and turn out your toes. I reckon you are as deff as a shad, do you hear there, "go ahead Old Clay." There now, he'd say, Squire aint that dreadful pretty? There's action. That looks about right – legs all under him – gathers all up snug – no bobbin of his head – no rollin of his shoulders – no wabblin of his hind parts, but steady as a pump bolt, and the motion all underneath. When he fairly lays himself to it, he trots like all vengeance. Then look at his ears, jist like rabbits, none o' your flop ears like them Amherst beasts, half horses, half pigs, but strait up and pineted, and not too near at the tips; for that are, I concait, always shews a horse aint true to draw. *There are only two things, Squire, worth lookin at in a horse, action and soundness, for I never saw a critter that had good action that was a bad beast.* Old Clay puts me in mind of one of our free and enlightened ———. Excuse me, said I, Mr. Slick, but really you appropriate that word "free" to your countrymen, as if you thought no other people in the world were entitled to it but yourselves. Neither be they, said he. We first sot the example. Look at our declaration of independence. It was writ by Jefferson, and he was the first man of the age, perhaps the world never seed his ditto. It's a beautiful piece of penmanship that, he gave the British the butt eend of his mind there. I calculate you could'nt falt it in no particular, it's generally allowed to be his cap shief. In the first page of it, second section, and first varse, are these words, "We hold this truth to be self-evident, that all men are created equal." I guess King George turned his quid when he read that. It was somethin to chaw on, he had'nt been used to the flavor of, I reckon. Jefferson forgot to insert – one little word, said I, he should have said, "all white men;" for, as it now stands, it is a practical untruth, in a country which tolerates domestic slavery in its worst and most forbidding form. It is a declaration of *shame*, and not of *independence*. It is as perfect a misnomer as ever I knew. Well, said he, I must admit there is a screw loose somewhere thereabouts, and I wish it would convene to Congress, to do somethin or another about our niggers, but I am not quite certified how that is to be sot to rights – I concait that you don't understand us. But, said he, (evading the subject with his usual dexterity,) we deal only in niggers, – and those thick skulled, crooked shanked, flat footed, long heeled, wooly headed gentlemen, don't seem fit for much else but slavery, I do suppose. They aint fit to contrive for themselves. They are jist like grasshoppers; they dance and sing all summer, and when winter comes they have nothin provided for it, and lay down and die. They require some one to see arter them. Now, we deal in black niggers only, but the Blue Noses sell their own species – they trade in white slaves. Thank God, said I, slavery does not exist in any part of his Majesty's dominions now, we have at last wiped off that national stain. Not quite, I guess, said he, with an air of triumph, it tante done with in Nova Scotia, for I have seed these human cattle sales with my own eyes – I was availed of the truth of it up here to old Furlong's, last November. I'll tell you the story, said he; and as this story of the Clockmaker's contained some extraordinary statements, which I had never heard of before, I noted it in my journal, for the purpose of ascertaining their truth; and, if founded on fact, of laying them before the proper authorities.

Last fall, said he, I was on my way to Partridge Island, to ship off some truck and pro*duce* I had taken in, in the way of trade; and as I neared old Furlong's house, I seed an amazin crowd of folks about the door; I said to myself, says I, whose dead, and what's to pay now – what on airth is the meanin of all this? Is it a vandew, or a weddin, or a rolin frolic, or a religious stir, or what is it? Thinks I, I'll see, so I hitches Old Clay to the fence, and walks in. It was some time afore I was able to swiggle my way thro' the crowd, and get into the house. And when I did, who should I see but deacon Westfall, a smooth faced, slick haired, meechin lookin chap as you'd see in a hundred, a standin on a stool, with an auctioneer's hammer in his hand; and afore him was one Jerry Oaks and his wife, and two little orphan children, the prettiest little toads I ever beheld in all my born days. Gentlemen, said he, I will begin the sale by putting up Jerry Oaks, of Apple River, he's a considerable of a smart man yet, and can do many little chores besides feedin the children and pigs, I guess he's near about worth his keep. Will you warrant him sound, wind and limb? says a tall ragged lookin countryman, for he looks to me as if he was foundered in both feet, and had a string halt into the bargain. When you are as old as I be, says Jerry, mayhap you may be foundered too, young man. I have seen the day when you would'nt dare to pass that joke on me, big as you be. Will any gentleman bid for him, says the deacon, he's cheap at 7s. 6d. Why deacon, said Jerry, why surely your honor is'nt a goin for to sell me separate from my poor old wife, are you? Fifty years have we lived together as man and wife, and a good wife has she been to me, through all my troubles and trials, and God knows I have had enough of 'em. No one knows my ways and my ailments but her, and who can tend me so kind, or who will bear with the complaints of a poor old man but his wife. Do, deacon, and Heaven bless you for it, and yours, do sell us together. We have but a few days to live now, death will divide us soon enough. Leave her to close my old eyes, when the struggle comes, and when it comes to you, deacon, as come it must to us all, may this good deed rise up for you, as a memorial before God. I wish it had pleased him to have taken us afore it came to this, but his will be done; and he hung his head, as if he felt he had drained the cup of degradation to its dregs. Can't afford it, Jerry – can't afford it, old man, said the deacon, (with such a smile as a November sun gives, a passin atween clouds.) Last year they took oats for rates, now nothin but wheat will go down, and that's as good as cash, and you'll hang on as most of you do yet these many years. There's old Joe Crowe, I believe in my conscience he will live for ever. The biddin then went on, and he was sold for six shillings a week. Well, the poor critter gave one long loud deep groan, and then folded his arms over his breast, so tight that he seemed tryin to keep in his heart from bustin. I pitied the misfortinate wretch from my soul, I don't know as I ever felt so streaked afore. Not so his wife, she was all tongue. She begged and prayed, and cryed, and scolded, and talked at the very tip eend of her voice, till she became, poor critter, exhausted, and went off in a faintin fit, and they ketched her up and carried her out to the air, and she was sold in that condition. Well I could'nt make head or tail of all this, I could hardly believe my eyes and ears; so, says I, to John Porter, (him that has that catamount of a wife, that I had such a touss with,) John Porter, says I, who ever seed or heerd tell of the like of this, what under the sun does it all mean? What has that are critter done that he should be sold arter that fashion? Done, said he, why nothin, and that's the reason they sell him. This is town meetin day, and we always sell the poor for the year, to the lowest bidder. Them that will keep them for the lowest sum, gets them. Why, says I, that feller that bought him is a pauper himself, to my sartan knowledge. If you were to take him up by the heels and shake him for a week, you could'nt shake sixpence out of him. How can he keep him? it appears to me the poor buy the poor here, and that they all starve together. Says I, there was a very good man once lived to Liverpool, so good, he said he had'nt sinned for seven years; well he put a mill dam across the river, and stopt all the fish from goin up, and the court fined him fifty pounds for it, and this good man was so wrathy, he thought he should feel better to swear a little, but conscience told him it was wicked. So he compounded with conscience, and cheated the devil, by callin it a "dam fine business." Now, friend Porter, if this is your poor law, it is a damn poor law, I tell you, and no good can come of such hard-hearted doins. It's no wonder your country don't prosper, for who ever heerd of a blessin on such carryins on as this? Says I, did you ever hear tell of a sartan rich man, that had a beggar called Lazarus laid at his gate, and how the dogs had more compassion than he had, and came and licked his sores? cause if you have, look at that forehanded and sponsible man there, deacon Westfall, and you see the rich man. And then look at that are pauper, dragged away in that ox-cart from his wife for ever, like a feller to States' Prison, and you see Lazarus. Recollect what follered, John Porter, and have neither art nor part in it, as you are a Christian man. It fairly made me sick all day. John Porter follered me out of the house, and as I was a turnin Old Clay, said he, Mr. Slick, says he, I never seed it in that are light afore, for its our custom, and custom you know will reconcile one to most any thing. I must say, it does appear, as you lay it out, an unfeelin way of providin for the poor; but, as touchin the matter of dividen man and wife, why, (and he peered all round to see that no one was within hearin,) why I dont know, but if it was my allotment to be sold, I'd as lives they'd sell me separate from Jane as not, for it appears to me its about the best part of it.

Now, what I have told you Squire, said the Clockmaker, is the truth; and if members, instead of their everlasting politics, would only look into these matters a little, I guess it would be far better for the Country. So, as for our declaration of independence, I guess you need'nt twitt me with our slave-sales, for we deal only in blacks; but Blue Nose approbates no distinction in colours, and when reduced to poverty, is reduced to slavery, and is sold – *a White Nigger.*

FIRE IN THE DAIRY

As we approached within fifteen or twenty miles of Parrsboro, a sudden turn of the road brought us directly in front of a large wooden house, consisting of two stories and an immense roof, the heighth of which edifice was much increased by a stone foundation, rising several feet above ground. Now, did you ever see, said Mr. Slick, such a catamaran as that; there's a proper goney for you, for to go and raise such a buildin as that are, and he as much use for it, I do suppose, as my old waggon here has for a fifth wheel. Blue Nose always takes keer to have a big house, cause it shows a big man, and one that's considerable forehanded, and pretty well to do in the world. These Nova Scotians turn up their Blue Noses as a bottle nose porpoise turns up his snout, and puff and snort exactly like him at a small house. If neighbor Carrit has a two story house, all filled with winders, like Sandy Hook light house, neighbor Parsnip must add jist two feet more on to the post of hisn, and about as much more to the rafter, to go ahead of him; so all these long sarce gentlemen strive who can get the furdest in the sky, away from their farms. In New England our maxim is a small house, and a most an everlastin almighty big barn; but these critters revarse it, they have little hovels for their cattle, about the bigness of a good sizeable bear trap, and a house for the humans as grand as Noah's Ark. Well, jist look at it and see what a figur it does cut. An old hat stuffed into one pane of glass, and an old flannel petticoat, as yaller as jaundice, in another, finish off the front; an old pair of breeches, and the pad of a bran new cart saddle worn out, titivate the eend, while the backside is all closed up on account of the wind. When it rains, if there aint a pretty how-do-you-do, it's a pity – beds toated out of this room, and tubs set in tother to catch soft water to wash; while the clapboards, loose at the eends, go clap, clap, clap, like galls a hacklin flax, and the winders and doors keep a dancin to the music. The only dry place in the house is in the chimbley corner, where the folks all huddle up, as an old hen and her chickens do under a cart of a wet day. I wish I had the matter of half a dozen pound of nails, (you'll hear the old gentleman in the grand house say,) I'll be darned, if I don't, for if I had, I'd fix them are clapboards, I guess they'll go for it some o' these days. I wish you had, his wife would say, for they do make a most particular unhansum clatter, that's a fact; and so they let it be till the next tempestical time comes, and then they wish agin. Now this grand house has only two rooms down stairs, that are altogether slicked up and finished off complete, the other is jist petitioned off rough like, one half great dark entries, and tother half places that look a plaguy sight more like packin boxes than rooms. Well, all up stairs is a great onfarnished place, filled with every sort of good for nothin trumpery in natur – barrels without eends – corn cobs half husked – cast off clothes and bits of old harness, sheep skins, hides, and wool, apples, one half rotten, and tother half squashed – a thousand or two of shingles that have bust their withs, and broke loose all over the floor, hay rakes, forks and sickles, without handles or teeth; rusty scythes, and odds and eends without number. When any thing is wanted, then there is a general overhaul of the whole cargo, and away they get shifted forrard, one by one, all handled over and chucked into a heap together till the lost one is found; and the next time, away they get pitched to the starn agin, higglety pigglety, heels over head, like sheep taken a split for it over a wall; only they increase in number each move, cause some on 'em are sure to get broke into more pieces than they was afore. Whenever I see one of these grand houses, and a hat lookin out o' the winder, with nary head in it, thinks I, I'll be darned if that's a place for a wooden clock, nothin short of a London touch would go down with them folks, so I calculate I wont alight.

Whenever you come to such a grand place as this, Squire, depend on't the farm is all of a piece, great crops of thistles, and an everlastin yield of weeds, and cattle the best fed of any in the country, for they are always in the grain fields or mowin lands, and the pigs a rootin in the potatoe patches. A spic and span new gig at the door, shinin like the mud banks of Windsor, when the sun's on 'em, and an old wrack of a hay waggon, with its tongue onhitched, and stickin out behind, like a pig's tail, all indicate a big man. He's above thinkin of farmin tools, he sees to the bran new gig, and the hired helps look arter the carts. Catch him with his go-to-meetin clothes on, a rubbin agin their nasty greasy axles, like a tarry nigger; not he, indeed, he'd stick you up with it.

The last time I came by here, it was a little bit arter day light down, rainin cats and dogs, and as dark as Egypt; so, thinks I, I'll jist turn in here for shelter to Squire Bill Blake's. Well, I knocks away at the front door, till I thought I'd a split it in: but arter a rappin awhile to no purpose, and findin no one come, I gropes my way round to the back door, and opens it, and feelin all along the partition for the latch of the keepin room, without finding it, I knocks agin, when some one from inside calls out 'walk.' Thinks I, I don't cleverly know whether that indicates 'walk in,' or 'walk out,' its plaguy short metre, that's a fact; but I'll see any how. Well, arter gropin about awhile, at last I got hold of the string and lifted the latch and walked in, and there sot old Marm Blake, close into one corner of the chimbley fire place, a see-sawin in a rockin chair, and a half grown black house help, half asleep in tother corner, a scroudgin up over the embers. Who be you, said Marm Blake, for I can't see you. A stranger, said I. Beck, says she, speakin to the black heifer in the corner, Beck, says she agin, raisin her voice, I believe you are as def as a post, get up this minit and stir the coals, till I see the man. Arter the coals were stirred into a blaze, the old lady surveyed me from head to foot, then she axed me my name, and where I came from, where I was agoin, and what my business was. I guess, said she, you must be reasonable wet, sit to the fire and dry yourself, or mayhap your health may be endamnified p'raps.

So I sot down, and we soon got pretty considerably well acquainted, and quite sociable like, and her tongue when it fairly waked up, began to run like a mill race when the gate's up. I hadn't been talkin long, 'fore I well nigh lost sight of her alto-gether agin, for little Beck, began to flourish about her broom, right and left, in great style, a clearin up, and she did raise such an auful thick cloud o' dust, I didn't know if I should ever see or breathe either agin. Well when all was sot to rights and the fire made up, the old lady began to apologize for havin no candles; she said she'd had a grand tea party the night afore, and used them all up, and a whole sight of vittals too, the old man hadn't been well since, and had gone to bed airly. But, says she, I do wish with all my heart you had a come last night, for we had a most a special supper – punkin pies and dough-nuts, and apple sarce, and a roast goose stuffed with indian puddin, and a pig's harslet stewed in molasses and onions, and I dont know what all, and the fore part of to-day folks called to finish. I actilly have nothin left to set afore you; for it was none o' your skim-milk parties, but superfine uppercrust real jam, and we made clean work of it. But I'll make some tea, any how, for you, and perhaps, arter that, said she, alterin of her tone, perhaps you'll expound the Scriptures, for its one while since I've heerd them laid open powerfully. I hant been fairly lifted up since that good man Judas Oglethorp travelled this road, and then she gave a groan and hung down her head, and looked cornerways, to see how the land lay thereabouts. The tea kettle was accordingly put on, and some lard fried into oil and poured into a tumbler; which, with the aid of an inch of cotton wick, served as a make shift for a candle. Well, arter tea we sot and chatted awhile about fashions, and markets, and sarmons, and scandal, and all sorts o' things; and, in the midst of it, in runs the nigger wench, screemin out at the tip eend of her voice, oh Missus! Missus! there's a fire in the Dairy, fire in the Dairy! I'll give it to you for that, said the old lady, I'll give it you for that, you good for nothin hussy, that's all your carelessness, go and put it out this minit, how on airth did it get there? my night's milk gone, I dare say; run this minit and put it out and save the milk. I am dreadful afeard of fire, I always was from a boy, and seein the poor foolish critter seize a broom in her fright, I ups with the tea kettle and follows her; and away we clipt thro' the entry, she callin out mind the cellar door on the right, take kear of the close horse on the left, and so on, but as I could'nt see nothin, I kept right straight ahead. At last my foot kotched in somethin or another, that pitched me somewhat less than a rod or so, right agin the poor black critter, and away we went, heels over head. I heerd a splash and a groan, and I smelt somethin plaguy sour, but I couldnt see nothin; at last I got hold of her and lifted her up, for she didn't scream, but made a strange kind of choakin noise, and by this time up came Marm Blake with a light. If poor Beck didnt let go then in airnest, and sing out, for dear life, its a pity, for she had gone head first into the swill tub, and the tea kettle had scalded her feet. She kept a dancin right up and down, like one ravin distracted mad, and boohood like any thing, clawin away at her head the whole time, to clear away the stuff that stuck to her wool.

I held in as long as I could, till I thought I should have busted, for no soul could help a larfin, and at last I haw hawed right out. You good for nothin stupid slut you, said the old lady, to poor Beck, it sarves you right, you had no business to leave it there – I'll pay you. But, said I, interferin for the unfortunate critter, Good gracious Marm! you forget the fire. No I don't, said she, I see him, and seesin the broom that had fallen from the nigger's hand, she exclaimed, I see him, the nasty varmint, and began to belabor most onmarcifully a poor half starved cur that the noise had attracted to the entry. I'll teach you, said she, to drink milk; I'll larn you to steal into the dairy; and the besot critter joined chorus with Beck, and they both yelled together, till they fairly made the house ring agin. Presently old Squire Blake popt his head out of a door, and rubbin his eyes, half asleep and half awake, said, What the devil's to pay now, wife? Why nothin, says she, only "*fire's in the dairy*," and Beck's in the swill tub, that's all. Well, don't make such a touss, then, said he, if that's all, and he shot tu the door and went to bed agin. When we returned to the keepin room, the old lady told me that they always had had a dog called "*Fire,*" ever since her grandfather, Major Donald Fraser's time, and what was very odd, says she, every one on 'em would drink milk if he had a chance. By this time the shower was over, and the moon shinin so bright and clear that I thought I'd better be up and stirrin, and arter slippin a few cents into the poor nigger wench's hand, I took leave of the grand folks in the big house. Now, Squire, among these middlin sized farmers you may lay this down as a rule – *The bigger the house, the bigger the fools be that's in it.*

But, howsomever, I never call to mind that are go in the big house, up to the right, that I don't snicker when I think of "*Fire in the dairy.*"

A BODY WITHOUT A HEAD

I allot you had ought to visit our great country Squire, said the Clockmaker, afore you quit for good and all. I calculate you don't understand us. The most splendid location atween the Poles is the United States, and the first man alive is Gineral Jackson, the hero of the age, him that skeered the British out of their seven senses. Then there's the great Danel Webster, its generally allowed, he's the greatest orator on the face of the airth, by a long chalk, and Mr. Van Buren, and Mr. Clay, and Amos Kindle, and Judge White, and a whole raft of statesmen, up to every thing, and all manner of politics; there aint the beat of 'em to be found any where. If you was to hear 'em, I concait you'd hear genuine pure English for once, any how; for its generally allowed we speak English better than the British. They all know me to be an American citizen here, by my talk, for we speak it complete in New England.

Yes, if you want to see a free people – them that makes their own laws, accordin to their own notions – go to the States. Indeed, if you can falt them at all, they are a little grain too free. Our folks have their head a trifle too much, some-times, particularly in Elections, both in freedom of speech and freedom of Press. One hadnt ought to blart right out always all that comes uppermost. A horse that's too free frets himself and his rider too, and both on em lose flesh in the long run. I'd een a most as lives use the whip sometimes, as to be for everlastenly a pullin at the rein. One's arm gets plaguy tired, that's a fact. I often think of a lesson I larnt Jehiel Quirk once, for letten his tongue outrun his good manners. I was down to Rhode Island one summer to larn gilden and bronzin, so as to give the finishin touch to my clocks. Well, the folks elected me a hog reave, jist to poke fun at me, and Mr. Jehiel, a bean pole of a lawyer, was at the bottom of it. So one day, up to Town Hall, where there was an oration to be delivered on our Independence, jist afore the orator commenced, in runs Jehiel in a most allfired hurry; and, says he, I wonder, says he, if there's are a hog reave here, because if there be I require a turn of his office. And then, said he, a lookin up to me and callin out at the tip eend of his voice, Mr. Hogreave Slick, says he, here's a job out here for you. Folks snickered a good deal, and I felt my spunk a risen like half flood, that's a fact; but I bit in my breath, and spoke quite cool. Possible, says I; well duty, I do suppose, must be done, though it tante the most agreeable in the world. I've been a thinkin, says I, that I would be liable to a fine of fifty cents for sufferin a hog to run at large, and as you are the biggest one, I presume, in all Rhode Island, I'll jist begin by ringin your nose, to prevent you for the futur from pokin your snout where you hadnt ought to, and I seized him by the nose and nearly wrung it off. Well, you never heerd sich a shoutin and clappin of hands, and cheerin, in your life – they haw-hawed like thunder. Says I Jehiel Quirk that was a superb joke of yourn, how you made the folks larf didnt you? You are een amost the wittiest critter I ever seed. I guess you'll mind your parts o' speech, and study the *accidence* agin afore you let your clapper run arter that fashion, won't you?

I thought, said I, that among you republicans, there were no gradations of rank or office, and that all were equal, the Hogreave and the Governor, the Judge and the Crier, the master and his servant; and although, from the natur of things, more power might be entrusted to one than the other, yet that the rank of all was precisely the same. Well, said he, it is so in theory, but not always in practice; and when we do prac*tise* it, it seems to go a little agin the grain, as if it warnt quite right neither. When I was last to Baltimore there was a Court there, and Chief Justice Marshall was detailed there for duty. Well, with us in New England, the Sheriff attends the Judge to Court, and, says I to the Sheriff, why dont you escort that are venerable old Judge to the State House, he's a credit to our nation that man, he's actilly the first pot hook on the crane, the whole weight is on him, if it warnt for him the fat would be in the fire in no time; I wonder you dont show him that respect – it wouldnt hurt you one morsel, I guess. Says he, quite miffy like, don't he know the way to Court as well as I do? if I thought he didnt, I'd send one of my niggers to show him the road. I wonder who was his lackey last year, that he wants me to be hisn this time. It don't convene to one of our free and enlightened citizens, to tag arter any man, that's a fact; its too English and too foreign for our glorious institutions. He's bound by law to be there at 10 o'clock, and so be I, and we both know the way there I reckon.

I told the story to our minister, Mr. Hopewell (and he has some odd notions about him that man, though he don't always let out what he thinks), says he, Sam, that was in bad taste, (a great phrase of the old gentleman's that) in bad taste, Sam. That are Sheriff was a goney; don't cut your cloth arter his pattern, or your garment won't become you, I tell you. We are too enlightened, to worship our fellow citizens as the ancients did, but we ought to pay great respect to vartue and exalted talents in this life; and, arter their death, there should be statues of eminent men placed in our national temples, for the veneration of arter ages, and public ceremonies performed annually to their honor. Arter all, Sam, said he, (and he made a considerable of a long pause, as if he was dubersome whether he ought to speak out or not) arter all, Sam, said he, atween ourselves, (but you must not let on I said so, for the fullness of time han't yet come) half a yard of blue ribbon is a plaguy cheap way of rewarden merit, as the English do; and, although we larf at em, (for folks always will larf at what they hant got, and never can get,) yet titles aint bad things as objects of ambition, are they? Then, tappen me on the shoulder, and lookin up and smilin, as he always did when he was pleased with an idee, Sir Samuel Slick would not sound bad, I guess, would it Sam?

When I look at the English House of Lords, said he, and see so much larning, piety, talent, honor, vartue, and refinement, collected together, I ax myself this here question, can a system which produces and sustains such a body of men, as the world never saw before and never will see agin, be defective? Well, I answer myself, perhaps it is, for all human institutions are so, but I guess its een about the best arter all. It wouldn't do here now, Sam, nor perhaps for a century to come, but it will come sooner or later with some variations. Now the Newtown pippin, when transplanted to England, don't produce such fruit as it does in Long Island, and English fruits don't presarve their flavor here, neither; allowance must be made for difference of soil and climate – (Oh Lord! thinks I, if he turns in to his orchard, I'm done for; I'll have to give him the dodge some how or another through some hole in the fence, that's a fact – but he passed on that time.) So it is, said he, with constitutions; ourn will gradually approximate to theirn, and theirn to ourn. As they lose their strength of executive, they will varge to republicanism, and as we invigorate the form of government, (as we must do, or go to the old boy) we shall tend towards a monarchy. If this comes on gradually, like the changes in the human body, by the slow approach of old age, so much the better; but I fear we shall have fevers, and convulsion-fits, and cholics, and an everlastin gripin of the intestines first; you and I wont live to see it Sam, but our posteriors will, you may depend.

I don't go the whole figur with minister, said the Clockmaker, but I do opinionate with him in part. In our business relations we bely our political principles – we say every man is equal in the Union, and should have an equal vote and voice in the Government; but in our Banks, Rail Road Companies, Factory Corporations, and so on, every man's vote is regilated by his share and proportion of stock; and if it warnt so, no man would take hold on these things at all.

Natur ordained it so – a father of a family is head, and rules supreme in his household; his eldest son and darter are like first leftenants under him, and then there is an overseer over the niggers; it would not do for all to be equal there. So it is in the univarse, it is ruled by one Superior Power; if all the Angels had a voice in the Government I guess ———— Here I fell fast asleep; I had been nodding for some time, not in approbation of what he said, but in heaviness of slumber, for I had never before heard him so prosy since I first overtook him on the Colchester road. I hate politics as a subject of conversation, it is too wide a field for chit chat, and too often ends in angry discussion. How long he continued this train of speculation I do not know, but, judging by the different aspect of the country, I must have slept an hour.

I was at length aroused by the report of his rifle, which he had discharged from the waggon. The last I recollected of his conversation was, I think, about American angels having no voice in the Government, an assertion that struck my drowsy faculties as not strictly true; as I had often heard that the American ladies talked frequently and warmly on the subject of politics, and knew that one of them had very recently the credit of breaking up General Jackson's cabinet. – When I awoke, the first I heard was "well, I declare, if that aint an amazin fine shot, too, considerin how the critter was a runnin the whole blessed time; if I han't cut her head off with a ball, jist below the throat, that's a fact. There's no mistake in a good Kentucky rifle, I tell you. Whose head? said I, in great alarm, whose head, Mr. Slick? for heaven's sake what have you done? (for I had been dreaming of those angelic politicians the American ladies.) Why that are hen-partridge's head, to be sure, said he; don't you see how special wonderful wise it looks, a flutterin about arter its head. True, said I, rubbing my eyes, and opening them in time to see the last muscular spasms of the decapitated body; true, Mr. Slick, it is a happy illustration of our previous conversation – *a body without a head.*

A TALE OF BUNKER'S HILL

M r. Slick, like all his countrymen whom I have seen, felt that his own existence was involved in that of the Constitution of the United States, and that it was his duty to uphold it upon all occasions. He affected to consider its government and its institutions as perfect, and if any doubt was suggested as to the stability or character of either, would make the common reply of all Americans, "I guess you don't understand us," or else enter into a labored defence. When left, however, to the free expression of his own thoughts, he would often give utterance to those apprehensions which most men feel in the event of an experiment not yet fairly tried, and which has in many parts evidently disappointed the sanguine hopes of its friends. But, even on these occasions, when his vigilance seemed to slumber, he would generally cover them, by giving them as the remarks of others, or concealing them in a tale. It was this habit that gave his discourse rather the appearance of "thinking aloud," than a connected conversation.

We are a great nation, Squire, he said, that's sartain, but I'm afeard we didnt altogether start right. Its in politics as in racin, every thing depends upon a fair start. If you are off too quick, you have to pull up and turn back agin, and your beast gets out of wind and is baffled, and if you lose in the start you hant got a fair chance arterwards, and are plaguy apt to be jockied in the course. When we set up housekeepin, as it were for ourselves, we hated our step mother, Old England, so dreadful bad, we wouldnt foller any of her ways of managin at all, but made new receipts for ourselves. Well, we missed it in many things most consumedly, some how or another. Did you ever see, said he, a congregation split right in two by a quarrel, and one part go off and set up for themselves. I am sorry to say, said I, that I have seen some melancholy instances of the kind. Well, they shoot ahead, or drop astern, as the case may be, but they soon get on another tack, and leave the old ship clean out of sight. When folks once take to emigratin in religion in this way, they never know where to bide. First they try one location, and then they try another; some settle here and some improve there, but they dont hitch their horses together long. Some times they complain they *have too little water*, at other times that they *have too much*; they are never satisfied, and, wherever these separatists go, they onsettle others as bad as themselves. *I never look on a desarter as any great shakes.* My poor father used to say, "Sam, mind what I tell you, if a man don't agree in all particulars with his church, and can't go the whole hog with 'em, he aint justified on that account, no how, to separate from them, for Sam, "*Schism is a sin in the eye of God.*" The whole Christian world, he would say, is divided into two great families, the Catholic and Protestant. Well, the Catholic is a united family, a happy family, and a strong family, all governed by one head; and Sam, as sure as eggs is eggs, that are family will grub out tother one, stalk, branch and root, it won't so much as leave the seed of it in the ground, to grow by chance as a nateral curiosity. Now the Protestant family is like a bundle of refuse shingles, when withed up together, (which it never was and never will be to all etarnity) no great of a bundle arter all, you might take it up under one arm, and walk off with it without winkin. But, when all lyin loose as it always is, jist look at it, and see what a sight it is, all blowin about by every wind of doctrine, some away up een a most out of sight, others rollin over and over in the dirt, some split to pieces, and others so warped by the weather and cracked by the sun – no two of 'em will lie so as to make a close jint. They are all divided into sects, railin, quarrellin, separatin, and agreein in nothin, but hatin each other. It is awful to think on. Tother family will some day or other gather them all up, put them into a bundle and bind them up tight, and condemn 'em as fit for nothin under the sun, but the fire. Now he who splits one of these here sects by schism, or he who preaches schism, commits a grievous sin; and Sam, if you valy your own peace of mind, have nothin to do with such folks.

Its pretty much the same in politics. I aint quite clear in my conscience, Sam, about our glorious revolution. If that are blood was shed justly in the rebellion, then it was the Lord's doin, but if unlawfully, how am I to answer for my share in it. I was at Bunker's Hill (the most splendid battle its generally allowed that ever was fought); what effect my shots had, I can't tell, and I am glad I can't, all except one, Sam, and that shot ——— Here the Old Gentleman became dreadful agitated, he shook like an ague fit, and he walked up and down the room, and wrung his hands, and groaned bitterly. I have wrastled with the Lord, Sam, and have prayed to him to enlighten me on that pint, and to wash out the stain of that are blood from my hands. I never told you that are story, nor your mother neither, for she could not stand it, poor critter, she's kinder narvous.

Well, Doctor Warren, (the first soldier of his age, though he never fought afore,) commanded us all to resarve our fire till the British came within pint blank shot, and we could cleverly see the whites of their eyes, and we did so – and we mowed them down like grass, and we repeated our fire with awful effect. I was among the last that remained behind the breastwork, for most on 'em, arter the second shot, cut and run full split. The British were close to us; and an officer, with his sword drawn, was leading on his men and encouragin them to the charge. I could see his features, he was a rael handsum man, I can see him now with his white breeches and black gaiters, and red coat, and three cornered cocked hat, as plain as if it was yesterday, instead of the year '75. Well, I took a steady aim at him and fired. He did'nt move for a space, and I thought I had missed him, when all of a sudden, he sprung right straight up an eend, his sword slipt through his hands up to the pint, and then he fell flat on his face atop of the blade, and it came straight out through his back. He was fairly skivered. I never seed any thing so awful since I was raised, I actilly screamed out with horror – and I threw away my gun, and joined them that were retreatin over the neck to Charlestown. Sam, that are British officer, if our rebellion was onjust or onlawful, was murdered, that's a fact; and the idee, now I am growin old, haunts me day and night. Sometimes I begin with the Stamp Act, and I go over all our grievances, one by one, and say aint they a sufficient justification? Well, it makes a long list, and I get kinder satisfied, and it appears as clear as anything. But sometimes there come doubts in my mind, jist like a guest that's not invited or not expected, and takes you at a short like, and I say, warn't the Stamp Act repealed, and concessions made, and warn't offers sent to settle all fairly – and I get troubled an oneasy again? And then I say to myself, says I, oh yes, but them offers came too late. I do nothin now, when I am alone, but argue it over and over again. I actilly dream on that man in my sleep sometimes, and then I see him as plain as if he was afore me, and I go over it all agin till I come to that are shot, and then I leap right up in bed and scream like all vengeance, and your mother, poor old critter, says, Sam, says she, what on airth ails you to make you act so like Old Scratch in your sleep – I do believe there's somethin or another on your conscience. And I say, Polly dear, I guess we're a goin to have rain, for that plaguy cute rheumatis has seized my foot, and it does antagonize me so I have no peace. It always does so when it's like for a change. Dear heart, she says, (the poor simple critter,) then I guess I had better rub it, had'nt I, Sam? and she crawls out of bed and gets her red flannel petticoat, and rubs away at my foot ever so long. Oh, Sam, if she could rub it out of my heart as easy as she thinks she rubs it out of my foot, I should be in peace, that's a fact.

What's done, Sam, can't be helped, there is no use in cryin over spilt milk, but still one can't help a thinkin on it. But I dont love schisms and I dont love rebellion.

Our revolution has made us grow faster and grow richer; but Sam, when we were younger and poorer, we were more pious and more happy. We have nothin fixed either in religion or politics. What connection there ought to be atween Church and State, I am not availed, but some there ought to be as sure as the Lord made Moses. Religion when left to itself, as with us, grows too rank and luxuriant. Suckers and sprouts, and intersecting shoots, and superfluous wood make a nice shady tree to look at, but where's the fruit, Sam? that's the question – where's the fruit? No; the pride of human wisdom, and the presumption it breeds will ruinate us. Jefferson was an infidel, and avowed it, and gloried in it, and called it the enlightenment of the age. Cambridge College is Unitarian, cause it looks wise to doubt, and every drumstick of a boy ridicules the belief of his forefathers. If our country is to be darkened by infidelity, our Government defied by every State, and every State ruled by mobs – then, Sam, the blood we shed in our revolution will be atoned for in the blood and suffering of our fellow citizens. The murders of that civil war will be expiated by a political suicide of the State.

I am somewhat of father's opinion, said the Clockmaker, though I dont go the whole figur with him, but he needn't have made such an everlastin touss about fixin that are British officer's flint for him, for he'd a died of himself by this time, I do suppose, if he had a missed his shot at him. Praps we might have done a little better, and praps we mightn't, by sticken a little closer to the old constitution. But one thing I will say, I think arter all, your Colony Government is about as happy and as good a one as I know on. A man's life and property are well protected here at little cost, and he can go where he likes and do what he likes, provided he dont trespass on his neighbor.

I guess that's enough for any on us, now aint it?

GULLING A BLUE NOSE

I allot, said Mr. Slick, that the Blue Noses are the most gullible folks on the face of the airth – rigular soft horns, that's a fact. Politics and such stuff set 'em a gapin, like children in a chimbly corner listenen to tales of ghosts, Salem witches, and Nova Scotia snow storms; and while they stand starin and yawpin, all eyes and mouth, they get their pockets picked of every cent that's in 'em. One candidate chap says, "Feller citizens, this country is goin to the dogs hand over hand; look at your rivers, you have no bridges; at your wild lands, you have no roads; at your treasury, you hante got a cent in it; at your markets, things dont fetch nothin; at your fish, the Yankees ketch 'em all. There's nothin behind you but suf-ferin, around you but poverty, afore you, but slavery and death. What's the cause of this unheerd of awful state of things, ay, what's the cause? Why Judges, and Banks, and Lawyers, and great folks, have swallered all the money. They've got you down, and they'll keep you down to all eternity, you and your posteriors arter you. Rise up like men, arouse yourselves like freemen, and elect me to the Legislatur, and I'll lead on the small but patriotic band, I'll put the big wigs thro' their facins,

I'll make 'em shake in their shoes, I'll knock off your chains and make you free." Well, the goneys fall tu and elect him, and he desarts right away, with balls, rifle, powder horn and all. *He promised too much.*

Then comes a rael good man, and an everlastin fine preacher, a most a special spiritual man, renounces the world, the flesh, and the devil, preaches and prays day and night, so kind to the poor, and so humble, he has no more pride than a babe, and so short-handed he's no butter to his bread – all self denial, mortifyin the flesh. Well, as soon as he can work it, he marries the richest gall in all his flock, and then his bread is buttered on both sides. *He promised too much.*

Then comes a Doctor, and a prime article he is too, I've got, says he, a screw augur emetic and hot crop, and if I cant cure all sorts o' things in natur my name aint quack. Well he turns stomach and pocket, both inside out, and leaves poor Blue Nose – a dead man. *He promised too much.*

Then comes a Lawyer, an honest lawyer too, a rael wonder under the sun, as straight as a shingle in all his dealins. He's so honest he cant bear to hear tell of other lawyers, he writes agin 'em, raves agin 'em, votes agin 'em, they are all rogues but him. He's jist the man to take case in hand, cause *he* will see justice done. Well, he wins his case, and fobs all for costs, cause he's sworn to see justice done to – himself. *He promised too much.*

Then comes a Yankee Clockmaker, (and here Mr. Slick looked up and smiled,) with his "Soft Sawder," and "Human Natur," and he sells clocks warranted to run from July to Etarnity, stoppages included, and I must say they do run as long as – as long as wooden clocks commonly do, that's a fact. But I'll shew you presently how I put the leak into 'em, for here's a feller a little bit ahead on us, whose flint I've made up my mind to fix this while past. Here we were nearly thrown out of the waggon, by the breaking down of one of those small wooden bridges, which prove so annoying and so dangerous to travellers. Did you hear that are snap? said he, well as sure as fate, I'll break my clocks over them etarnal log bridges, if Old Clay clips over them arter that fashion. Them are poles are plaguy treacherous, they are jist like old Marm Patience Doesgood's teeth, that keeps the great United Independent Democratic Hotel, at Squaw Neck Creek, in Massachusetts, one half gone, and tother half rotten eends. I thought you had disposed of your last clock, said I, at Colchester, to Deacon Flint. So I did, he replied, the last one I had to sell to *him*, but I got a few left for other folks yet. Now there is a man on this road, one Zeb Allen, a real genu*ine* skinflint, a proper close fisted customer as you'll amost see any where, and one that's not altogether the straight thing in his dealin neither. He dont want no one to live but himself, and he's mighty handsum to me, sayin my clocks are all a cheat, and that we ruinate the country, a drainin every drop of money out of it, a callin me a Yankee broom and what not. But it tante all jist Gospel that he says. Now I'll put a clock on him afore he knows it, I'll go right into him as slick as a whistle, and play him to the eend of my line like a trout. I'll have a hook in his gills, while he's a thinkin he's only smellin at the bait. There he is now, I'll be darned if he aint, standin afore his shop door, lookin as strong as high proof Jamaiky; I guess I'll whip it out o' the bung while he's a lookin arter the spicket, and praps he'll be none o' the wiser till he finds it out, neither.

Well Squire, how do you do, said he, how's all to home? Reasonable well, I give you thanks, wont you alight? Cant to-day, said Mr. Slick, I'm in a considerable of a hurry to katch the Packet, have you any commands for Sow West? I'm goin to the Island, and across the Bay to Windsor. Any word that way? No says Mr. Allen, none that I can think on, unless it be to enquire how butter's goin; they tell me cheese is down and pro*duce* of all kind particular dull this fall. Well, I'm glad I can tell you that question, said Slick, for I dont calculate to return to these parts, butter is risin a cent or two; I put mine off mind at 10 pence. Dont return! possible! why how you talk? have you done with the clock trade? I guess I have, it tante worth follerin now. Most time, said the other, laughing, for by all accounts the clocks warnt worth havin, and most infarnal dear too, folks begin to get their eyes open. It warnt needed in your case, said Mr. Slick, with that peculiarly composed manner, that indicates suppressed feeling, for you were always wide awake, if all the folks had cut their eye teeth as airly as you did, their'd be plaguy few clocks sold in these parts, I reckon; but you are right, Squire, you may say that, they actilly were *not* worth havin, and that's the truth. The fact is, said he, throwing down his reins, and affecting a most confidential tone, I felt almost ashamed of them myself, I tell you. The long and short of the matter is jist this, they dont make no good ones now-a-days, no more, for they calculate 'em for shippin and not for home use. I was all struck up of a heap when I see'd the last lot I got from the States; I was properly bit by them, you may depend; they didnt pay cost, for I couldnt recommend them with a clear conscience, and I must say I do like a fair deal, for I'm strait up and down, and love to go right ahead, that's a fact. Did you ever see them I fetched when I first came, them I sold over the Bay? No, said Mr. Allen, I cant say I did. Well, continued he, they *were* a prime article, I tell you, no mistake there, fit for any market, its generally allowed there aint the beat of them to be found any where. If you want a clock, and *can* lay your hands on one of them, I advise you not to let go the chance; you'll know 'em by the 'Lowell' mark, for they were all made at Judge Beler's factory. Squire Shepody, down to Five Islands, axed me to get him one, and a special job I had of it, near about more sarch arter it than it was worth, but I did get him one, and a particular handsum one it is, copald and gilt superior. I guess its worth ary half dozen in these parts, let tothers be where they may. If I could a got supplied with the like o' them, I could a made a grand spec out of them, for they took at once, and went off quick. Have you got it with you, said Mr. Allen, I should like to see it. Yes, I have it here, all done up in tow, as snug as a bird's egg, to keep it from jarrin, for it hurts 'em consumedly to jolt 'em over them are etarnal wooden bridges. But its no use to take it out, it aint for sale, its bespoke, and I would'nt take the same trouble to get another for twenty dollars. The only one that I know of that there's any chance of gettin, is one that Increase Crane has up to Wilmot, they say he's a sellin off.

After a good deal of persuasion, Mr. Slick unpacked the clock, but protested against his asking for it, for it was not for sale. It was then exhibited, every part explained and praised, as new in invention and perfect in workmanship. Now Mr. Allen had a very exalted opinion of Squire Shepody's taste, judgment, and saving knowledge; and, as it was the last and only chance of getting a clock, of such superior quality, he offered to take it at the price the Squire was to have it, at seven pounds ten shillings. But Mr. Slick vowed he could'nt part with it at no rate, he didn't know where he could get the like agin, (for he warnt quite sure about Increase Crane's) and the Squire would be confounded disappointed, he could'nt think of it. In proportion to the difficulties, rose the ardor of Mr. Allen, his offers advanced to £8, £8 10, to £9. I vow, said Mr. Slick, I wish I had'nt let on that I had it at all. I dont like to refuse you, but where am I to get the like. After much discussion of a similar nature, he consented to part with the clock, though with great apparent reluctance, and pocketed the money with a protest that, cost what it would, he should have to procure another, for he could'nt think of putting the Squire's pipe out arter that fashion, for he was a very clever man, and as fair as a boot jack. Now, said Mr. Slick, as we proceeded on our way, that are feller is properly sarved, he got the most inferior article I had, and I jist doubled the price on him. Its a pity he should be a tellin of lies of the Yankees all the time, this will help him now to a little grain of truth. Then mimicking his voice and manner, he repeated Allen's words with a strong nasal twang, "Most time for you to give over the clock trade, I guess, for by all accounts they aint worth havin, and most infarnel dear too, folks begin to get their eyes open." Better for you, if you'd a had yourn open, I reckon, a joke is a joke, but I concait you'll find that no joke. The next time you tell stories about Yankee pedlars, put the wooden clock in with the wooden punkin seeds, and Hickory hams, will you? The Blue Noses, Squire, are all like Zeb Allen, they think they know every thing, but they get gulled from years' eend to years' eend. They expect too much from others, and do too little for themselves. They actilly expect the sun to shine, and the rain to fall, through their little House of Assembly. What have you done for us? they keep axin their members. Who did you spunk up to last Session? jist as if all legislation consisted in attackin some half dozen puss proud folks at Halifax, who are jist as big noodles as they be themselves. You hear nothin but politics, politics, politics, one everlastin sound of give, give, give. If I was Governor I'd give 'em the butt eend of my mind on the subject, I'd crack their pates till I let some light in 'em, if it was me, I know. I'd say to the members, don't come down here to Halifax with your long lockrums about politics, makin a great touss about nothin; but open the country, foster agricultur, encourage trade, incorporate companies, make bridges, facilitate conveyance, and above all things make a rail road from Windsor to Halifax; and mind what I tell you now, write it down for fear you should forget it, for it's a fact; and if you don't believe me, I'll lick you till you do, for there aint a word of a lie in it, by Gum: *"One such work as the Windsor Bridge is worth all your laws, votes, speeches and resolutions, for the last ten years, if tied up and put into a meal bag together. If it tante I hope I may be shot."*

TOO MANY IRONS IN THE FIRE

We had a pleasant sail of three hours from Parrsboro to Windsor. The arrivals and departures by water, are regulated at this place by the tide, and it was sunset before we reached Mrs. Wilcox's comfortable inn. Here, as at other places, Mr. Slick seemed to be perfectly at home; and he pointed to a wooden clock, as a proof of his successful and extended trade, and of the universal influence of "soft sawder," and a knowledge of "human natur." Taking out a pen knife, he cut off a splinter from a stick of firewood, and balancing himself on one leg of his chair, by the aid of his right foot, commenced his favorite amusement of whitling, which he generally pursued in silence. Indeed it appeared to have become with him an indispensible accompaniment of reflection. He sat in this abstracted manner, until he had manufactured into delicate shavings the whole of his raw materiel, when he very deliberately resumed a position of more ease and security, by resting his chair on two legs instead of one, and putting both his feet on the mantel piece. Then, lighting his cigar, he said in his usual quiet manner, there's a plaguy sight of truth in them are old proverbs. They are distilled facts steamed down to an essence. They are like portable soup, an amazin deal of matter in a small compass. They are what I valy most, experience. Father used to say I'd as lives have an old homespun self taught doctor as are a Professor in the College at Philadelphia or New York to attend me; for what they do know, they know by experience, and not by books; and experience is every thing, its hearin and seein and tryin, and arter that a feller must be a born fool if he dont know. That's the beauty of old proverbs; they are as true as a plum line, and as short and sweet as sugar candy. Now when you come to see all about this Country you'll find the truth of that are one – "*a man that has too many irons in the fire, is plaguy apt to get some on 'em burnt.*"

Do you recollect that are tree I show'd you to Parrsboro, it was all covered with *black knobs*, like a wart rubbed with caustic. Well, the plum trees had the same disease a few years ago, and they all died, and the cherry trees I concait will go for it too. The farms here are all covered with the same "*black knobs*," and they do look like old scratch. If you see a place all gone to wrack and ruin, its mortgaged you may depend. The "*black knob*" is on it. My plan, you know, is to ax leave to put a clock in a house, and let it be till I return. I never say a word about sellin it, for I know when I come back, they wont let it go arter they are once used to it. Well, when I first came, I knowed no one, and I was forced to enquire whether a man was good for it, afore I left it with him; so I made a pint of axin all about every man's place that lived on the road. Who lives up there in the big house, says I? its a nice location that, pretty considerable improvements them. Why Sir, that's A.B.'s; he was well to do in the world once, carried a stiff upper lip and keerd for no one; he was one of our grand aristocrats, wore a long tailed coat, and a ruffled shirt, but he must take to ship buildin, and has gone to the dogs. Oh, said I, too many irons in the fire. Well, the next farm, where the pigs are in the potatoe field, whose is that? Oh, Sir, that's C.D.'s; he was a considerable fore handed farmer, as any in our place, but he sot up for an Assembly man, and opened a Store, and things went agin him some how, he had no luck arterwards. I hear his place is mortgaged, and they've got him cited in chancery. "*The black knob*" is on him, said I. The black what, Sir, says Blue Nose? nothin says I. But the next, who improves that house? Why that's E.F.'s he was the greatest farmer in these parts, another of the aristocracy, had a most a noble stock o' cattle, and the matter of some hundreds out in jint notes; well he took the contract for beef with the troops; and he fell astarn so, I guess its a gone goose with him. He's heavy mortgaged. "Too many irons" agin, said I. Who lives to the left there? that man has a most special fine intervale, and a grand orchard too, he must be a good mark that. Well he was once, Sir, a few years ago; but he built a fullin mill, and a cardin mill, and put up a lumber establishment, and speculated in the West Indy line, but the dam was carried away by the freshets, the lumber fell, and faith he fell too; he's shot up, he hant been see'd these two years, his farm is a common, and fairly run out. Oh, said I, I understand now, my man, these folks had too many irons in the fire you see, and some on 'em have got burnt. I never heerd tell of it, says Blue Nose; they might, but not to my knowledge; and he scratched his head, and looked as if he would ask the meanin of it, but didn't like too. Arter that I axed no more questions; I knew a mortgaged farm as far as I could see it. There was a strong family likeness in 'em all – the same ugly featurs, the same cast o' countenance. The "black knob" was discernible – there was no mistake – barn doors broken off, fences burnt up – glass out of windows – more white crops than green – and both lookin poor and weedy – no wood pile, no sarse garden, no compost, no stock – moss in the mowin lands, thistles in the ploughed lands, and neglect every where – skinnin had commenced – takin all out and puttin nothin in – gittin ready for a move, *so as to leave nothin behind.* Flittin time had come. Fore gatherin, for foreclosin. Preparin to curse and quit. – That beautiful river we came up to-day, what superfine farms it has on both sides of it, hante it? its a sight to behold. Our folks have no notion of such a country so far down east, beyond creation most, as Nova Scotia is. If I was to draw up an account of it for the Slickville Gazette, I guess few would accept it as a bona fide draft, without some spon-sible man to indorse it, that warnt given to flammin. They'd say there was a land speculation to the bottom of it, or a water privilege to put into the market, or a plaister rock to get off, or some such scheme. They would, I snore. But I hope I may never see daylight agin, if there's sich a country in all our great nation, as the *vi*-cinity of Windsor.

Now its jist as like as not, some goney of a Blue Nose, that see'd us from his fields, sailin up full split, with a fair wind on the packet, went right off home and said to his wife, "now do for gracious sake, mother, jist look here, and see how slick them folks go along; and that Captain has nothin to do all day, but sit straddle legs across his tiller, and order about his sailors, or talk like a gentleman to his passengers; he's got most as easy a time of it as Ami Cuttle has, since he took up the fur trade, a snarin rabbits. I guess I'll buy a vessel, and leave the lads to do the plowin and little chores, they've growd up now to be considerable lumps of boys. Well, away he'll go, hot foot, (for I know the critters better nor they know themselves) and he'll go and buy some old wrack of a vessel, to carry plaister, and mortgage his farm to pay for her. The vessel will jam him up tight for repairs and new riggin, and the Sheriff will soon pay him a visit (and he's a most particular troublesome visitor that; if he once only gets a slight how-d'ye-do acquaintance, he becomes so amazin intimate arterwards, a comin in without knockin, and a runnin in and out at all hours, and makin so plaguy free and easy, its about as much as a bargain if you can get clear of him arterwards.) Benipt by the tide, and benipt by the Sheriff, the vessel makes short work with him. Well, the upshot is, the farm gets neglected, while Captain Cuddy is to sea a drogin of plaister. The thistles run over his grain fields, his cattle run over his hay land, the interest runs over its time, the mortgage runs over all, and at last he jist runs over to the lines to Eastport, himself. And when he finds himself there, a standin in the street, near Major Pine's tavern, with his hands in his trowser pockets, a chasin of a stray shillin from one eend of 'em to another, afore he can catch it to swap for a dinner, wont he look like a ravin distracted fool, that's all? He'll feel about as streaked as I did once, a ridin down the St. John river. It was the fore part of March – I'd been up to Fredericton a speculatin in a small matter of lumber, and was returnin to the city, a gallopin along on one of old Buntin's horses, on the ice, and all at one I missed my horse, he went right slap in and slid under the ice out of sight as quick as wink, and there I was a standin all alone. Well, says I, what the dogs has become of my horse and port mantle? they have given me a proper dodge, that's a fact. That is a narrer squeak, it fairly bangs all. Well, I guess he'll feel near about as ugly, when he finds himself brought up all standin that way; and it will come so sudden on him, he'll say, why it aint possible I've lost farm and vessel both, in tu tu's that way, but I dont see neither on 'em. Eastport is near about all made up of folks who have had to cut and run for it.

I was down there last fall, and who should I see but Thomas Rigby, of Windsor. He knew me the minit he laid eyes upon me, for I had sold him a clock the summer afore. (I got paid for it, though, for I see'd he had too many irons in the fire not to get some on 'em burnt; and besides, I knew every fall and spring the wind set in for the lines, from Windsor, very strong – a regular trade wind – a sort of mon-shune, that blows all one way, for a long time without shiftin.) Well, I felt proper sorry for him, for he was a very clever man, and looked cut up dreadfully, and amazin down in the mouth. Why, says I, possible! is that you, Mr. Rigby? why, as I am alive! if that aint my old friend – why how do you do? Hearty, I thank you, said he, how be you? Reasonable well, I give you thanks, says I; but what on airth brought you here? Why, says he, Mr. Slick, I couldn't well avoid it; times are uncommon dull over the bay; there's nothin stirrin there this year, and never will I'm thinkin. No mortal soul *can* live in Nova Scotia. I do believe that our country was made of a Saturday night, arter all the rest of the Universe was finished. One half of it has got all the ballast of Noah's ark thrown out there; and the other half is eat up by Bankers, Lawyers, and other great folks. All our money goes to pay salaries, and a poor man has no chance at all. Well, says I, are you done up stock and fluke – a total wrack? No, says he, I have two hundred pounds left yet to the good, but my farm, stock and utensils, them young blood horses, and the bran new vessel I was a buildin, are all gone to pot, swept as clean as a thrashin floor, that's a fact; Shark & Co. took all. Well, says I, do you know the reason of all that misfortin? Oh, says he, any fool can tell that; bad times to be sure – every thing has turned agin the country, the banks have it all their own way, and much good may it do 'em. Well, says I, what's the reason the banks don't eat us up too, for I guess they are as hungry as yourn be, and no way particular about their food neither; considerable sharp set – cut like razors, you may depend. I'll tell you, says I, how you got that are slide, that sent you heels over head – "*You had too many irons in the fire.*" You hadn't ought to have taken hold of ship buildin at all, you knowed nothin about it; you should have stuck to your farm, and your farm would have stuck to you. Now go back, afore you spend your money, go up to Douglas, and you'll buy as good a farm for two hundred pounds as what you lost, and see to that, and to that only, and you'll grow rich. As for Banks, they can't hurt a country no great, I guess, except by breakin, and I concait there's no fear of yourn breakin; and as for lawyers, and them kind o' heavy coaches, give 'em half the road, and if they run agin you, take the law of 'em. *Undivided, unremittin attention paid to one thing, in ninety-nine cases out of a hundred, will ensure success; but you know the old sayin about "too many irons."*

Now, says I, Mr. Rigby, what o'clock is it? Why, says he, the moon is up a piece, I guess its seven o'clock or thereabouts. I suppose its time to be a movin. Stop, says I, jist come with me, I got a rael nateral curiosity to show you – such a thing as you never laid your eyes on in Nova Scotia, I know. So we walked along towards the beach; now, says I, look at that are man, old Lunar, and his son, a sawin plank by moonlight, for that are vessel on the stocks there; come agin to-morrow mornin, afore you can cleverly discarn objects the matter of a yard or so afore you, and you'll find 'em at it agin. I guess that vessel won't ruinate those folks. *They know their business and stick to it.* Well, away went Rigby, considerable sulky, (for he had no notion that it was his own fault, he laid all the blame on the folks to Halifax,) but I guess he was a little grain posed, for back he went and bought to Sowack, where I hear he has a better farm than he had afore.

I mind once we had an Irish gall as a dairy help; well, we had a wicked devil of a cow, and she kicked over the milk pail, and in ran Dora, and swore the Bogle did it; jist so, poor Rigby, he wouldnt allow it was nateral causes, but laid it all to politics. Talkin of Dora, puts me in mind of the galls, for she warnt a bad lookin heifer that; my! what an eye she had, and I concaited she had a particular small foot and ankle too, when I helped her up once into the hay mow, to sarch for eggs; but I cant exactly say, for when she brought em in, mother shook her head and said it was dangerous; she said she might fall through and hurt herself, and always sent old Snow arterwards. She was a considerable of a long headed woman, was mother, she could see as far ahead as most folks. She warn't born yesterday, I guess. But that are proverb is true as respects the galls too. Whenever you see one on 'em with a whole lot of sweet hearts, its an even chance if she gets married to any on em. One cools off, and another cools off, and before she brings any one on em to the right weldin heat, the coal is gone and the fire is out. Then she may blow and blow till she's tired; she may blow up a dust, but the deuce of a flame can she blow up agin, to save her soul alive. I never see a clever lookin gall in danger of that, I dont long to whisper in her ear, you dear little critter, you, take care, *you have too many irons in the fire, some on 'em will get stone cold, and tother ones will get burnt so, they'll never be no good in natur.*

WINDSOR AND THE FAR WEST

The next morning the Clockmaker proposed to take a drive round the neighborhood. You hadn't ought, says he, to be in a hurry; you should see the *vi*cinity of this location; there aint the beat of it to be found anywhere. While the servants were harnessing Old Clay, we went to see a new bridge, which had recently been erected over the Avon River. That, said he, is a splendid thing. A New Yorker built it, and the folks in St. John paid for it. You mean of Halifax, said I; St. John is in the other province. I mean what I say, he replied, and it is a credit to New Brunswick. No, Sir, the Halifax folks neither know nor keer much about the country – they wouldnt take hold on it, and if they had a waited for them, it would have been one while afore they got a bridge, I tell you. They've no spirit, and plaguy little sympathy with the country, and I'll tell you the reason on it. There are a good many people there from other parts, and always have been, who come to make money and nothin else, who don't call it home, and don't feel to home, and who intend to up killoch and off, as soon as they have made their ned out of the Blue Noses. They have got about as much regard for the country as a pedlar has, who trudges along with a pack on his back. He *walks*, cause he intends to *ride* at last; *trusts*, cause he intends to *sue* at last; *smiles*, cause he intends to *cheat* at last; *saves all*, cause he intends to *move all* at last. Its actilly overrun with transient paupers, and transient speculators, and these last grumble and growl like a bear with a sore head, the whole blessed time, at every thing; and can hardly keep a civil tongue in their head, while they're fobbin your money hand over hand. These critters feel no interest in any thing but cent per cent; they deaden public spirit; they han't got none themselves, and they larf at it in others; and when you add their numbers to the timid ones, the stingy ones, the ignorant ones, and the poor ones that are to be found in every place, why the few smart spirited ones that's left, are too few to do any thing, and so nothin is done. It appears to me if I was a Blue Nose I'd ———; but thank fortin I aint, so I says nothin – but there is somethin that aint altogether jist right in this country, that's a fact.

But what a country this Bay country is, isn't it? Look at that medder, beant it lovely? The Prayer Eyes of Illanoy are the top of the ladder with us, but these dykes take the shine off them by a long chalk, that's sartin. The land in our far west, it is generally allowed, can't be no better; what you plant is sure to grow and yield well, and food is so cheap you can live there for half nothin. But it don't agree with us New England folks; we don't enjoy good health there; and what in the world is the use of food, if you have such an etarnal dyspepsy you can't digest it. A man can hardly live there till next grass afore he is in the yaller leaf. Just like one of our bran new vessels built down in Maine, of best hackmatack, or what's better still, of our rael American live oak, (and that's allowed to be about the best in the world) send her off to the West Indies, and let her lie there awhile, and the worms will riddle her bottom all full of holes like a tin cullender, or a board with a grist of duck shot thro it, you wouldn't believe what a *bore* they be. Well, that's jist the case with the western climate. The heat takes the solder out of the knees and elbows, weakens the joints and makes the frame ricketty. Besides, we like the smell of the Salt Water, it seems kinder nateral to us New Englanders. We can make more a plowin of the seas, than plowin of a prayer eye. It would take a bottom near about as long as Connecticut River, to raise wheat enough to buy the cargo of a Nantucket whaler, or a Salem tea ship. And then to leave one's folks, and na*tive* place where one was raised, halter broke, and trained to go in gear, and exchange all the comforts of the old States, for them are new ones, dont seem to go down well at all. Why the very sight of the Yankee galls is good for sore eyes, the dear little critters, they do look so scrumptious, I tell you, with their cheeks bloomin like a red rose budded on a white one, and their eyes like Mrs. Adams's diamonds, (that folks say shine as well in the dark as in the light,) neck like a swan, lips chock full of kisses – lick! it fairly makes one's mouth water to think on 'em. But its no use talkin, they are just made critters that's a fact, full of health and life and beauty, – now, to change them are splendid white water lillies of Connecticut and Rhode Island, for the yaller crocusses of Illanoy, is what we dont like. It goes most confoundedly agin the grain, I tell you. Poor critters, when they get away back there, they grow as thin as a sawed lath, their little peepers are as dull as a boiled codfish, their skin looks like yaller fever, and they seem all mouth like a crocodile. And that's not the worst of it neither, for when a woman begins to grow saller its all over with her; she's up a tree then you may depend, there's no mistake. You can no more bring back her bloom than you can the color to a leaf the frost has touched in the fall. It's gone goose with her, that's a fact.

And that's not all, for the temper is plaguy apt to change with the cheek too. When the freshness of youth is on the move, the sweetness of temper is amazin apt to start along with it. A bilious cheek and a sour temper are like the Siamese twins, there's a nateral cord of union atween them. The one is a sign board, with the name of the firm written on it in big letters. He that dont know this, cant read, I guess. It's no use to cry over spilt milk, we all know, but its easier said than done that. Women kind, and especially single folks, will take on dreadful at the fadin of their roses, and their frettin only seems to make the thorns look sharper. Our minister used to say to sister Sall, (and when she was young she was a rael witch, a most an everlastin sweet girl,) Sally, he used to say, now's the time to larn, when you are young; store your mind well, dear, and the fragrance will remain long arter the rose has shed its leaves. *The otter of roses is stronger than the rose, and a plaguy sight more valuable.* Sall wrote it down, she said it warnt a bad idee that; but father larfed, he said he guessed minister's courtin days warnt over, when he made such pretty speeches as that are to the galls. Now, who would go to expose his wife or his darters, or himself, to the dangers of such a climate, for the sake of 30 bushels of wheat to the acre, instead of 15. There seems a kinder somethin in us that rises in our throat when we think on it, and wont let us. We dont like it. Give me the shore, and let them that like the Far West go there, I say.

This place is as fartile as Illanoy or Ohio, as healthy as any part of the Globe, and right along side of the salt water; but the folks want three things – *Industry, Enterprise, Economy*; these Blue Noses dont know how to valy this location – only look at it, and see what a place for bisness it is – the centre of the Province – the nateral capital of the Basin of Minas, and part of the Bay of Fundy – the great thoroughfare to St. John,

Canada, and the United States – the exports of lime, gypsum, freestone and grindstone – the dykes – but it's no use talkin; I wish we had it, that's all. Our folks are like a rock maple tree – stick 'em in any where, but eend up and top down, and they will take root and grow; but put 'em in a rael good soil like this, and give 'em a fair chance, and they will go ahead and thrive right off, most amazin fast, that's a fact. Yes, if we had it we would make another guess place of it from what it is. *In one year we would have a rail road to Halifax, which, unlike the stone that killed two birds, would be the makin of both places.* I often tell the folks this, but all they can say is, oh we are too poor and too young. Says I, you put me in mind of a great long legged, long tailed colt, father had. He never changed his name of colt as long as he lived, and he was as old as the hills; and though he had the best of feed, was as thin as a whippin post. He was colt all his days – always young – always poor; and young and poor you'll be, I guess to the eend of the chapter.

On our return to the Inn the weather, which had been threatening for some time past, became very tempestuous. It rained for three successive days, and the roads were almost impassible. To continue my journey was wholly out of the question. I determined, therefore, to take a seat in the coach for Halifax, and defer until next year the remaining part of my tour. Mr. Slick agreed to meet me here in June, and to provide for me the same conveyance I had used from Amherst. I look forward with much pleasure to our meeting again. His manner and idiom were to me perfectly new and very amusing; while his good sound sense, searching observation, and queer humor, rendered his conversation at once valuable and interesting. There are many subjects on which I should like to draw him out; and I promise myself a fund of amusement in his remarks on the state of society and manners at Halifax, and the machinery of the local government, on both of which he appears to entertain many original and some very just opinions.

As he took leave of me in the coach, he whispered, "Inside of your great big cloak you will find wrapped up a box, containin a thousand rael genuine first chop Havanahs – no mistake – the clear thing. When you smoke 'em think sometimes of your old companion, SAM SLICK THE CLOCKMAKER."

THE END

AFTERWORD

BY ROBERT L. McDOUGALL

A newspaper clipping pasted to the inside cover of an early American edition of *The Clockmaker* reads as follows:

ORIGINAL "SAM SLICK" DEAD

A despatch from Bangor, Maine, to the Montreal "Star" states: Jackson Young, known throughout New England as the original of "Sam Slick, the Yankee Clockmaker," written by Judge Thomas Chandler Haliburton, is dead here, aged 87 years. . . .

Mr. Young was one of four brothers who came to Maine from Vermont and travelled the State selling Yankee notions in peddlers' carts. Later they took up the clock business, and thousands of the old-fashioned brass clocks still doing duty in the farm-houses of Maine and the provinces were bought from the Young brothers.

Samuel J. Young was the last surviving of the four, the others of whom became millionaires in Western and

Canadian lumbering and lands, all getting their start from peddling clocks.

Was Samuel Jackson Young in fact the "original" of Thomas Chandler Haliburton's Sam Slick? Probably not. The news item is dated 1908 – which means that the Mr. Young who died "aged 87 years" could have been no more than a teenager, with (as Sam would say) many rings to grow on his horns yet, at the time when Mr. Slick made his first bow to the public in the pages of *The Novascotian* in 1835. Moreover, the best authorities, including Haliburton himself on one occasion, are agreed that there was no "original" for Sam in this narrow sense.

What the clipping does establish, on the other hand, is the remarkable vitality of Haliburton's portrait of the Clockmaker – and at the same time, of course, its faithfulness to a real-life background of clock-peddling and Yankee enterprise. Sam Slick of Slickville, Connecticut, became a legend in his own time. When Haliburton visited England in 1838, Lord Abinger is reported to have raised himself on one elbow from a sickbed long enough to ask the author if it was not true (as he firmly believed) "that there is a veritable Sam Slick in the flesh now selling clocks to the Blue Noses." To which Haliburton replied no, it was not true. But the point is that Sam was the kind of person one read about and was promptly sure that one knew, or that someone knew, in the flesh. Such vitality is proof against time. If Samuel Jackson Young, therefore, is very much dead today, Samuel Slick is not. It seems likely, in fact, that he will outlive even the very durable brass clocks which those of his calling are said to have sold by the thousands to Maritimers more than a century ago.

More specifically, Sam Slick has survived because the man who created him was a capable humorist – and the tricks of making people laugh change little with the years. Reports of Haliburton refer often to his lively wit, and tradition has it that he had a special fondness for off-colour jokes. The off-colour jokes had to remain for the most part private; but the rest of his comic spirit (with just a touch of bawdiness for sauce) Haliburton successfully incorporated in the one memorable character that was to come from his pen. Above all, he made this character a reflection of his own remarkable energy of mind and imagination. His methods were the standard ones of comedy: exaggeration and disruptive turns of speech and action.

Yet universal laughter can have a special ring to it, and it is worth recalling that the American humorist Artemus Ward is said to have named Haliburton "the father of American humour." The claim, like all of its kind, is open to debate. It is certainly not one that has found much favour with American critics since Ward's time, who have generally preferred that their founding father be homegrown. But however the case is argued, there is at any rate no disputing the fact that Haliburton is often funny in a recognizably North American way. Sam's democratic brashness, his "calculatin'" shrewdness, his colossal assurance and resourcefulness in argument, his readiness with homespun comments, with anecdotes and tall tales – all these traits were already connected with popular conceptions of the Yankee character in Haliburton's time, and most of them were well suited to humorous treatment. It is true that they are traits which occur (though usually with a different twist) in English humour. But their aggregate in Sam is a distinctive mark. Davy Crockett, type of the "ring-tailed roarer" of the West, is his blood brother, and so also is Jack Downing, Seba Smith's dispenser of axe-handles and cracker-barrel philosophy who had a wide following in these years throughout the eastern states. The legendary Paul Bunyan is a not-too-distant relative.

Certainly, if I were asked to name the qualities of *The Clockmaker* which attracted me most, I would choose two which seem somehow more native to the New World than the Old – audacity and energy. If these are not noticeably Canadian qualities, it is perhaps because Haliburton wrote long before national self-consciousness gave birth, in the strange Canadian way, to national diffidence. The qualities are of course Sam's, but they are easily transferred into a feeling one has about the whole book. The kind of spawning of comic situation that goes on in *The Clockmaker* is part of this feeling, but much more it is a matter of language – the colourful and inexhaustible speech which flows from page to page, and which in sum makes up one of the most remarkable monologues ever written. Sober critics (mostly Canadian) of Haliburton's time complained of murders committed on grammar and the proper use of words. They found that Sam, like his friend January Snow, knew English "real well," and could do "near about anything but speak it." But in the wake of slaughtered forms rise lively words and phrases, and altogether as fine an array of imagery as one could hope for in a shelfload of contemporary writing.

Is a man crestfallen, put out, downhearted? Well, says Sam, he's "streaked" or "chop-fallen." Or, better still, he's "wamblecropt." And the words stream out into images – images bred in the barnyards, the inns, the farm-kitchens, the seacoast villages of Nova Scotia. A pettifogging justice, says Sam, is "a regular suck egg." "They ought to pay his passage, as we do such critters, tell him his place is taken in the Mail Coach, and if he is found here after twenty four hours, they'd make a carpenter's plumb-bob of him, and hang him outside the church steeple, to try if it was perpendicular." Small matter who the Grahamites were, but the man who belonged to this sect catches the eye. "I once travelled all through the State of Maine with one of them are chaps," Sam says. "He was as thin as a whippin post. His skin looked like a blown bladder arter some of the air had leaked out, kinder wrinkled and rumpled like, and his eye as dim as a lamp that's livin on a short allowance of ile. He put me in mind of a pair of kitchen tongs, all legs, shaft and head, and no belly; a real gander gutted lookin critter, as holler as a bamboo walkin cane, and twice as yaller." See also, in one of many unflattering poses, the Blue Nose – "with his go-to-meetin clothes on, coat tails pinned up behind like a leather blind of a Shay, an old spur on one heel, and pipe stuck through his hat band, mounted on one of these limber tim-bered critters, that moves its hind legs like a hen scratchin gravel." Turbulent, sometimes overwrought, but always bold and vigorous, this language is probably the heart of the book's attraction for the present-day reader.

The passages quoted, however, will suggest that Sam Slick is often funny, not in an empty-headed way, but with a purpose. Most amusement is at someone else's expense, and the fact is that Haliburton, in his own person a bold and ener-getic thinker, was very much bent on satiric business when he created Mr. Slick. Indeed there were to be times in Sam's later career when this satiric business fairly drained the lifeblood out of him, so that he became no more than the vehicle for political argument on questions frequently clouded with contemporary reference. Fortunately, what is published in this reprint (which is only the first of three series of *The Clockmaker*) contains little that needs to be explained in terms of political and social developments in the Nova Scotia of Haliburton's time. An allusion, for example, to a project much favoured by Haliburton for building a railroad from Halifax through to the Minas Basin is manageable enough in its own context, and if not, there is no great loss. And for the rest, we shall do well enough if we simply approach the satirical side of the book at the ground-floor level of an attack upon pride and laziness and greed – upon human traits, in other words, as recognizable today as they were in 1835. Still, since a specific design controlled the conception of *The Clockmaker*, it is perhaps worth doing a little more than this to pin down Haliburton's intentions.

Like the best satire, Haliburton's comes from clearly defined opinions strongly held in the face of opposing values. Haliburton was a Tory of an old and rigorous school – a school so completely overwhelmed subsequently by the triumphs of labour and democratic thought as to be almost a museum-piece now. Yet the line is pure from Burke, whom Haliburton greatly admired.

It should not at any rate be difficult for the present-day reader to make the necessary distinction between this outlook and that of a narrow-minded reactionary. Haliburton fashioned his convictions into a coherent and, in its own way, enterprising political philosophy. He came by his Tory principles honestly: from his parents, who were Loyalist stock transplanted from New England to Nova Scotia about the time of the American Revolution; from his studies and associations at King's College, Windsor, which was in his day the seat of established Anglicanism and social privilege in higher learning; and, perhaps most notably, from his own thoughtful appraisals of the British and American constitutions. On the Bench and in the House of Assembly, it is true, he showed a certain amount of concern for political justice and human rights. Contrary to a commonly held opinion, however, such a concern is by no means incompatible with the viewpoint of a true-blue Tory. With as much consistency as can be demanded of any man, Haliburton made Tory principles the cornerstone of his thinking from the time of his first entry into provincial politics in 1826 to the time of his death in England in 1865. He stood for the British constitution and the perpetuation of colonial ties with the mother country; he opposed mob rule, the levelling tendencies of his age, and the swing towards responsible government in the Canadian provinces.

It was the particular issue of responsible government that awoke the satirist in Haliburton. History, which saw the achievement of responsible government in the Maritimes by 1848 and the course of all the provinces set steadily in the direction of the national independence which Canada now enjoys, has put the satirist on the wrong side of the fence. Yet Haliburton's mistrust of the initial gesture towards independence was shared by some of the best minds of the period. When he came up to Halifax in 1826 as a member of the provincial assembly for Annapolis Royal, he found the House of Assembly at odds with the appointed Executive Council. By the terms of the colonial constitution, this Council, acting in conjunction with the Governor, could block any legislation passed on to it by the House of Assembly. And the Council, being on the whole a body of special privilege whose members were tied to the Crown by the strings of appointment, was beginning to make notorious use of these powers. For a time, when the stand taken by the Assembly seemed to be a simple one against injustice and oppression at the hands of a privileged few, Haliburton supported the call for reform. But it was a different matter when the Reformers (as they came to be called) began to argue that the ministers of provincial government should be responsible, not to the Crown of England, but to the people of Nova Scotia. To Haliburton, as to Lord John Russell, such a conception of colonial government was completely at variance with the conception of a continued connection between the colony and the mother country. The logical outcome could only be independence, and Haliburton, perhaps because of his realistic insight into the American experiment and an accompanying fear that the United States might in course of time simply engulf the British provinces, could see no future in independence for Nova Scotia. He split with the Reformers and sharpened his quill for the attack.

Thus, Sam Slick was born. Since the satire of the first series of *The Clockmaker* was veiled, and since Joseph Howe, though the leader of the reform movement, was still a good friend of the author, it was not wholly inappropriate that the sketches should appear in the columns of Howe's *The Novascotian*. There arose, nevertheless, the pleasant paradox of this Yankee democrat, Mr. Slick, being fathered by a Tory die-hard and presented to the public in the pages of a liberal newspaper.

As originally conceived (for he was to prove unwieldy in later books), Sam Slick was a brilliant choice of weapon. The crux of the matter, as Haliburton saw it, was that the Blue Noses spent far too much time agitating for political reform and laying the ills of their depressed economic condition at anyone's door but their own. Nova Scotia, he argued, was a country of immense natural resources, strategically located on the sea lanes, and a good farming province to boot, provided hard work and the right methods were applied. What better stick with which to beat the Blue Noses than Sam? He was an outsider with a plausible knowledge of the country and a plausible interest in its welfare. At the same time, he had the credentials of a "grassroots" representative of a people already renowned for their industriousness and shrewd application to practical affairs, for their bold speech and love of exaggeration. Sam was a natural for the job. It mattered little in these early days of the first series that a Yankee democrat was being put to work in the interests of Tory ideals, for Haliburton was not at this stage inclined to press the more strictly political side of his views. The ideals of Benjamin Franklin, already implanted in the American conscience as national characteristics, were the ideals of frugality, industry, and practicality. And these were ideals admirably suited to Haliburton's vision of a revived agrarian economy for Nova Scotia. The arch-Tory Swift is their common denominator.

But the best of Sam was that he could be used to beat more heads than one. If Sam could say that *The Clockmaker* "wipes up the Blue Noses considerable hard," he could say also, perhaps with more truth than he knew, that it "don't let off the Yankees so very easy neither." The balance of the Yankee criticism was a difficult one to maintain, since ridicule of Sam, once out of hand, could quickly damage his authority as the homespun prosecutor of the case against the Nova Scotians. A few touches must suffice – a little inflation in Sam under the pressure of some of his own hot air about the prowess of the American eagle; a little deflation, as needed, from the Squire. It was better that the rest of the criticism be cleared out of Sam's way and dropped in the lap of the Rev. Mr. Hopewell. And the third target was the British – chiefly for the pride and bull-headedness which produced what Haliburton came more and more to see as a badly informed and unintelligent colonial policy. In this case, of course, it was not the problem of keeping Sam in character (which was no problem at all), but the much stronger check of Haliburton's fundamental sympathies that set the curb on ridicule. Over the whole of this first series of sketches, therefore, the play of satire is remarkably rich and complex. It provides an interesting glimpse, if only a glimpse, of a way Canadians would later develop of looking in upon themselves with reasonable clarity by looking out upon John Bull and Uncle Sam. By the same token, it prophesies faintly our later commitment to the uninspiring but useful middle course. In his subsequent work, Haliburton foresaw specifically something of the nature and function of the Commonwealth as we know it today. It is certainly a fair guess that he would have understood very well Canada's role in NATO.

Satire and humour, then, combine to make *The Clockmaker* a book well worth keeping in print. It was, in fact, by far the most creditable piece of writing in this line to be produced in Canada for many years to come. The winning of responsible government, without the severance of ties with the parent state, must be counted one of the great events in Canadian history – perhaps even in the history of the western world. But it took the sharp taste out of the nation's drink. Extremes had found their cue in compromise and were soon, duly moderated, to make a holy alliance with Victorian seriousness. Thus, the springs which feed such writing as Haliburton's were pretty well dried up at their source. The country's centre of settlement and development shifted westward, moreover, and it was to be a long time before new writers could experience the benefits Haliburton enjoyed from being deeply rooted in a distinctive cultural environment. Whatever the reasons, nearly a hundred years were to pass before Canadians took freely to laughter and mockery again. Stephen Leacock was a long way off.